SIZZLING COLD CASE

(The Legend of Lori London)

A Barnaby Jones Novel

Buddy Ebsen

with
Darlene Quinn

Bloomington, IN Milton Keynes, UK
authorHOUSE

AuthorHouse™
1663 Liberty Drive, Suite 200
Bloomington, IN 47403
www.authorhouse.com
Phone: 1-800-839-8640

AuthorHouse™ UK Ltd.
500 Avebury Boulevard
Central Milton Keynes, MK9 2BE
www.authorhouse.co.uk
Phone: 08001974150

First published by AuthorHouse 6/28/2006

ISBN: 1-4259-4051-X (e)
ISBN: 1-4259-4049-8 (sc)
ISBN: 1-4259-4050-1 (dj)

Library of Congress Control Number: 2006904748

Printed in the United States of America
Bloomington, Indiana

This book is printed on acid-free paper.

To Dorothy Ebsen, whose loving support
is the backbone of this novel.

ACKNOWLEDGMENTS

Dorothy Ebsen—Whose dedication and
  unwavering support made this novel possible
Jack Quinn—Art Consultant—The best natured
  and most supportive man on the planet
Raymond P. Lombardo, Lieutenant— Officer
  in charge Los Angeles Police Department
  Hollywood Precinct, Detective Section
Joy Tierney, Costume Consultant—Quinn
  Martin Productions (*Barnaby Jones*)
Eileen Moore, Associate Justice—California
  Court of Appeals
Steve Fama, Attorney—Prison Law Office, San
  Francisco
Jennifer L. Keller—Certified Specialist in
  Criminal Law
Stuart Anderson, MD (Anesthesiologist)
James Barger, MD (Psychiatrist)
Gainer Pillsbury, MD—Hospital Administrator,
  Long Beach Memorial Hospital
James Wells, MD
Richard Wigod, MD (Internal Medicine)
Elliot Schwartz, Pharmacist
Dave Wilcox—Correctional Officer, Pelican Bay
  State Prison
Pam Wilcox—Administrative Assistant,
  Chamber of Commerce-, Crescent City
Michael Heusser—President, Sunset Ford
Paul Leone—Service Manager, Sunset Ford
Roswitha Bohme—Barnaby Jones Fan Club
  Consultant

Michael Hanrahan—Analyst
Lisa deVincint—Writer
Wesla Kerr—Writer
Robert S. Telford—Director, Actor, Writer
Jim Burgum—President of Smart Reps USA
A. Daniel McIntosh—Genius-at-Large
Eric Watson—Ocean Club Security
Lorraine Leabo—Musical Consultant
Margaret Page—Musical Consultant
Charles Stafford—For his support, and the
    use of his name for an attractive fictional
    character.

FOREWORD

Blessed with a high energy level, a positive outlook, and keen interest in many areas, Buddy gathered a wealth of material to set pen to paper.

Buddy had several works in progress at the time of his death. One that was close to his heart was this *Barnaby Jones* novel, starring the cool-headed PI he portrayed on TV for eight seasons

Buddy was taken from all of us who loved and admired him before finishing this book. Darlene Quinn, who worked with Buddy on his previous novel, *Kelly's Quest,* and other writing projects, completed this mystery novel .

The *Barnaby Jones Fan Club* is still in existence—one of *Barnaby's* loyal fans was President Richard Nixon. A synopsis of each *Barnaby Jones* TV episode is available.

Go to sizzlingcoldcase.com, buddyebsenmuseum.com, buddyebsen.com, unclejedcountry.com and darlenequinn.net for links to *Barnaby Jones* and for Buddy Ebsen.

BARNABY LYRICS

Though many dangers now surround you

And evil lurks beneath the night,

One man will fight the wrong around you

And strike a blow to make it right.

When naked terror rides the highways

And sudden death waits in the street,

One man alone will roam the byways

Confronting crime he must defeat.

Barnaby, Barnaby—what driving force has
set your pace?

Barnaby, Barnaby—can one man save the
human race?

No knight of old in shining armor.

No seeker for the Holy Grail.

Just Barnaby the crook disarmer.

His destiny, <u>he must not fail!</u>

PROLOGUE

I dropped the receiver back into the cradle, fully aware that I'd told a flat-out lie. No denying it. I had no intention of turning in early tonight, and yet, unaccustomed as I was to keeping Betty in the dark, I rationalized that I had no choice. No point in getting my daughter-in-law all riled up at this stage of the investigation. We'd had more than our share of false starts and disappointing leads over the past eighteen years, and this could be another.

But I honestly didn't think so.

Deep in thought, I smoothed the creases of the tattered *Los Angeles Times* article on my kitchen counter. The article, written nearly a year ago, had given me hope and what I considered the first real lead in years.

I glanced down at the article. The headlines danced before my eyes, and once again I wondered how much of the article was fact and how much was a heap of creative fiction. I prayed that tonight would lead me down a new path. One that would prove that Lori London's death was no suicide.

I checked the clock above the counter. It was only quarter to nine—I'd have to cool my heels for at least another three hours. I reached for my unfinished glass of milk, still pondering exactly what effect my reopening this particular case might have on my daughter-in-law. She'd have a strong reaction—that was for sure. But for the life of me I couldn't predict what that might be. Would she support a full-speed-ahead approach or would she still be afraid to have me reopen the case?

This unsolved case remained an open wound; one I felt had been relegated to the back burner for far too long. Now was the time to bring it front and center. Betty was resilient, but the thought of her slipping back into the uncharacteristic kind of depression that overtook her following my son, Hal's, senseless murder filled me with more than a bit of unease. Would reopening the Lori London case bring it all spiraling back to her?

I shook my head.

I knew deep in my soul that no matter what the night had in store, this case was now my number-one priority.

CHAPTER 1.

Around 11:30 p.m., I pulled out of the garage and headed for Hollywood Boulevard. Luck was on my side and I found a parking spot less than two blocks from Lori London's special star. A good start for this long-awaited night as I made my way down the street.

A lifetime of memories wove its spell as my long legs propelled me past a good portion of the five acres of bronze stars embedded in pink terrazzo that lined the celebrated Walk of Fame. I'd taken in the famous names of movie icons of the past, such as Gloria Swanson, Charlie Chaplin, Marilyn Monroe, right up to the present, and yet their contributions barely registered. I strode across the stars of Orson Welles, Jack Benny, Red Skelton, right on past Boris Karloff, George Burns, and Gracie Allen, as I approached the corner of Hollywood and Las Palmas. But my mind was fixed on only one. Thoughts of Lori London overshadowed all others.

As I reached the corner, I realized this was no ordinary newspaper machine; the papers were free for the taking. I dropped the coins I'd held ready to deposit back into my pocket and lifted the metal door of the bright-red contraption. The paper listed a wide range of jobs, along with scores of advertisements. I glanced at the paper, then retraced my steps to the shelter of the broad concrete column outside the neon lights of the tattoo and body-piercing establishment. I'd scoped out this dubious business a bit earlier and decided my best bet was to pick up a newspaper and wait to see what I could discover from this obscure vantage point.

Just inside the doorway of this specialized business of body mutilation, on a high stool, at an equally high counter, sat the slim young man with the flaming-red hair, six rings in each ear, and tattoos covering both arms as if they were long sleeves. When I'd spoken to him earlier, he told me the establishment remained open until 3 a.m. "Later if we have a late-night client." Now, I'd hardly describe a 3 a.m. customer as "late-night," but that's what the young fellow said.

Leaning against a flat surface on the five-sided concrete column, I tried to get somewhat less uncomfortable as I casually opened the newspaper, but my interest lay elsewhere.

*****

Shoving his hands deep into the pockets of his leather jacket and turning up his collar against the December chill, Detective Craig Scott picked up his pace. This three-quarter-mile strip of Hollywood Boulevard had recently been targeted by the LAPD's Crime Analysis Detail, and Detective Scott had drawn an assignment a few blocks west of the unusual array of costumed spectacles lining the street across from the El Capitan Theater.

Scott could think of a hell of a lot better places to be on a night like this. Promoted to Detective I not quite three weeks ago and here he was back on the street, the steamiest street in Los Angeles. Only difference was he no longer wore a uniform. Thank God for small favors.

Pausing beside the Egyptian Theater, Scott observed a stately, silver-haired man in a pristine gray suit, who strode purposefully toward the newspaper vending machine at the corner of Hollywood Boulevard and North Las Palmas Avenue.

Noting the total incongruity of the polished gentleman and the tawdry surroundings, Scott shortened his stride and headed toward the man. He glanced down at his wristwatch. It was just a few minutes before midnight. He couldn't believe the gentleman might actually be seeking the type of job offered in one of those throwaway rags, and he sure as hell was no candidate for tattooing or body piercing. So why was he lingering?

*****

Hollywood Boulevard, though still ablaze in a backwash of ambient light from the ubiquitous marquees up and down the renowned Walk of Fame, was relatively quiet, and relatively deserted. Relatively was the only way I could describe this section of Hollywood, a part of the infamous city that never seemed to sleep.

But now, away from the area near the El Capitan Theater, there were only the soft whispers of tires from the occasional automobile or the light tread of a lone pedestrian. A cold silence wrapped around me. I hadn't realized how darn cold it was until I'd stopped walking. Then from somewhere in the night, the sweet, poignant loneliness of an alto saxophone drifted into my consciousness but lingered for only a moment.

Alerted by the deep-throated vibrations of a powerful engine, my focus rapidly shifted. A red Ferrari had crossed the white line a yard or so in front of me and pulled up to the curb on the opposite side of the street. It was facing in the direction of oncoming traffic, had there been any. The driver's door stood ajar as the Ferrari's powerful idle pierced the early morning air.

Knowing this might be just who I'd been waiting for, I tucked the unread newspaper under my arm but stood rock steady, taking a moment or so to observe.

A dinner-jacketed young man, shirt collar open, tie dangling, emerged from the Ferrari and stared pensively down at the sidewalk—the very spot that housed that special bronze star. The instant I caught a glimpse of the something red in the young man's hand, I knew I had my man. The time for observation had come to an end. It was time for action. In one long stride, I reached the large, circular trash container beside the cement bus bench, dumped the newspaper, and raced toward the reflective young man.

The young man stooped and laid a red rose gently on the sidewalk, then stood for a moment, head bowed, seemingly oblivious to anything other than his mission. I sprinted toward him.

*****

Scott felt a wave of familiarity wash over him as he approached the man in the gray suit and took in his ramrod-straight posture. Who was he? A military officer, out of uniform? A politician? A high-powered businessman? Or perhaps some shrewd criminal he might have come face to face with at the Hollywood precinct? Whoever this distinguished looking gentleman might be, Scott knew he'd seen the man before. But where? He couldn't put his finger on it. One thing was certain: the man had lingered far too long in this tough, crime-ridden neighborhood not to have something specific on his mind, and he'd damn sure find out what it was.

Scott rubbed his hands together briskly to ward off the cold, flexed his fingers, and cleared his throat, ready to ask some very pointed questions. But before he had a chance to utter a single syllable, the man tossed the paper in the trash and bolted into the street.

"Hold it!" Scott called out as he took off after the man.

The man paused, looked in his direction, but continued across the street at a rapid pace.

"Halt!" Detective Scott boomed, sprinting to and stepping in front of the man while flashing his badge.

The man stopped mid-stride and blinked, as if the detective had appeared from thin air. "Sorry," the silver-haired man said. But his words did not ring true. Hell, the man hadn't even met his gaze—a gaze intended to bore straight through to his soul.

With his badge a mere few inches from the man's face, there could be little doubt he meant business. Damned if this long-legged jerk wasn't attempting to peer around him. Hell, he was flat-out ignoring him, his attention clearly riveted on the man who'd stepped from the Ferrari.

Feeling a wave of heat rise from the base of his collar bone and travel the width of his forehead, his gaze froze. And as the man distractedly reached inside the pocket of his gray suit, Scott's hand inched down to the butt of his Beretta.

*****

I reached inside my jacket and withdrew my wallet. Dang poor timing, I nearly said aloud, as the detective stood in front of me, blocking a good portion of my view. I knew the detective had a job to do, but so did I, and I was still a good three yards from the young man in the Ferrari. The officer deserved my undivided attention, but I couldn't afford even the few precious seconds it would take to explain the situation. There was no time; it was ticking away at a breathtaking pace, and I wasn't about to let another year slip by. As these thoughts tumbled through my head, I peered around the detective in time to see the dinner-jacketed young man ooze back into the Ferrari, make a slow illegal U-turn, and head east at a speed that could be described as nothing short of excessive.

Risking the detective's rising ire, I took a few more seconds to ponder the license plate as the Ferrari slipped out of sight. No numbers. Just five letters: M-O-R-G-U-E. I smiled. I, too, had once had personalized license plates. No numbers. Just seven letters: B-A-R-N-A-B-Y.

As the detective looked over my ID, I decided it was about time to focus my full attention on him. "My name is Barnaby Jones. I'm a private investigator, and you are Detective…?" I paused.

The officer looked up from my ID, pulled a business card from his jacket pocket, and handed it to me. "Detective Scott, Hollywood Precinct," he said. His gaze remained on my face briefly, and then returned to my ID. "Bar-na-by Jones," he repeated, pronouncing each syllable slowly and deliberately. Then a smile of familiarity spread across the features on his ruddy, round face. "You're that legendary PI who's worked some cases with Lieutenant Biddle." It wasn't a question.

"Legendary?" I felt my lips turn up in a smile, and found I had to tilt my head to meet the detective's eyes. At six foot four, I seldom had need to look up to meet anyone's gaze, but this barrel-chested detective must have been a good six foot seven or so. "Not sure whether to take that as a compliment or consider it as a polite way of telling me I'm old."

"No. Not at all," Detective Scott said at lightning speed, his face glowing bright red rivaling the red of the lettering on the nearby marquee. "Lieutenant Biddle touts your skills as an investigator, and says your deductive reasoning is top drawer. Tells us if we master even a portion of your skills of logic, we'll be up for promotion."

"He does, does he?" I couldn't help but smile. Lieutenant Biddle and I had been friends for eons. We shared a mutual respect and I knew we were good together, but neither of us had a tendency to gild the lily. Compliments had never been a part of our MO. Challenges were a lot more like it. "Well, don't—"

Before I could finish, Scott asked, "You want to tell me what brings you out to this part of our fair city at this late hour?"

CHAPTER 2.

Knowing the detective had observed my every move, just as I had those of the man in the red Ferrari, I said, "I think it's about time the death of Lori London was finally put to rest, and the true story brought to light."

"Lori London?" Scott's forehead creased into a series of shallow lines. "The name rings a bell, but...."

Scott's gaze followed my index finger as I pointed to the marquee outside the Egyptian Theater. Just like a cotton-pickin' light bulb in the comic strips, I saw the detective's memory kick in. His mouth stretched into a wide grin. His recollections began to spew forth. "Right. You mean that dead actress in this recent surge of retro films?"

I nodded. "Heard about the legend of the red rose?"

"Yeah."

It was clear that Scott's thoughts were now focused. It made me wonder if he didn't know a lot more about the case than he first let on.

"Think I read something about the so-called mystery caller and the single red rose in that *Times* article. The one that appeared a month or so ago." Scott hesitated; then added, as if it just occurred to him, "You'd think someone would have put their finger on the identity of that mystery dude by now. Like, how tough could that be?"

I nodded. "Well, since you probably read the same article I did, you might recall that the owner of that shop," I gestured to the green awning of the food market then paused, "Mirabelle Reese, I believe." Yeah, that was it, I silently confirmed. "Apparently she's been picking up a single rose from Lori's star for many years—the past eighteen years would be my guess. Said she never made a connection between the rose and the anniversary of Lori London's death until last year, when a reporter interviewed her and the shop owner next door for one of those retro pieces on Lori. Since it was the day following the anniversary of Lori London's death, and Ms. Reese remembered picking up another red rose from Lori's star that very morning, the pieces came together for her." Had the reporter not come on that very day, it might never have come to light.

Scott raised a brow. "Shades of Joe DiMaggio and Marilyn Monroe," Scott said with a flare of drama. Then a pinched expression flittered across his broad forehead as he pulled from his memory bank. "Don't believe Joe confined his floral deliveries to a single rose.

Not even just for anniversaries. Joe went the 'whole nine yards.' I understand Marilyn's gravesite is reminiscent of a blooming rose garden." Both brows arched as he reconsidered. "Well, some kind of flower garden, anyway."

I nodded, no longer listening. I knew the story. Darn near everybody knew the story. They'd most likely also heard DiMaggio had arranged for eternal floral deliveries—these deliveries had already gone beyond Joe's own lifetime—a visceral bond with his former wife, stretching in perpetuity. But this was not the story I needed to ponder. My thoughts were fleeting, and as gently as possible I set about shutting down Scott's litany of recollections. I quickly but politely interjected, "Only in this case nobody knows the identity of Lori London's gentleman caller. The supposition that a single red rose has actually appeared on her star on the anniversary of her death for the past eighteen years only surfaced last year."

"Surprised there aren't a fistful of reporters here to check it out this year." Scott's look was direct.

"I wouldn't have been surprised to see one or two. But maybe they wrote the whole thing off as an old woman's fantasy or need for attention." I hesitated; then said, "Would have been even less surprised if I'd caught Ms. Reese pulling a late-night vigil." My own gaze held Scott's as I gave him my take. "Now, as for myself, I tend to check things out before discrediting. That's what brought me out tonight—this morning—or whatever in tarnation you might choose to call it. I'd sort of hoped to find out whether this red rose ritual was fact or fantasy. Might even have had something concrete, provided I hadn't been detained at the crucial moment and could have spoken to the gentleman caller." I raised a brow and gave Scott an amused smile, hoping to telegraph my lack of desire to place blame on the detective, who was merely doing his job. I had to admit to myself, though, that I might not have been so amiable or forgiving had I not spotted the personalized license plate, which, with my resources, would lead me right to the door of Lori London's devoted admirer.

"Sorry about that," Scott said with a momentary note of chagrin.

I held up my hand. "No problem. I didn't get a chance to chat with Lori London's admirer, but I got what I needed."

"Which was?" Scott asked.

"His oddly personalized license plate. Although I have no idea why anyone would choose the letters M-O-R-G-U-E as a personal ID, it should be easy to trace."

"Maybe some ghoulish coroner," Scott shot back with amusement.

"A medical examiner in a flaming-red Ferrari? I don't think so." I paused; then said, "Well, as long as I keep putting one size-13 shoe in front of the other, all will be revealed in time. One thing is already crystal clear. This particular gentleman admirer is not in hiding. That is, unless he's of the school that the best place to hide is in plain sight."

Scott appeared perplexed. Assumptions about the license plate apparently no longer filled his mind, as he asked, "So why, after all these years, does someone want you to trace the identity of the man behind the red rose ritual and look into the cause of Ms. London's death?" Then, without a pause, as his right brow lifted, he asked, "Didn't she kill herself?"

"That's one theory. But not one I put much stock in."

Just as I was about to put an end to the idle chit-chat, Scott asked, "So who, after some fifteen-odd years, would want to dig into this?"

"Are you asking who hired me?" I asked, not bothering to correct him. The odd years he spoke of added up to exactly three. Lori had been taken from all of us who loved her, as well as her multitude of adoring fans, exactly eighteen years ago tonight. Or would it be more accurate to say this morning? A frown most likely crossed my brow as I pondered the semantics.

Scott shot back quickly, "Not exactly. I know you private dicks—I mean investigators aren't always free to divulge the identity of your clients. But it piques my curiosity when I see a case that's been closed … and dormant for more than a decade…. It just seems to me—"

Stepping on Scott's unfinished sentence, I said, "In this case, my client's identity is no mystery. I'm the client." I paused for a beat, and then said. "I've hired myself. This is something personal."

CHAPTER 3.

My feet were itching to get a close-up view of Lori's bronze star and the legendary red rose, but first I'd give Detective Scott an abbreviated background of my interest in solving the Lori London case. A case I believed to the depth of my soul should never have been closed. Lori London's death had been no suicide.

"My son, Hal Jones, was part of the initial investigation. He didn't believe it was a suicide, and neither do I."

"Do either of you have any new leads?" Scott asked.

I paused for a beat, and then said, "My son was killed while working on another case. Killed by his own client, Terry McCormack."

"Sorry. Losing a son has got to be one of life's greatest tragedies," Scott said, sincerity and empathy mirrored in his dark eyes. Then in a nearly imperceptible flash, he said, "Terry McCormack? Wasn't he running for some sort of political office a few years back? Up to his eyeballs in blackmail, as I recall."

"Right," I said. "McCormack is now serving a life sentence."

"Not on death row?"

"No. Can't say I think much of taking another life. It wouldn't have brought Hal back. I'd say it's like puttin' up a fence after the horses have reached the hills."

"Hal's gone, and there's no way of changing that now. Can't say I didn't think of revenge, along the lines of 'an eye for an eye,' when I first learned of my son's senseless murder. It took time, but as they say, time, if we use it to our advantage, is the greatest healer. I've also come to believe that a life sentence is a heck of a lot more retribution than most folks get. In the long run, a life in prison seems a lot tougher on the perpetrator. Might even give him time for remorse. Even with time off for good behavior McCormack will be a pretty old man before he sees the light of day."

"Did you say McCormack was his client?"

I nodded.

"So why—?"

Not wanting to drag this out, I said, "McCormack was filled with some sort of gung-ho ambition and got in way over his head. His judgment went haywire and he thought Hal had betrayed him. Couldn't have been further from the truth, but without taking the time to check it out, McCormack saw Hal in a public phone booth carrying McCormack's briefcase filled with his blackmail money. He took aim and fired. End of story," I said with finality.

I'd lived with the loss and the endless questions that could never be put to rest and had no desire to rehash the details with the detective.

I'd come to terms with the things that couldn't be changed and moved on. Before Scott could ask any further questions, I switched back to my interest in discovering the true cause of Lori London's death.

"While my son had a burning desire to solve this case, he couldn't afford to let his other cases fall by the wayside. With a wife and plans for a family, Hal had to concentrate on making a living. So when the LAPD closed the case, labeling it a suicide, and Hal had temporarily run out of leads, he was forced to put the case on the back burner. And yet he knew Lori had not committed suicide, so he never closed his Lori London file, nor did he stop attempting to carve out time to pursue possible links."

Before Scott could interject, I continued, "I've always known that one day I would devote all my time to solving this case. This mysterious rose-dropping gentleman is the first new lead to surface in the past several years.

"And as you point out, the trail has been untraveled for nearly two decades, so digging up new leads is no part-time job. Fortunately, I have a competent staff. My associate, Jedediah Jones, who recently passed the bar, has a good handle on the business. Along with the help of my secretary—" I hesitated, and then made the kind of correction that Betty would have made had she been here. "I should say, my administrative assistant—I'm confident my business is in capable hands."

Scott stared at me for a beat, then smiled and said, "We sure could use a few more Don Quixote types around here." Scott gave an expansive gesture, taking in the surrounding area. "Sure would make our job a lot easier."

Again, while I realized Scott's somewhat flippant statement was meant as a compliment, I figured there might be a subtle undercurrent indicating that I might be chasing windmills. No matter; I had a mission. Now was the time to pursue it.

Not many people knew the vulnerable and sensitive side of Lori London. But I had known it, and so had Hal. Throughout the years, Hal and Lori had become very close. It was not a romantic relationship, but it was a strong one. Though Hal was a good four years younger than Lori, he had metamorphosed into the big brother Lori never had in her troubled young life. It had been Hal she turned to when things went wrong. Hal was also the one with whom she shared her fears and her secrets, and just before her death he was the one she wanted to share in her newfound happiness. Hal told me she'd been absolutely euphoric when he'd talked to her for the very last time. Everything in her life was perfect, she'd told him. Her career had reached new heights and at last she'd found the man of her dreams. She said she was finally free, and everything was going to work out. She'd arranged to have Hal and his wife, Betty, meet the man she planned to marry and had set up a lunch date for the following weekend at the Sports Lounge in Hollywood. She'd also told Hal that she had something she wanted him to look into. Something really big. Lori said it involved a part of her life that she'd never been able to share with him. They hadn't discussed what that something was. Hal said he'd been curious, but chalked it up to Lori's flare for drama and suspense, and set it aside thinking they were to meet in less than a week's time. A meeting that never took place. That conversation was the before day Lori supposedly committed suicide.

CHAPTER 4.

Not much point in spelling out all my theories to the detective. He was probably as ready as I was to bring this to a close, so I kept the dialogue to a minimum.

Catching me slightly off guard, Scott asked, "How about a cup of java?" Tilting his head in the direction of Starbuck's just a few yards down the street, he said, "I could use something hot; how about you?" Then, without so much as a pause, Scott sighed and muttered, almost to himself, "Good old Sunny California."

"Thanks, but I'd like to take a closer look at Lori London's star and this so-called legendary red rose, then beat a trail back home." A glass of milk would sure hit the spot, but it could wait.

We quickly said our good-byes, and Scott set off for Starbuck's. He would most likely skip the fancy designer coffees, order a strong black Colombian, and take it along as he returned to his mission of keeping criminals off Hollywood's star-studded Walk of Fame—

the world's most famous sidewalk and the city's most widely visited tourist attraction.

As Detective Scott walked away, I quickly strode the remaining few yards to Lori London's star. The rose lay nestled against a bronze movie camera near the top of the cast bronze star, in vivid contrast to the pink terrazzo background.

Tiny droplets of dew on the rose petals caught the light, and once again the blaze of lights that were once Lori's due danced in my head.

Lori London. The name exploded in my mind, a memory like a string of fire crackers.

"Lori London," I spoke her name aloud and felt a shift in my heart as I thought of the living, laughing, loving spirit I'd known so well.

A dancing shadow on a million screens—enticing, enthralling, commanding, a worldwide cult of men worshiping her image. That was the Lori London the public knew and adored—that image, light years away from the vulnerable young girl I'd known so well.

When Lori was eleven or so she'd beg to be allowed to baby-sit for my son, Hal, a bright, precocious seven-year-old. She was mature for her age and oh-so-willing. In the beginning, perhaps being a bit overprotective since my wife's death, I didn't feel right about leaving my son with someone so young. But I'd bring Lori along to my office, where she would entertain Hal for hours in the reception area. No matter how long I plodded along in my private office, she never seemed to tire of the task and never ran out of fun activities.

I stooped down to pick up the delicate red rose and thought of that neglected little rich girl who had grown up a stone's throw from my office. A little girl who had grown up far too fast, wanting, needing, and seeking attention. She yearned to be noticed and wanted to please, but it didn't always serve her well. Once she made it in Hollywood, the tabloids had a field day at her expense, exploiting her every move. Any time she failed to dot an i or cross a t, she'd hit the front page.

As I gazed down at this famous sidewalk, I imagined the sparkle of lights that danced in young Lori's eyes. "One day, I'll have my own star," she'd told me. She was only twelve or thirteen at the time, long before this famous street became the trashy thing that it is today—an amalgam of glamour and tawdry businesses.

"How did she die?" I murmured aloud. I knew it was no suicide, but could it have been an accident? Or, as the Hollywood "whisperers" dared to put into words, "was it murder?" Hal was sure it was a murder, and my gut told me he hadn't been wrong.

I looked down the boulevard to where the red Ferrari had disappeared and heard the clatter of an early morning dump truck. It was picking up trash and losing some as it worked its way down the now-deserted boulevard. I walked past steel-shuttered storefronts, crossed the street, and rounded the corner to my car.

A black cat emerged from the darkness. I paused, my gaze fixed on the nubile feline as I watched it slowly disappear between buildings. The distant saxophone played on.

CHAPTER 5.

Betty Jones, Barnaby's widowed daughter-in-law, pulled into the familiar underground parking structure at the unusually early hour of 8:15 on Monday morning.

Slipping into the slot beside Barnaby's black Lincoln, she involuntarily shook her head. She'd hoped to arrive before him and catch up on some paperwork before he gave her a basket full of new priorities.

Since the senseless murder of her husband, Hal, Barnaby's only son, they'd formed a strong, unbreakable bond, and working with him had kept her from slipping back into the deep depression that swept over her when Hal was taken from her.

Betty had become more than a secretary, more than a mere daughter-in-law; she was Barnaby's family, his confidant, and had become an active part of the agency, greatly expanding her involvement in the day-to-day business.

As she stepped into the recently renovated elevator and pushed the button for the sixth floor, she marveled at how their own offices had escaped the many major renovations throughout the building and remained relatively unchanged. Even when Barnaby retired to his horse ranch and her husband had taken over the business, Hal said, "Dad set these offices up just the way they should be. I see no reason to change a single thing." And so other than routine maintenance, that was the way they stayed.

Now, as Betty strode into her normally well-ordered domain, she stopped statue-still. The contents of three filing cabinets were strewn about the floor, and her usually cool-tempered boss addressed her with some heat.

"Where," he demanded, "is the complete Lori London file?"

"The Lori London file?" Betty's heart sank down to the carpet. She'd known this day was bound to come, especially after she'd seen the article in the *L.A. Times* featuring the mystery of Lori London's death and the supposition that it might not have been a suicide. This case had been Hal's obsession, and she had always known it was only a matter of time before Barnaby picked up where Hal left off.

"The Lori London file." He gestured toward the filing cabinets. "It used to be here."

"I put it with all that old stuff in storage in the basement," she said, and then quickly added, "the way you asked me to, remember? "

✶✶✶✶✶✶

"Oh," I remembered grudgingly. I'd kept the initial file in the bottom drawer of my own desk, knowing that one day I'd clear Lori London's name. Free it from the suicide label that it never deserved.

I took a ring of keys from my top desk drawer, checked them, started for the door, stopped, and turned back to Betty.

"By the way," I paused, "good morning."

Betty laughed. "Good morning, Barnaby." Her gaze fell to my empty glass of milk. "Shall I make coffee?"

Preoccupied, I replied, "Why not?"

On my way to the door, I paused again. "One other thing. Call your friend, Martha, at Motor Vehicles. Check out a red Ferrari, no plate numbers, just the letters M-O-R-G-U-E. Got it?"

"Got it," she echoed as she scribbled on her lined yellow pad. Then came her raised-eyebrow reaction as she studied her notes. "Did you say M-O-R-G-U-E? The place where dead bodies are stored?"

Her voice reached me just as I stepped into the elevator.

*****

Betty watched Barnaby disappear behind the closed doors of the elevator and turned back to the disordered office. She sighed, shook her head, and felt somewhat like a doting parent surveying the destruction of a particularly rambunctious child. A smile lifted the corners of her mouth. But she quickly refocused, temporarily ignored the mess, and picked up the phone. She dialed the number of her friend Martha at DMV.

*****

I took one of the fancy redecorated elevators to the lobby. There was always some sort of renovation going on in one part of the building or another. Some good, some not so good. The building had been designed with a great deal of forward thinking by none other than Bertram Goethe, the renowned L.A. architect. However, the elevator system to the basement left much to be desired. I stepped out of the plush public elevator and pushed the button for the freight elevator. It seemed to take forever, but eventually it ground to a stop in front of me. I took it down two more floors to a sub-basement, which was fitted with lockers for storing the overflow from filing cabinets in the offices above.

I finally arrived in front of my dusty locker and fumbled for the right key. On my third try I hit the right one and unlocked the door. It swung open on somewhat rusty hinges and I reached in and rifled though a number of sealed and labeled bags before coming to a carton marked Lori London. I placed it on a convenient packing crate and spilled out the contents: one Hollywood High School yearbook circa 1976; a packet of brittle yellowed newspaper clippings; one front-page story encased in plastic, its headlines screaming, "Lori London Dead! Death Ruled a Suicide"; and a clipping captioned "Where Lori London Died," with a picture of the open garage at the Montcreif Estate. Nigel Montcreif, Lori's mentor and decades-older lover, had been credited with boosting Lori to the big time through a number of breathtaking overnight successes.

Opening the dusty yearbook to a flagged page, I browsed through the graduating class pictures and saw the rather plain-looking Shirley Demstead—a far cry from Lori London, the glamorous movie star she was to become.

There were a couple of fingerprint samples. Hal had most likely worked these up in the lab following Lori's death. But apparently they'd taken him nowhere. Not many notes. Typical. Hal's uncomplicated style mirrored my own. He tended to carry most everything in his head. But now that he was no longer here to lead the way, I'd need to start back at the beginning.

I pondered this for a moment and was about to secure the other items in the locker when I noticed two penciled notes on yellow Post-its. They were attached to the inside of the manila file folders. The first read, "Recheck ignition when car is released from LAPD," and the second, "No sand in Lori's shoes."

CHAPTER 6.

Back in my office, Betty was ready and waiting.

"That license plate," she announced, "M-O-R-G-U-E, is registered to Tommy Morgan. I'm sure you must have heard of him—the international playboy who was heavily into polo, girls, and race cars," Betty rattled off. "Then somewhere in his mid-thirties he got himself a trophy wife, and disappeared from the jet set and began dabbling in various business enterprises. His current kick is movie production. His studio is called Universal Enterprises."

The lettered license plate began to fall into place, but remained odd and still a bit of a stretch. M-O-R-G could be for Morgan and the U-E for his movie company. I pondered for a beat, wondering why some rich playboy would chose to ride around with a personal identification that spelled out morgue.

"He has several addresses in various parts of the world," Betty continued. "Locally, 15015 Mar Vista, Truesdale Estates." She paused, most likely sensing my mind had slipped into contemplation.

Caught in the act, I smiled. "I'm with you. Go on."

"Here is his address. His phone is unlisted, but I'm working on it."

I took the memorandum.

"Sorry I haven't made the coffee yet."

"Oh, that's all right. I'll just grab another glass of milk."

I felt Betty's eyes on me as I crossed to the small pantry beside her reception area and pulled out a carton of milk. With the milk in one hand, a glass in the other, and the file folders tucked under my arm, I stepped into my private office.

Although somewhat preoccupied, I realized Betty was hungry for information but knew better than to ask. She also knew I was prone to be a long looker and a slow thinker, and, in time, I'd bring her into the picture, and all would be revealed. I heard her voice as she resumed her telephone inquires.

Still pondering the two notations Hal had scribbled on the yellow post-its, I poured the milk into my glass, took a long sip, leaned back in my high-backed desk chair, and rested my eyes. My mind was far from clear as I thought back over the years.

I was well aware that Hal was not the only person to question why no sand was found in Lori's sandals. How she could have walked through two or three yards of sand to her car with no traces of sand on her feet or in her shoes remained a mystery. One that I felt should have been looked into more thoroughly, and should have been cause to keep the case open.

When Lori's body was discovered, I was on an extended fishing trip with a few of my old cronies. It was before the advent of cell phones, so I had been out of touch. Still don't have one of those blasted cell phones and don't intend to get one. Before drifting farther off track, I commanded my mind to stay focused.

With absolute clarity, undiminished over time, I remembered returning to the ranch to a heap of newspapers whose delivery I'd failed to cancel. I bent to pick up the pile of unread newspapers on the front stoop and carried them to the trash bin at the side of the house. It was a mighty tall pile, and as I struggled to open the lid, the headline "Lori London Found Dead in the Garage of Her Married Lover's Home" leapt from the front page of the sun-yellowed newspaper. The shock and sense of loss I felt then has continued to bubble to the surface in waves over long stretches of time for the past eighteen years. It wasn't just the recent newspaper articles that had sparked my interest. I knew I would never rest until I put this case to bed. I could hardly believe I'd allowed business and life to stand in my way for such a long time.

I took another swig of milk, remembering my call to Hal as if it were yesterday. The instant Hal heard my voice, he said, "I've been trying to reach you for days."

Not bothering to explain what Hal was too distressed to recall, I said, "Just got back to the ranch about ten minutes ago. I know about Lori." That was all I had a chance to say.

Hal was talking in a non-stop gallop. He told me about Lori's sandals: "Not even a single grain of sand," he said. "LAPD has followed through on a line of inquiry, but Detective Armor told me they might have to let it go. I've done a rather exhaustive investigation myself, but so far it's leading me nowhere. As well as the lack of sand in Lori's shoes or car, the police found traces of skin under her fingernails. They know it's not hers, but even that new DNA technology falls flat when there's nothing to match it to. At this point, the police are leaning toward suicide,"

"How about Montcreif?" I asked.

"Apparently, the police are satisfied with his alibi. He claims he was on his yacht, somewhere mid-Atlantic, between the U.S. and France."

"And you?"

"He has the means to get witnesses to swear to whatever cockamamie story he chooses."

"You want me to check it out?" I asked.

"Not yet. Maybe if I run into a dead end." Somehow I knew Hal needed to be the one to nail this down.

"How in tarnation do the detectives assigned to this case explain the skin fragments under Lori's nails?" I asked.

"Well, the bartender at the Hilltop Café in Santa Monica—that's where Lori was most of that evening before she died," Hal explained. "Anyway, he said he told the detectives Lori spent the better part of the evening in the bar area. He said she wasn't drinking, despite what all those tabloids claim. And I believe him, though I'm not sure how that went down with the detectives assigned to the case."

"And you believe that because…?" We both knew that Lori was known to have a drinking problem.

"Dad, Lori was on top of the world when she called me, the same day as this so-called suicide. She told me she had cleaned up her act and…." He paused, and then said, "I'll fill you in on that later; just let me give you the bartender's take. He said Lori took her glass of tonic and lemon." This time Hal paused to make sure I got it. "Yeah, I said tonic and lemon, not gin and tonic. He said she chose one of those dark, secluded booths on the wall opposite the bar area. She sat down across from some tall man who wore an overcoat. He said he remembered the coat because you seldom see them in Southern California. The bartender said they talked for only a short time, and when the man left, he saw Lori give the man a sisterly sort of hug, and heard her say something like, 'You've made me so happy. You're the best,' and 'No,' he said, 'I couldn't describe the man, other than that he was tall. About a head taller than Miss London. The lighting is dim in that area and I was busy with other customers.' I thought he had come to the end of his recollections of Lori's last night, but he went on to say, 'A young guy who comes in now and then decided to get chummy with Miss London, but she wasn't having any. The guy seemed to be unable to take no for an answer.' The bartender said Miss London put up with it for a while, and then it seems the guy went too far and she hauled off and slapped him across the face, leaving long red welts. To the bartender and apparently the detectives, that could explain

33

the skin fragments, since there were no signs that Lori had put up any kind of a struggle."

"Have the police checked out the identity of the young man?" I asked

"Sure. But he has another of those pretty air-tight alibis. The bartender told us the guy didn't leave until long after Lori did. He was still there when the bar closed at 2 a.m. and he was in the company of a young woman who is a regular at the Hilltop Café. I've talked to both the young man, a longshoreman by the name of Chad Sawyer, and his lady friend, Julie Hart. She vouches for him. Said they were together until 10 a.m. the next morning. The detectives are satisfied on that particular point, and I guess I am too.

"Dad, I'm afraid the police are getting ready to close the case and label Lori's death a suicide. No way is that true, but I've got such a heavy caseload right now, I can't afford to give this my full attention."

Again I wanted to offer my help, and again I knew I had to let Hal take the lead.

"But," Hal continued, "Lori did not commit suicide and I aim to prove it. I'll never consider this case closed until I uncover the truth behind Lori's death and can back it up with hard, indisputable evidence."

Chapter 7.

I heaved an audible sigh. If only I could turn back the clock. If only—

I stopped mid-thought. "If onlys" would get me nowhere. I gulped down the remainder of the milk and smacked the glass down on my desk. I needed a few minutes to clear my head—to clear it completely. Allowing too much time for rehashing was bound to lead to even deeper conundrums.

I gazed around my walnut-paneled inner office. Nothing much had changed. Even when Hal had taken over so that I could indulge my fantasy of actually running our horse ranch, he hadn't changed much. Hal had grown up in this office suite; from childhood through law school, he'd spent more time here than in our home.

Feeling restless and set on clearing my mind, I decided to stretch my long legs, just surveying my own territory. The walls that were not covered by floor-to-ceiling library shelves were decorated with photographs, mementos, and plaques, which hung side by side, like proud marching soldiers. Unlike many of my colleagues, I had not come from a background on the police force. My expertise was in forensics. However, I'd worked in tandem with the police force, not as a policeman or a detective, but as a consultant, most often with the Hollywood Division of the LAPD. That was before I set up the offices of Barnaby Jones Private Investigations.

On my desk were four photographs, mounted in silver frames. Two were pictures of loved ones who had gone before me: my wife, Helen, and my son, Hal. The other two were of my current family and associates: my daughter-in-law, Betty, and my cousin's son Jedediah, who asks any and everyone to call him J. R. the first chance he gets.

I sat back down in my overstuffed chair and refocused my attention. The time for clearing my head had come to an end. I picked up the second yellow note: "Recheck car ignition."

Where was the car where Lori London's body had been discovered? It was unlikely that the 1985 Cadillac convertible would still be around. Had Hal ever reexamined it? What could he have been looking into that he or the police hadn't discovered the first time around? Why had he jotted down his questions? Like me, he tended to keep most of his speculations in his head. When did Hal put pencil to paper? Had it been during the original investigation? I gave myself a mental headshake. It must have been after the case had been officially closed.

I couldn't come up with any good answers, just an endless litany of questions.

Feeling time was a-wasting, I slipped the two notes into my top desk drawer and reached for the files from the Lucite tray labeled Current. There was an insurance claim for a jewel theft that required an investigation for my steady client, California Meridian Insurance; a celebrity stalking case; and three missing-person's cases I was working on with my longtime friend Lieutenant Biddle in the Hollywood Division of the LAPD.

My intercom buzzed and I flipped the switch.

Betty's voice came through the proverbial static. "I have Morgan's private number now and another piece of information I think you'll find most interesting."

"Well, spit it out," I said, tapping my fingers on the desktop.

"It seems that Tommy Morgan has purchased the movie rights for *The Legend of Lori London.*"

"Good girl." It was no empty compliment; Betty was a gem, always up for a new challenge, and could be counted on to dig a little deeper than requested. This news was dynamite and I was itching to get a move on. "Try Morgan's private number," I said, attempting to monitor my enthusiasm.

"I did, and got a recording."

I switched off the intercom, and immediately switched it back on. "See who has the literary rights for Montcreif's novel."

Betty did not respond, so I clarified, "Nigel Montcreif was the author of *The Legend of Lori London.* Only, I think that was the subtitle. There's a much longer title—something about life and death."

"Wouldn't the rights belong to the family?"

"Usually, but it seems to me that there were no heirs. See if the publisher has the rights or if it somehow reverted to the literary agent."

"Will do," Betty said, apparently up for another challenge.

As I clicked off for the second time, I pondered this new development. What was Morgan's motivation?

I glanced back down at the stack of file folders. There was no urgent need to work on these routine cases. I would turn some of them over to Jedediah; I was too preoccupied to do them justice. I'd take the rest of the day and focus on the case I'd hired myself to solve.

Last night's missed encounter with the mysterious rose-dropping admirer, a Tommy Morgan of Universal Enterprises, gave way to a burning knot of anxiety. The added dimension of Morgan buying the movie rights shed a whole new light on the case. Why now, after all these years, did Morgan decide to make the Lori London story into a movie? If he filmed it as Montcreif penned it, it would be blasphemous. How in tarnation did Morgan fit in? Had he actually been dropping a rose on Lori London's star all these years? Had Lori known Morgan? Had he known her personally? Or was he among her throng of admirers who'd allowed his worship from afar to develop into some kind of fetish? Or could he possibly be the man who'd turned Lori's world upside down? Hal had suspected the man in Lori's life at the time of her death might also have had an unfortunate accident;

otherwise, why hadn't he come forward at the time of her death. Unless, perhaps, he had something to hide. I shut my thoughts off abruptly. No more time for supposition; it was time I got crackin'.

Pushing back from my desk, I rose and strode to the bookcase on the wall adjacent to my desk. I scanned the titles, until I came across the one I was looking for: *The Life and Tragic Death of the Greatest Star of this Century,* subtitled, *The Legend of Lori London,* by Nigel Montcreif. It would be oh-so-wrong to depict Lori London's death as a senseless suicide, as Montcreif had done in this overrated novel. I felt the gnawing rebirth of my old obsession. The mysterious death of Lori London. I needed closure, and Lori deserved to have her reputation cleared.

CHAPTER 8.

I studied the Truesdale Estates address Betty had given me, glad it wasn't Bel Air, where the streets are an over-planted labyrinth—a place where I always managed to get lost. The 15015 El Morino address turned out to be walled and gated.

About ten yards from the ten-foot-tall double gates, I pulled to the side of the road and punched the office number into the car phone. Betty answered on the second ring. As she began her customary greeting, I cut in. "Were you able to reach Morgan?" I asked. She told me she hadn't, so I said, "Forget it. I'm within a stone's throw of his impressive entrance, so will just proceed unannounced."

Returning the phone to the cradle, I pulled up to the kiosk in front of the massive gates and rolled down the window. A portly, uniformed guard greeted me. He stepped out of the kiosk, walked over to my car, and looked in expectantly. "May I help you?" he asked. Then before I had a chance to a reply, a happy dawn of recognition spread across his round face. His features were reminiscent of a map of Ireland. "Well, as I live and breathe. If it isn't none other than Barnaby Jones."

I grinned. "Hi, Murph. So this is what you fell into after you quit the force. Pretty soft I'd say."

"Yeah. Well, it sure beats patrolling the L.A. war zones. Besides, a cop's retirement pay doesn't go far." His tone was somewhat defensive.

"Nice work if you can get it. Looks like a pretty formidable place."

Murphy nodded, his amiable manner returning. "Anyway, good to see you. What can I do for you?"

I looked around, then seeking confirmation, I said, "This Tommy Morgan's pad?"

Murphy nodded. "That it 'tis, and a broth of a lad, Mister Morgan is. An honest-to-goodness prince." Then Murphy continued suspiciously, "You're not here to give him any kind of grief, are you?"

I laughed. "No, Murph." I hesitated for want of a glib response. "It's a private matter. I just want to chat with Mr. Morgan."

Murphy's tone changed abruptly. With an air of suspicion he asked, "I take this job seriously, Barnaby. I want to hang onto it. So what am I supposed to tell Mr. Morgan?"

"You can tell him," I replied with what might be taken as a supercilious grin, "that I want his autograph."

The guard wrinkled his nose and snorted his disbelief. "In a pig's eye."

"No, really," I responded. "I saw him play polo once in Santa Barbara. Very good, too, as I remember. He had a three-goal rating."

"I don't believe you for a minute," Murphy said. "So what really brings you here?"

"Look, Murph, I admire the man, and I have a few questions that I think he might be able to clear up on a case I'm working on."

"And what might that be?" He wasn't giving an inch.

"Hey, Murph," I said, "Morgan is not a suspect. And you know I can't—"

"Right you are," Murphy said, completing my sentence in his head. "I'll call in your name, but if you get me fired, me and the whole family'll be movin' in with ya," he added as he stepped into the gatehouse.

I saw him pick up the phone. It seemed a lengthy conversation, but finally when it came to an end, Murphy placed the phone receiver back on the wall hook. "Remember what I said," Murphy warned, his bushy eyebrows raised in jest. "If you do anything to endanger my livelihood, it's me and all the kids." He pressed a button and the massive iron gate swung open.

"Thanks, Murph. I'll keep that in mind." I gave a mock salute to my friend, drove in, and twisted and turned up a winding driveway. It led toward an edifice, obviously architecturally inspired by some medieval castle. There was no moat, but over the massive, iron-studded door the spikes of a portcullis threatened invaders. I wondered if it were in working order or just there to lend an air of authenticity. My bet would be that, working or not, the iron grating had never been lowered. But that was just my uneducated guess. Maybe Tommy Morgan was a real nutcase.

CHAPTER 9.

I parked the Lincoln beside the manicured lawn to the left of the Morgan Estate. Its castle-like facade was a bit ostentatious, and as I approached the entrance I noticed that there was no doorbell. There wasn't even one of those old fashioned door knockers. There was an imposing, heavy, gold-linked chain. Not knowing what else to do, I pulled down on it, sending the clapper of a suspended bronze bell into rhythmic spasms of low-pitched clangs.

After a short wait, I heard a muffled sound indicating the door was being unbarred from the inside. Curious. I wondered what kind of precautions this Morgan character took for an unannounced visitor.

The door swung open, and an Asian houseboy greeted me without a hint of warmth, then said, "Sir, come with me, please."

I followed his soft-shoed steps through the foyer and down a long dark hall populated by six burnished suits of armor. They were positioned a few feet apart, like sentinels lining both sides of the walls.

The houseboy opened the massive oak door to a rosewood-paneled library and gestured me inside.

"Wait here," he said, then disappeared like a puff of smoke.

Alone in the cold, unheated room, I took the opportunity to snoop around. The glass-enclosed bookshelves supported a deluxe set of embossed, leather-bound editions of the classics. I read some of the titles: *The Rise and Fall of the Roman Empire*, the works of Joseph Conrad, Dickens, Tolstoy, the *Encyclopedia Britannica from A to Z*, the ten-volume review edition of Matthew Brady's photographs of the Civil War.

Continuing to take in the contents of the room, I noted a paperback volume that lay on a coffee table. It was conspicuous among the literary treasure I'd seen on the shelves. It was a work entitled *Soul Mate* by a writer named Jess Stern. I read the byline: "A world-renowned authority on spirituality who can merge beyond the limits of space, time of life, and death to create <u>a perfect union of body and soul</u>." Though there were notes in the margins throughout the book, only those last seven words of the introduction had been underlined.

Before I had a chance to ponder the significance, I sensed the presence of someone besides myself in the room. I put the book down and turned to face the handsome young man who had silently entered the room. Though casually dressed in corduroys, a pullover sweater, and loafers, I recognized Morgan as the dinner-jacketed man from the night before.

I was immediately impressed with Tommy Morgan's easy manner and boyish good looks, while recognizing that he was considerably older than I'd assumed when I'd seen him on the Walk of Fame delivering the rose to Lori London's bronze star.

Morgan was of medium height and had chiseled features, a full head of dark well-groomed hair, blue eyes, and a well-proportioned body. He had strong shoulders, his biceps bulging in the sleeves of his sweater, most likely a result of his days on the polo field—swinging a polo mallet with one arm as he controlled a prancing polo mount with the other.

He eyed me with a fair amount of curiosity and suspicion as he abruptly halted his progress into the room. His dark eyes were cold, telegraphing his patent resentment at being interrupted to receive an uninvited stranger. That was obvious.

Reading his mood, I spoke without delay.

"Mr. Morgan, I am Barnaby Jones." As I reached in my pocket to take out a business card, I continued, "I apologize for this intrusion, but last night I witnessed your touching gesture marking the anniversary of Lori London's death."

There was a silence. The unexpected had blindsided Morgan. He was thunderstruck and angry.

"You did what?" His voice was harsh, but after he paused for an almost imperceptible beat, he raised it an octave and asked, "Are you another of those goddamned reporters?"

"No, I'm a private investigator." I handed him my card. "I saw you drop the rose on Lori's star."

"So you just happened to be strolling on Hollywood Boulevard, just after midnight?" Before I could answer he said, "Fat chance."

"No. It wasn't by chance, I—"

"You read that goddamned article in the *Times*, right?" Abruptly, Morgan walked the length of the room and back. He fixed me with a cold glare.

"Mr. Jones, I let you in here as a favor to my gatekeeper, Pat Murphy. I think a great deal of him, but had I known that that decision would result in an unwelcome invasion of my privacy I would never have made it. Now, sir, have the good manners to get out of my house and off my property."

I took the dismissal calmly, but had no intention of leaving. "Certainly, Mr. Morgan. I'll go," I said, "but before I do there is something you ought to know. It's just come to my attention that you've invested a fortune to do a movie entitled *The Legend of Lori London*, based on the book by Nigel Montcreif. I've read that book three times," I continued at an unusually rapid pace for fear of getting cut off mid-message. "If you stick to his story, Lori's suicide, which most everyone has accepted for fact, you have no finish, and your picture will bomb at the box office."

"So you're a movie critic as well as a PI? And I presume you also think yourself to be some kind of psychic. Well, this time, Mr. Jones, you're way off track."

Although thrown somewhat off balance, I let it go. Traveling down that path could easily spin me way off course. Besides it was clear my minutes were ticking away at a rapid clip. "Mr. Morgan, my son worked on the Lori London case for years, officially, and unofficially, not letting it rest even after it was officially closed," I inserted. "I can't prove it yet, but I know in my heart that Lori London did not commit suicide."

I paused to watch his expression and let my words sink in. I had a lot more to say, but was stopped cold by his harsh, corrosive tone.

"Damn right. No way did she commit suicide. She had everything to live for. Lori London was murdered."

Somewhat taken aback, I said, "So you are not following the storyline of Montcreif's novel?"

"Hell no." His gaze bore into mine. "Montcreif was a monster; if I knew for sure that he was still alive, I'd kill the bastard myself. I just bought the rights to his book so I—"

Baffled, I cut in mid-sentence. "And your relationship with Miss London was...?"

He countered with a question of his own. "Who in the hell is your client?"

"Mind if we sit down?" I asked. "Seems we both have a lot to get off our chests."

CHAPTER 10.

Morgan gestured to the cushy, ebony leather sofa, which sat directly across from a matching armchair. He warily eased into the chair and swung his feet onto the ottoman without taking his eyes off me.

I sank down into the couch but resisted the temptation to stretch out my long legs. I sat facing the movie mogul, curious but willing to take my time.

"Your client's name?" Morgan demanded.

"No client, other than myself."

Suspicion creased Morgan's forehead.

I struck quickly before he had an opportunity to broadside me again. "Hear me out," I said, leaving no space for his retort. "It's obvious that we both have more than a passing interest in the true cause of Lori London's death. I'd like to know yours," I said, then hurriedly added, "but I'm willing to begin with mine, if you prefer."

"Go ahead," he said, his voice still iced over.

I hadn't gotten far in my story of how Lori had come into our lives when my son, Hal, was knee-high to a grass hopper, when Morgan leapt from the chair. "Jesus," he said. "Your son was Hal Jones?"

It wasn't really a question, but I responded anyway, my head spinning with more than a bit of shock and a jillion unanswered questions battling for dominance in my head. Did Morgan know Hal? And even more important, did Hal know Morgan? And what was the relationship between Lori and this playboy—turned-movie producer? "Yes, Hal was my son. Did you know him?"

"Holy shit," Morgan said, the polish vanishing from his speech. Smacking his head with the heel of his hand, he said, "I intended to look him up, but—oh shit."

CHAPTER 11.

Morgan got up and paced the room, deep in thought. He stopped at the side bar and fondled the neck of a whiskey decanter. "Would you like a drink, Mr. Jones?" he asked as he filled his glass.

"Do you have any milk?"

Morgan smiled, and then pressed the intercom switch in the wall next to the side bar.

"Yes, Mr. Morgan?" The houseboy's voice was crisp and clear.

"Do we have any milk, Kip Lee?"

"Yes, Mr. Morgan."

"Bring Mr. Jones a glass, please."

Morgan switched off the intercom and eased back into the overstuffed armchair.

As I observed Morgan from the adjoining divan, I noticed he had undergone a 180-degree attitude shift since entering the room. His frown lines had disappeared, and he looked to be in his early forties, about the same age that Lori would have been.

There was now respect in his tone. "Lori told me you and Hal were like family."

"In a way, we were family. With no father, and a mother who had no time for her, Lori spent a great portion of her early years as part of our small family. At first she'd entertain Hal for endless periods so I could get some work done; then as the two of them grew older and the age difference was not so great, Lori's role became more like a big sister. Lori's mother took off with one wealthy boyfriend after another, leaving little Shirley—" I paused. "I mean Lori, at home with a sullen housekeeper who couldn't be any more bothered than her own mother would with the maturing young girl. So naturally...."

Morgan gave a sad thoughtful smile. "Shirley Demstead," his voice had a faraway tone and his eyes seemed as if they were focused elsewhere. "She told me that was her given name. She hated it and it sure didn't suit her, but—"

"I'm sorry, Mr. Morgan," I cut in.

"Call me Tommy."

"All right, Tommy. I need to know how you fit into Lori's life. Did you know her personally? And what do you mean by you intended to look Hal up?"

Kip Lee entered the library and delivered a tall, frosted glass of milk in the center of a filigreed silver tray. As he offered the tray to me, he unfolded a linen place mat with his other hand and placed it on the coffee table. Most likely picking up on his employer's more relaxed demeanor, Kip Lee flashed me a toothy grin.

I raised my glass but held my gaze squarely on Morgan's handsome features.

"Cheers." We clinked glasses and sipped our drinks in silence. I waited for Morgan to respond.

Morgan gazed up to the high ceiling as if assembling his thoughts. Straightening up in the chair, he crossed one ankle over the opposite knee and readjusted his position. "Lori and I were to be married."

He stopped waiting for my reaction.

When I made no attempt to fill the silence, he continued, his discomfort transparent.

"This is so damn hard, Mr. Jones."

"The name is Barnaby, Tommy."

"Thanks, Barnaby. Please bear with me. I have so much to say and there's no good place to begin."

"How about at the beginning?"

Tommy Morgan gave me a little-boy grin and sank back into the plump leather armchair. "You know, it's great to have someone who was close to Lori to talk to. She was the best. Sweet, funny, and just as beautiful on the inside as the outside. Those damn tabloids didn't know shit about the real Lori London."

His face held a wistful quality, and I knew he was slipping back in time, much as I found myself doing when my thoughts turned to Lori. I'm a patient man, but I found myself wanting to prod him. He was privy to a great deal, parts of Lori's life that I knew nothing about. I had so much to uncover, not just about Lori, but also how Hal fit in. How much had he known? I forced myself to lean back and just take it one step at a time—or in this case, one word at a time—until I learned all Morgan had to reveal.

"You see, Barnaby, when Lori and I met I was married, and Montcreif had her scared almost out of her mind. He haunted her every move. She told me it seemed every time she turned around he was there. But things were coming together for us."

"You were already married when you made plans with Lori?"

He nodded, his look full of remorse.

"Did Lori know you were married?" I tried not to sound judgmental.

"Of course." His gaze did not waver from mine. "Lori and I had no secrets. We both had a lot of baggage to clear up, but we were working toward a life together. One that would have been a forever commitment, not one of the typical Hollywood flings."

Morgan rose slowly to his feet, picked up his scotch from the end table, and began pacing. In what seemed like a long time, but was more likely less than a full minute, he returned his gaze to mine. "I was working on encouraging Sandy, my wife at that time, to file for divorce, but I couldn't let her know about Lori. If she'd gotten wind of that…. Well, anyway, I had to play it cool, make Sandy believe it was her idea. You know, women have their pride. All that bullshit about a woman scorned. So if Sandy thought she was being dumped for another woman…." He trailed off again. "You see, after I met Lori, things changed. My playboy lifestyle had to go. That's when I gave up other women, my heavy drinking, and instead of just playing polo for fun, I bought and sponsored a first-class polo team. I had a fair amount of money but had to play it cool with Sandy. Lori was the lady I wanted to take care of and in a style even better than the one she'd already become accustomed to."

"So you had no actual wedding plans," I interjected.

"We sure did. We just hadn't worked out the time line. As well as my situation, we had to bide our time until Lori could convince Montcreif to let her go."

"Are you talking movie contracts or their personal situation?"

"Both," Morgan said as he drained the remaining scotch from his glass and stepped back to the side bar to pour another. "Can I pour you something a little stronger?" he asked, eyeing my glass of milk.

"I'm fine," I said. "Go on."

"Well, the week of Lori's trumped-up suicide, I was in Thailand putting together one of the biggest transactions ever for polo ponies and team members. I didn't like the idea of leaving Lori here to meet with Montcreif on her own, but she told me that was the way it had to be. Even if I'd been in the States, she said this was something she had to do on her own. I understood, but I didn't like it. My deal in Thailand involved big bucks, far more than enough to bankroll all of Lori's future films. Each night while I was away we talked on the phone for an hour or so. She told me she'd met with Montcreif and he confided to her he was too old to keep up with her, she was free to do as she liked, and he was returning to France. Lori was elated and said she was sure he was going back to his wife to try to make a go of their marriage."

Morgan paused, deep lines creasing his forehead. "I'd have sworn she talked to him in person a day or so before she died. She said he was gaunt and did not look at all well. Finally looked his age." Morgan's body stiffened, and through gritted teeth he said, "But he had one hell of an alibi."

I nodded. I knew all about the alibi.

"He was supposedly somewhere in the mid-Atlantic on his 125-foot yacht."

"I take it you don't believe he was."

"Hell no." Morgan said through gritted teeth. "No way in hell he could have had his chat with Lori and been traveling on his yacht from the East Coast to the mid-Atlantic. I haven't been able to prove it, but I'd be willing to bet he had a helicopter at his disposal for covert transport."

Chapter 12.

"You sound pretty adamant." I said, unable to shift my gaze from his flushed face. "So what have you done about it?" If this Tommy Morgan was so broken up over Lori's murder, why had he been sitting on his hands for the past eighteen years?

Morgan plunked down on the arm of the leather chair, and, not quite meeting my eyes, he said, "I tried. God knows I tried. I couldn't go to the police."

"Because?" I demanded. Now I was getting steamed. Was this guy all flash and no substance? Nothing but a rich phony?

"I told you," he shot back, "I was married and in the midst of a big deal." Before I could interject, Morgan continued. "First I tried to get hold of Hal Jones." He smiled, most likely self-conscious over his formality. "Lori set up a meeting with Hal and his wife for a late lunch at the Sports Lounge in Hollywood for the weekend I was scheduled to return from Thailand. She'd said, 'You just have to meet Hal; he's like family, and my very dearest friend. I've only met his wife once but she's a real looker, and she's got to be pretty terrific or she never would have landed Hal.' But when I got back...." His voice trailed off.

"When you got back, Lori was already dead," I filled in.

"Yeah. Lori was gone, and if screwing up my life at that point would have brought her back, I'd have risked everything. But with her gone there was no fucking point."

"So you just let it go?"

"Hell no, I didn't just let it go. As I said, the first person I tried to get in touch with was Hal, since I thought that's what Lori would have wanted. But Hal was out every time I called—two or three times I think—and I didn't want to leave my name."

"Because?"

"Barnaby, I know you must think I'm a shallow sort of bastard." He set his drink on the end table and slipped into the armchair. "Well, maybe that's true, but not when it came to Lori. There was nothing I wouldn't have done if I could have turned back the clock. I kept telling myself that I should have been with her." He shook his head as if trying to shut out the self-recrimination, then continued. "Lori not only wanted me to meet Hal, she also said he was the only one she trusted to be discreet about the business she wanted him to look into."

Before I had a chance to ask what business Lori wanted Hal to look into, I saw the anxiety in Morgan's eyes—a plea for understanding.

"I doubted that Lori told Hal much about me, since there were only a few days between their talk and our plans to hook up. You know how Lori loved to stretch out a feeling of intrigue and anticipation."

I did indeed. Secrets and mystery were her forte`.

"After those few failed attempts to reach Hal, I sort of talked myself out of getting in touch. I was pretty sure from all Lori had told me that Hal would do his damnedest to discover the truth about Lori's death, which was no damn suicide. Besides, I was in no position at that time to take the chance of making myself one of the suspects. But I hired the PI firm of Sloane, Porter, and Bramble and kept them on retainer for years. But when it seemed the PIs were just taking my money and chasing their tails, I severed their contract. By that time my wife had divorced me and I was ready to contact Hal. That's when I discovered he'd been murdered." His gaze had been cast down toward the carpet, but now he looked directly back into my eyes. "I know that had to be one hell of a loss. Even though we never met, I felt like I knew your son. Lori was so fond of him, and I envied the close, brotherly love she had for him. I'm an only child and—" Morgan broke off, waving his hand in the air between us as if trying to erase his off-track wanderings. "Sorry, I have only myself to blame for not taking the opportunity to get to know Hal. He was my last visceral link to Lori."

No point in telling Morgan he should have gone to Hal. Maybe if they'd pooled their information … I aborted those thoughts. Nothing could be gained by traveling the path of if-onlys. Or maybes.

I was barely conscious of the fact that Morgan was still talking, but when he came back to his initial question, I was on full alert.

"Who is my client?" I repeated. "As I said, there is no client other than myself. Like you, I feel that Lori London's name has been dragged through the mud far too long. No darn point in going into why it's taken the two of us so long to get off our backsides and down to the business of solving this case."

Before Morgan could slip in another thought, I held up my hand, palm out to ward off his verbiage. "So tell me about this movie you intend to make."

CHAPTER 13.

"Barnaby, I've got good vibes about you. I feel you're someone I should and can trust. So before I go into my plot line and the new ending for this movie, I've got to let you know that everything I tell you about this movie has got to be kept under wraps. Not even the cast has the scripted ending."

"Does this mean you're not using Montcreif's ending?" I said this for confirmation, only. It wasn't actually a question. This past half-hour's worth of conversation left no doubt that Morgan didn't buy the suicide theory any more than I did.

"What do you think?" Morgan didn't bother to wait for my response. Apparently, we'd both learned enough this morning to let these rhetorical questions die in the air; there was no need for further comments.

He glanced at the library clock above his desk, and then checked his wristwatch. "Hey, this is no short story, so how about lunch?"

I also glanced up at the clock. It was 12:15. I could use something to eat but pondered a second, having no desire to waste time in some fancy Hollywood restaurant.

"The cook can prepare just about anything you might want in a nanosecond, straight from the kitchen," he said, as if reading my hesitation.

"Thanks. Sounds good. I do have a spot that could do with some filling." I gestured to the area just below my waistline.

He grinned and asked, "What's your pleasure?" as if he were a waiter ready to take my order rather than the master of this modern castle.

"I can eat anything as long as I can wash it down with milk." After a brief hesitation, I said, "I'll have whatever the cook wants to rustle up."

Morgan walked over to his desk, reached down, pressed the intercom, and mumbled into the receiver. At least it seemed like mumbling to my distracted ears. My mind was scattered over a full array of new thoughts and possible pathways, but I assumed that Kip Lee would soon appear with something edible.

Morgan slipped back into the armchair. "Before we get into the details on my version of *The Legend of Lori London*, I'd like to hire you. Just name your price."

"That's mighty flattering, Mr. Morgan—"

"Tommy," Morgan jumped in.

"Yes, Tommy. That's a mighty generous offer, but on this case I'm not for hire. But since we're after the same thing, we can work together. Pooling our information could save us a lot of time and might produce insights that would be hard to come by otherwise. It seems there was a big hunk of Lori's life that Hal and I weren't up to speed on."

"Look, Barnaby," he waved his arms to encompass the whole of his domain, "I can afford it. Since Lori's gone—"

I stepped in and said, "It's not a matter of money. This is personal."

Morgan's hands shot up in the air in a gesture of surrender. "We can talk about this later, but I want you to know that Lori was set to hire Hal to look into some personal business that I'd just as soon not get into at the moment. We'll talk about it later. Then you can decide if it's something you're willing to do on my payroll."

"Fair enough," I said, wanting to move on.

Kip Lee moved into the room in his silent, soft shoes and delivered our lunch. The two sandwiches were brought in on separate trays and appeared plump, full of whatever it is that goes into the variety that's called a clubhouse. A glass of merlot was on Morgan's tray and another tall glass of milk on mine.

Kip Lee delivered our lunch with ease and quickly vanished from sight.

Morgan took a bite from his three-inch-high sandwich, washed it down with a long sip of wine, and was ready to start.

"Years ago, I got this idea to make a movie on Lori's life that would wind up with her murder," he began. "Like you, I read Montcreif's novel more than once and was determined to set things right. Though the ending of Montcreif's prose sucked, he'd done a pretty fair job of revealing Lori's past. At least he depicted her softer side—not the trashy tabloid version. I thought I'd known a lot about Lori's early years, but I hadn't even begun to learn as much as I wish I had. We were young and in love and just didn't do much talking about the past. Most of our conversations were about our dreams for the future." He stopped, leaving a sizable gap of silence, then finally said, "I'll try not to take too many side roads. The bottom line is it took me years to actually track down and buy the rights to Montcreif's novel."

"Who owned the rights?" I couldn't keep from asking.

"His literary agent. But we'll get to that later. Although I bought the movie rights, there's a rather ugly catch."

"Which is?" I prompted, leaning toward him.

"I signed a contract saying that the ending could not be changed."

"But you plan to change it." Again it wasn't really a question; it was more of a statement in need of confirmation.

"Damn right. We're shooting the movie with a different ending; the true one. But we're shooting in secret. The only person other than myself who's privy to the ending is the actress who plays the part of Lori London. No one else but the cameramen and the technicians will learn of the new twist prior to it being revealed at the premier."

"And the new ending will be?" I queried.

"She was murdered," Morgan replied, as if speaking to a rather slow child.

"I presume you have the by whom part all figured out." Again, I knew the answer but I had to have him put it into words.

"By her jealous, discarded, psychopathic lover, Nigel Montcreif, of course."

"You'll no doubt have a blockbuster," I said, more than a bit uncomfortable with the lack of any kind of solid proof to that effect. Although, even if we hadn't been of like minds, I would have encouraged Tommy Morgan to end the movie with Lori being murdered rather than Montcreif's misdiagnosis of suicide. Without something darn concrete, I'd never have had the guts to outright point the finger at Montcreif and say that he had not died at sea, nor that he was the actual murderer.

"What are the ramifications?" I had to ask.

"Montcreif could sue," came Morgan's rapid retort.

I looked straight into Morgan's intense gaze, which was almost a challenge, leaving no doubt in my mind that he didn't much care about the consequences. "How could Montcreif sue? Even if he wasn't dead at the time of Lori's death, he's probably dead by now." My mind was jumping around like a rabbit. "Besides, if he is alive, he can hardly come out in the open to sue."

"I don't think he's dead. I never put any stock in Montcreif's alibi of being at sea at the time of Lori's murder, nor do I believe that he later died at sea. And you're right. I can't prove it. But if he's alive, this just might smoke him out of whatever sinkhole he dropped into."

"Hal was of a similar mind. But if Montcreif is still alive, he'd have to be on the downhill side of ninety by now."

"So?" Morgan challenged.

I dropped the suppositions that neither of us could prove one way or the other, but added, "His family could sue. That is, if he has any family."

Morgan stared at me, offering no additional information. It appeared that he expected me to fill in the silence, so I obliged. "Is his wife still alive?" Unless she was a lot younger than Montcreif, she'd be about ninety. But then I thought back to Montcreif's MO and realized she might be a good twenty to thirty years younger.

"It seems that Germaine Montcreif jumped out of the window of their fourteenth-floor flat while on vacation with Montcreif in Antibes. Again, Montcreif had the perfect alibi. It seems he had to leave Antibes for a couple of days to attend board meetings in Paris. Germaine's suicide was reported about six months after Lori's. The Sloane, Porter, and Bramble PI firm I had on retainer also ferreted out another suicide. It seems the young starlet whom Montcreif was fooling around with before he latched onto Lori was found dead in her bathtub, with both wrists slashed. Of course, Montcreif was out of town when it happened, with a cartload of witnesses to vouch for him. Three goddamned suicides that I know of, and who knows how many more. It wasn't remotely possible to tie Montcreif to any one of the three I know of. Montcreif claimed to be nowhere in the vicinity of any of the deaths, and his whereabouts in other places were always well documented."

Flinging his arms in the air, Morgan exclaimed, "Holy shit. For any lady snared in Monsieur Nigel Montcreif's tangled web, suicide was like some goddamned contagious disease."

CHAPTER 14.

"Tommy. I guess I owe you an apology. You haven't exactly let the grass grow high around Lori's grave."

"Not exactly," Morgan said, "but I still haven't been able to prove Montcreif's complicity in Lori's death or bring him out in the open. He seemed to have disappeared from the face of the earth for about four months after Lori's death, and again for about five months following his wife's 'suicide,'" he said with disgust, holding up the index and middle fingers of both hands in a gesture of quote marks as suicide slipped from his lips. "I had PIs working here and in France, but Montcreif's movements were damn near impossible to trace, until his novel hit the bookshelves. My private investigators kept him under surveillance and covered all of his book signings here and in various parts of France, but we learned diddly-squat—nothing concrete to bring him in. We couldn't disprove his alibi, though we sure as hell tried. Couldn't find one goddamned person to admit that Montcreif was not where he claimed he was. I'm damned sure they'd been paid off, though each and every last one of his crew members were questioned twice and nothing leaked from a single pair of lips. The first time 'round, Larry Bramble, the detective who was full time on my payroll, was out to verify Montcreif's presence or absence on the Mid-Atlantic voyage at the time of Lori's death. Lots of places to hide on a 125-foot yacht, and yet we could get no one to admit that he had been out of sight for any period of time on the yacht or that he wasn't exactly where he claimed he'd been at the time of Lori's demise.

"The second time was to check out whether anyone had seen a helicopter or any type of transport boat that might have pulled alongside the yacht. No dice. Nada.

"Finally, about three months after *The Legend of Lori London* hit the stands, that trumped-up story surfaced about how he'd taken the boat out on his own and was lost at sea." Morgan shot from his chair and began pacing. "He could be dead by now, but not then. Like Montcreif, who had to have been in his late seventies or early eighties by then, would take his seventy-foot sailboat out without at least a couple of crew members." His eyes met mine. "Give me a break."

Before I had a chance to interject a thought or two, the blare of Morgan's intercom shattered the atmosphere. He stepped over to his desk and switched on the speaker.

"Tell her I'm tied up right now. I'll give her a call within the next hour or two."

I glanced up at the clock, as Morgan perched on the overhang of his massive mahogany desk. "Well, Mr.—Tommy—even if Montcreif is still alive today, it seems that you've about run out of options for ferreting out his past alibis. It would be—"

"Not all of them," Morgan interjected. "If Montcreif is still alive, he won't be able to ignore the hoopla following the release of my take on Lori's death. As I said, my movie version of *The Legend of Lori London* will tell the true story. The story of how and by whom she was murdered."

"Which is Montcreif?" I stated. I wondered just how far he'd go. Would Montcreif's alibi, along with our speculations of where he actually was, be part of the film? Just how much of Morgan's take on the truth would be revealed? "And you're not worried about any slander or defamation of character suits that might bubble up from these revelations?" I asked.

"I'd love to have Montcreif or a member of his family sue. Nothing I'd like better," Morgan countered with a credible display of conviction.

"Family?" I was perplexed, knowing Montcreif's wife was reported to have committed suicide. I'd never heard anything about the former movie mogul having any offspring. "Were their any children?"

Pressing his hands to his temples, Morgan was silent for one of those interminable bouts of time. Distress registered across his chiseled features, making him look a good ten years older.

"Yes," Morgan said, his voice barely above a whisper. "That's what Lori wanted your son to look into."

CHAPTER 15.

"Come again?" I heard myself say, as a string of possible scenarios buzzed though my head.

Morgan had a faraway look in his eyes, and again he sat wordlessly for what seemed a long time. He slid down from his desktop and again sank into his cushy armchair. "Where to start?"

Morgan's voice was little more than a whisper. I waited in silence for him to begin, then again suggested he start at the beginning.

By the time Morgan came to the end of his sad tale, my heart went out to Lori. Montcreif was indeed a monster. "If only she'd come to Hal or me years before," I said, "maybe we could have helped her."

"Barnaby, I don't think you understand." His tone was accusatory. "As I said, Lori was at the peak of her career when she found out she was pregnant. But she didn't want an abortion; she wanted to have her baby more than anything. Although things were far from rosy between Lori and Montcreif, when she found out she was going to have his baby, she committed herself to getting the relationship back on track. She believed Montcreif loved her and that he'd already filed for divorce. She had no doubt that soon after the baby was born she would become his legal wife."

Looking straight into my eyes, Morgan said, "Being as close as you were to Lori, you most likely remember how the tabloids went wild with speculation during her six- or seven-month hiatus from the screen."

"Yes, I remember." I'd forgotten all about that period of time until just this moment, but my memory is terrific once it's been jogged. Morgan wasn't exaggerating. The tabloids had had another field day at Lori's expense.

"But Montcreif," Morgan continued, "insisted they keep everything confidential until he was granted his divorce." He stopped talking and brushed his hand across his forehead. "Oh God," he murmured.

He was most likely thinking of his own situation at the time of Lori's death. "Go on," I prodded.

"Anyway, Montcreif whisked Lori off to the south of France to await the birth of their baby. Lori said she'd made it clear to Montcreif that she had no intention of pursuing her career a single day longer, at least not until after their child was five or so. She said she was determined to be a good mother and would not be tripping off to the studio or on location. She wanted her baby to have a real mother and to feel her love."

I nodded. It made perfect sense considering the lack of love and caring young Lori had felt during her lonely childhood.

"Lori told me Montcreif had been just as adamant that she must return to the silver screen, telling her that she did not need to choose. She could be a good mother and a brilliant star at the same time. But Lori wasn't buying; she remained rock solid in her opinion that it wasn't possible to do both, at least not before her child was in school. That's when Lori said she felt a shift in Montcreif's attitude toward her and their life together. In hindsight, she felt that was when he cooked up the plot with the hospital to report the birth of her baby as stillborn."

Outraged, I said, "How in tarnation did he convince a doctor and entire hospital staff to go along with that?" It sounded ludicrous and again my heart ached for Lori.

"Money," Morgan said.

Sensing he was about to go on, I held up a hand and said, "Hold on. It would take more than money—"

"Barnaby," Morgan interjected, "You'd be right under normal circumstances, but as Lori explained it, this was a small hospital, financed entirely by the Montcreif trust. Lori said she arrived at the hospital somewhere around 11:00 in the evening. She couldn't come up with the exact time span or sequence, but as she vaguely remembered, the doctor came into the recovery room with Montcreif. She thought they arrived almost immediately after she'd been wheeled out of the delivery room and before she'd fully recovered from the anesthetics."

"She wasn't at least semiconscious at the time of the birth?" The words popped out before I'd taken my usual time to mull over the significance.

"Not sure," Morgan replied, brushing it off as irrelevant, which it was, I realized a beat too late.

"She just told me it seemed as if she was out of the hospital and back at the Montcreif Estate the next day. She said she must have been taken when she was still sleeping, most likely she'd been sent to 'never-never land' with some sort of powerful drug. She didn't remember leaving the hospital or arriving at the estate; just remembered waking up in the bedroom where she'd been before Montcreif had taken her to the hospital. She was young and trusting. That monster Montcreif did a real number on her. He held a private memorial service at a nearby churchyard, where they buried a beautiful child-size coffin. Lori believed it contained the body of their baby. She told me she'd gone into a deep depression, but before she knew it Montcreif had bought the rights to *Rude Awakening* and financed the movie package, with her in the starring role, of course. And as I'm sure you know it turned out to be a blockbuster, but personally Lori was falling apart." Morgan waved his hands in front of his face as if erasing the picture.

"I'm going into too much detail. The point is, Lori's child was five years old before she learned that she had not delivered a stillborn and learned of the terrible pack of lies she'd been fed. That was only a couple of months before her death."

"And how did she come to find this out?" I asked, feeling the heat of rage again begin to bubble to the surface at yet another injustice done to the vulnerable child inside the widely acclaimed superstar. Lori has been taken far away from her own country, and put her career on hold, while anticipating the birth of the baby she'd wanted with all her heart. She'd carried this baby in her petite little body for nine months and had received nothing in return. Nothing but a bushel of raw pain.

"I met Lori about three years or so after *Rude Awakening* hit the screen," Morgan continued. "Like they say in those romance novels, sparks ignited and we made an instant connection. I knew then I'd met my soul mate. About three months later we slipped away to Paris for a little R&R. I had some business to conduct, and I'd dropped Lori off at that shopping area by the Arc de Triomphe."

"The Champs-Elysées."

"Yeah, that's it," Morgan said, then murmured with a note of melancholy. "It was the first and only time we ever dared to go out together in public."

"So how had you managed to get so close?" I asked before my memory kicked in.

Morgan gave an ironic chuckle. "Didn't I mention our cozy little pad tucked up in the Hollywood Hills? That was—"

I nodded, remembering the covert comings and goings Morgan had described a bit earlier. "Sorry," I said, "please go on."

Morgan just looked at me for a beat, then said, "Well, aren't you going to ask if we were in disguise while in Paris?"

I smiled. "Since Lori was an international star and you weren't exactly an unknown, wouldn't that be one of those rhetorical questions?"

Morgan returned my smile and continued. "Well, after I'd shopped till, as Lori observed, I was ready to drop, she said, 'I guess we'd better call it a day.' But I said I'd just stop and get a cappuccino and pointed to a table at the sidewalk café beside us and told her to take her time. When she disappeared from sight, I picked up a newspaper that had been left on the table—one that was in English—and as I scanned it, I saw a picture of Montcreif and his wife, with a young boy and his nanny in the society section. The article touted Montcreif as a genius on two continents. It went on to say that little Nigel Montcreif III was being sent abroad and was to be placed in one of those fancy English boarding schools, 'to fully develop his own genius potential.'" Morgan walked back to the bar and poured himself a jigger of scotch and downed it in one gulp, then picked up the bottle of Dewar's and poured more in a tall glass with just a splash of water.

I was beginning to wonder just how much liquor Tommy Morgan could consume and still stay coherent.

"The kid had just celebrated his fifth birthday on October 15," Morgan continued. "I did a speedy backwards calculation and figured that was about the time Lori supposedly gave birth to a stillborn. In Montcreif's presence, the doctor told Lori that the baby had been a girl. But it was too much of a coincidence to consider that Montcreif's wife could have delivered a baby boy the very same month Lori supposedly delivered a stillborn. I wanted to do what was best for Lori and was wondering whether I should show her the article or not, when she strolled up to my table. I'm ashamed to say that I considered concealing the paper, but quickly decided that that kind of behavior had no place in the world we were creating for ourselves. I could never hide anything from Lori. She is my soul mate, and ours was a relationship based on total trust and honesty.

"When I handed the paper to Lori, she just stared at it for the longest time. She showed little emotion at first; just kept staring at the picture and rereading the article. As I look back I'm sure she saw little more than a sea of words. It didn't seem to register at first. The first words out of her mouth were, 'During our time in the south of France, Nigel was with me full time; no board of director's meeting or meetings of any kind.' Then she crumpled; her body just seemed to fold in on itself. I yelled out to one of the onlookers to hail a taxi so I could get Lori back to the hotel. I didn't want to leave her side.

"When she finally got hold of her emotions, she cried out, 'Holy Mother of God!' And in gulping sentence fragments, she said. 'At the funeral—the baby—what was inside that tiny little coffin?' I'd never seen Lori cry before. Hell, I'd never seen anyone cry themselves into a near-coma like she had that day. Soon the taxi pulled up to the curb and I took her straight back to our hotel. I think she slept for a good fifteen or sixteen hours. Hell, she was damned near comatose.

"When she finally came to, she said, 'No way are they going to send my son off to any boarding school.' She said it seemed like déjà vu, sweeping back to her childhood. Although she had never been sent off to a boarding school, she'd known what it was like to be abandoned, to be surrounded by material things but deprived of love and affection." He paused. "I held her close for a long time. Seeing her like that damn near broke my heart."

I swallowed hard, unable to say a single word. As Morgan continued to paint the scene, my mind was stuck on the instant replay. I couldn't stop the visions of that vulnerable child I knew to be wrapped inside the superstar image known as Lori London. It seemed as if a block of ice had made its way to the pit of my stomach.

Morgan's emotions were close to the surface, and I felt them right down to the soles of my shoes. There was so much I hadn't known, but now I would let nothing stand in the way of proving that Lori had not committed suicide. She had every reason to live. She was in love and had a child in need of rescuing.

CHAPTER 16.

I observed Tommy Morgan, who looked as if someone had hit him with an electric cattle prod squarely in the solar plexus. I felt that blow.

Morgan continued in his own colorful way. "The impact of Lori's loss over her stillborn child had never dulled. But knowing she'd been lied to was a shock, and the fact that another woman had taken Lori's baby as her own had the impact of a freight train. She ran the whole gambit of emotions, from sadness all the way to a fiery rage. If it had not been for our solid bond she might have again slipped into deep depression. But together we planned a strategy, and she felt confident that Hal would find a way to get her little boy back. Lori's child would become 'our' child. We were a united team, determined to right the wrong that had been done to her." He paused, and with a trace of chagrin said, "Excuse the drama."

I quickly assessed this initial meeting with Tommy Morgan. I'd learned a great deal, and I knew I'd found an ally. Most likely we'd brainstorm numerous times in the days to come, but it was time to take my leave. "This will always haunt me, Mr. Morgan," I said, not bothering to correct my slip back into formal address. There was no point—Morgan's expression was remote. He had slipped somewhere far beyond my reach.

"I intend to leave no stone unturned. With your help, I intend to prove the true cause of Lori's death, and remove that ugly suicide label from her name."

I cut off, knowing I must also sound like a modern-day Don Quixote.

After allowing a suitable time for Morgan to unwind, I stood. "Thank you for your time," I said. "I'll see myself out."

Abruptly, Morgan rose. "Don't leave now; I have something I'd like you to see. Come with me," he commanded.

It didn't sound much like something I should refuse.

Leaving his glass on the coffee table, Morgan led the way. I followed him back down the long, dimly lit corridor, past the suits of armor, and beyond. We climbed up a short flight of stairs to an entryway with a wide, mahogany door.

Morgan took a key from his pocket and unlocked the door. We entered a dark room. Morgan activated a dimmer switch. I stood just inside the doorway as the lights slowly came up, but the overhead lighting failed to cast anything but dim illumination.

Still standing beside the doorway, I could make out objects. I was essentially in what appeared to be a gallery housing a multitude of portraits. There were paintings done in oil and some impressionistic-style watercolors. There were colored photographs, black-and-whites, as well as several in sepia tones. There were also theatrical placards. All were artistically displayed and individually lighted. All featured Lori London. There were expansive close-ups—head shots and full body—many showing her lips seductively parted; and more demure shots featuring a haunting sad-eyed soulfulness. There were some wild, action dancing shots, and finally a life-sized cutout mounted and framed. It was her famous nude calendar shot that had achieved worldwide exposure. It was a classic example of successful personal exploitation.

This cornucopia of Lori London images was much more than a collection of super-fan mementos. Gauged by its depth, volume, artistic organization—and even more so by the beatific look on Morgan's face as he revealed it—this was a shrine.

After allowing me a proper moment to drink it all in, Morgan spoke. "What do you think?"

It was so darn intimate that I felt like an interloper. Not quite certain how to reply, I chose a single word.

"Impressive." I doubted Morgan even heard what I said. So I added, "You loved her very much."

Morgan responded with classic simplicity and a faraway quality in his voice. "She is my soul mate."

I noted the tense. He said she is—not she was.

CHAPTER 17.

I wound my way down the serpentine drive and stopped in front of the guard kiosk. Murphy popped out and gave me one of his wide Irish grins. As he approached, I spotted that unmistakable glint in his eyes. "Well, me lad, since ye didn't get tossed out on your bloody ear, I'll assume me job is secure. It seems ye won't be needin' to add that wee extension to your house."

I laughed then, adopting his hokey combination of Irish/English lingo, I said, "Right you are, laddie. No wee tussle anywhere afoot."

As I bid Murphy farewell, my mind began mulling over the day's new tidbits of information as well as the confirmations of what I'd known or suspected. I tried to string the pieces together, but came up with far too many blanks.

I wondered why the tabloids hadn't picked up some sort of romantic link between Morgan and Lori. I'd followed the case from the beginning, and nothing of their relationship ever hit the press. Though strange with such high-profile figures, it could be explained.

Morgan's marital status with a big business transaction at risk along with Lori's fear of Montcreif had caused them to be somewhat paranoid and absolutely covert. Although Montcreif spent as much time in France as in the U.S., Lori had never dared to have Morgan step one foot into the Montcreif Estate, not even when she'd been assured that the Frenchman was out of the country. They'd been uncompromising in their desire to avoid being seen together. And miraculously their names had never been linked. Incredible in this Tinseltown where, whether true or false, there were always whispers of romance or the latest affairs. Hollywood was a town of few secrets. But, miraculously, not even a hint of the Morgan-London affair had surfaced in the tabloids, even though stories were usually splashed across their pages before a hint of concrete evidence could be corroborated. One of Hal's greatest frustrations had been his inability to track down the identity of the man Lori arranged for him and Betty to meet the very week her life had come to such a cruel end.

As I drove out of the Truesdale Estates, I gave myself a mental headshake, and yet the kaleidoscope of possibilities continued to rattle though my head. If only Lori had at least mentioned the mystery man's name to Hal. But as soon as that thought flitted across my mind, I shut it down. With the day of their meeting set a mere few days after the phone call, Lori most likely wanted to keep Hal in suspense. That was her way—her quirky desire to keep others guessing. Now knowing the identity and reputation of her mystery man, I knew that was a definite possibility.

A few blocks from my office, another thought whispered through my brain. After Hal's initial all-out effort to uncover the true cause of Lori's death and clear the misdiagnosed suicide label from her name, the LAPD had closed the case. Hal had little choice but to take care of his paying clients. After a few months, the subject had faded from our frequent chats. To discuss it only sent Hal into a frustrated depression, and I'd sensed it was not yet time for me to step in.

Pulling into the underground parking of my office building, I wondered if Betty, reluctant as she appeared to be, might be able to fill in some of the blanks. I'd give it a whirl, but for now I willed my mind to give it a rest.

CHAPTER 18.

I strode into the office, looking forward to sitting down with Betty and getting things out in the open. I was sorry I hadn't taken the time earlier this morning when her distress was so evident. Now we'd have a real honest-to-goodness talk. No point in going to sleep tonight with anything left unsaid. I knew a little about what was troubling her, but I wouldn't get a wink of sleep until I knew exactly what was on her mind. The last thing I wanted to do was cause my daughter-in-law any undue pain.

"Betty," I called out when I saw that she was not at her desk.

"In here, Barnaby," she called from inside my adjoining office, but before I managed to stride more than a few feet, she appeared in the doorway, her trusty watering can in her hand and a quizzical expression on her lovely features. Still youthful and lovely as the day my son brought her home to meet me, I thought. Over the years I'm afraid I'd started taking Betty for granted, never taking the time to notice what a beauty she was; a beauty that went far deeper than her outward appearance. In my opinion, Betty had been a widow far too long and deserved more in her life. I hoped her loyalty to me was not standing in her way. She was too young and had too much to give to settle for a life without the special love of a man of her own. I enjoyed her company for an occasional dinner and movie but she deserved so much more. But tonight I wanted to clear any unsettling qualms she might have over my taking on the Lori London investigation.

"Any plans for dinner tonight?" I asked.

She hesitated, her expression a tad more than quizzical as she shook her head. "What did you have in mind?"

"How about us taking off around five?

She nodded. "And…."

"I thought we'd have a nice leisurely dinner over at the Sports Lounge."

"Barnaby, I'd love it. But—"

"But what? Can't a man take his daughter-in-law out for a nice dinner?"

Again she nodded. "I guess I'm just waiting for the other shoe to drop." Her gaze was steady as she said, "This morning you didn't seem to have enough hours in the day, and now—"

Cut mid-sentence by Jedediah's flamboyant entrance, both of us looked toward the outer door. "Boy have I got news for you."

Before I could tell Jedediah he was interrupting, he tossed his briefcase and blue blazer on one of the upholstered client chairs and exclaimed, "I nailed that smarmy forger."

Distracted, I said, "Good job. We were just arranging dinner plans, so why don't you," I paused, trying to remember Jedediah's standard "make-it-short" phrase, "just cut to the chase."

Jedediah ran a hand through his tousled dark hair and proceeded to fill us in, then asked, "What's this about dinner?"

"We're going to the Sports Lounge," Betty said.

I'd really planned on having a private conversation, but Jedediah was family and I'd be bringing him into the picture fairly quickly, so what the heck. "Sure. Join us. We're leaving here around five, and I'll make dinner reservations for six."

"Five," Jedediah said. "Guess I'll have to pass. Too much paperwork to process before tomorrow morning. I've got to file this motion," he patted the manila file folder, "over at L.A. Municipal before ten."

"Well, you've got to eat," Betty said, a maternal quality to her tone.

Jedediah grinned, looking about sixteen. "I'll eat, but right now I've got to strike while the fire's still blazing."

"Don't let anyone quench that blaze," I said, somewhat relieved that I'd have some time alone with Betty. Although she hadn't said anything this morning when I let her know I was digging into the Lori London file, wariness spread across her lovely features, and her body language mirrored her unease. I hadn't taken the time this morning, but the time to clear the air was now, and that's what I intended to do.

CHAPTER 19.

We arrived in the parking lot adjoining the Sports Lounge at about six o'clock as planned. Betty and I had engaged in small talk on the drive from her apartment. I purposely avoided the topic centermost in my mind. Usually not one to play cat-and-mouse, I was just biding my time. I had no intention of leaving anything unsaid or unexplored before we left the Sports Lounge that night, but figured it was best to wait until we had a period of uninterrupted time.

The moment we stepped out of the car, the blustery winds of December were upon us, ruffling Betty's long dark hair in a becoming air of casualness; a casualness that her serious expression belied.

Once inside, I helped Betty slip out of her cashmere coat as the maître d', Mr. Charles, greeted us with a welcoming smile. "I have a nice table for you beside the fireplace," he said.

As he led the way to our table, I was pleased with his choice, somewhat secluded to afford us a fair amount of privacy, with the blazing fire adding warmth to the atmosphere. On the journey to our table I noticed that my attractive daughter-in-law in a simple black dress with a single strand of pearls still caused more than a few heads to turn in our direction.

In a flash the waiter appeared. He delivered our menus, filled our glasses from the carafe of chardonnay that Mr. Charles had arranged to have placed on our table, and silently disappeared.

Betty appeared apprehensive as we clinked our glasses and made the usual toast to good health and happiness, so I didn't beat around the bush but plunged right in. "Betty, tell me your thoughts on my digging into the Lori London case." My gaze locked directly on hers.

"What can I say, Barnaby? I know once you make up your mind, you're like a dog with a big juicy bone. But this case is not like any other, and I'm afraid—"

"Afraid of what?" I cut in. I sort of knew where this was going, but we had to get it out in the open.

Betty took a sip of her wine and looked at me over the rim of her glass. "Well, do you want me to just blurt it out?" She paused, waiting for my reaction. When I wordlessly met her gaze, she continued, "Hal was so absorbed and distracted with trying to discover the true cause of Lori's death, that...." She flipped back an errant strand of hair. "Barnaby, it was nothing less than an obsession. Although he said he couldn't devote all his time to solving Lori's death, it was never far from his mind. He took on other cases and threw himself into solving each and every one of them, but he was distracted. If he hadn't been, I don't think he'd ever have been taken in by Terry McCormack."

"You don't think he'd have been killed?"

Setting the wine glass on the table, she leaned forward, her eyes misty. "No, that's not what I meant." She hesitated. "Well, maybe it is. Barnaby, you know McCormack was not Hal's usual kind of client. Ordinarily, Hal would have dropped any client who even suggested he might be part of any kind of cover-up."

I nodded, wondering just where Betty was headed. Hal had indeed inadvertently gotten in over his head with McCormack, and Betty and I knew exactly how that had come about. The night Hal was killed he'd been on the phone with Frank Cannon, a well-respected private investigator with an LAPD background, who had been Hal's closest friend and confidant. They'd planned to meet that night at Cannon's condo and come up with a plan. Hal wanted out but had not yet found a way to extricate himself from the crafty politician. Somehow Terry McCormack always seemed to manage to pull him back in.

Betty rested her chin on her folded hands, her elbows resting on the arms of her chair. "I guess I'm going off on a tangent."

Just then the waiter appeared to take our order. Neither of us had even looked at the menu, but we knew what we wanted. "Prime rib?" I asked Betty for confirmation.

Betty nodded. "I'll have the salad with Dijon vinaigrette dressing," she recited.

After I ordered my usual clam chowder, the waiter again vanished and we were alone again.

"Barnaby," Betty said, "please be careful."

I smiled. "That's my MO."

Betty frowned. "I know I've told you this before, but Hal was sure that nothing would happen to him. If I got worried, he always told me, 'Honey, they don't shoot people like me. Worst I might get is a traffic ticket or a punch in the face.' But that turned out to be false."

"Betty, we're not talking about the McCormack case. Terry McCormack is serving a life sentence."

"I know," Betty said, "but there's a connection."

Stunned, I repeated, "A connection?"

CHAPTER 20.

Betty sank back in her chair, her eyes fixed on the ceiling for a reflective moment, and then she reluctantly explained. "About a week before Hal was killed, he heard that McCormack's campaign was being backed by the Montcreif trust."

I was puzzled. As far as I knew, the Frenchman had no political ties in the U.S. My mental calculator spun back to the time of Hal's murder. Montcreif had to have been dead or been thought to be dead for a decade or more. It was clear that Hal hadn't had a chance to pass this information on to me, and there was no point in asking Betty why she hadn't.

"Are you saying Hal was looking into that tie when he was killed?"

Betty shook her head. "He never got a chance, but I know it was on his mind and he intended to look into it ASAP."

If there was a tie between McCormick and Montcreif, it had little to do with Lori London's death. She'd died a year or so before

Montcreif's reported fatal boating accident, and that was a good ten years or so before McCormick's aborted campaign. But if a connection could be proven, it might validate the fact that Montcreif had not been lost at sea. And if he'd been able to fake a death at sea, it wouldn't be much of a stretch to imagine he was not at sea at the time of Lori's reported suicide. Even more to the point, who, if not Montcreif, was running his so-called trust?

In the midst of my contemplation, our dinner arrived. The waiter, a pleasant-appearing young man with a clean-shaven face and wide smile, engaged Betty in a brief conversation. Or more accurately, it was Betty who initiated the conversation, discovering the young man had worked his way through college and was now in pre-med at USC. Betty had an uncanny way of drawing anyone into conversation, but as I listened to her somewhat benign conversation with the waiter, I wondered if she was merely shifting her focus from unpleasant memories.

When we were once again alone, I raised my glass to hers and said, "Bon appe`tit."

Following the clink of our glasses we both tucked into our prime rib. But I wasn't really hungry for food. I was hungry for information, so I picked up our conversation where we left off.

"Betty, how deeply were you involved with Hal's investigation into Lori London's death?"

She looked up, her fork poised midway between her plate and her mouth. "Not much, Barnaby. My role was that of receptionist and secretary. But, of course, Hal and I usually discussed his cases at the end of the day."

"And you objected to the time he was spending on the Lori London case?"

Shaking her head, she said, "Not at first. I knew how close they were, and I'd been looking forward to seeing her. I'd only met...." Betty twisted the ring on her finger, then raised her chin until her eyes met mine. "I wasn't jealous, if that's what you're asking."

"No, not at all," I cut in. "That thought never crossed my mind." And it hadn't. Hal and Betty had something very special, which included total honesty and trust. Betty had nothing to fear from any other woman, least of all Lori. With another man, maybe; but not with Hal. He and Lori were like brother and sister. "What I'd really like is for you to fill me in on everything you know about Hal's investigation."

"Barnaby...."

"Betty, I'm not about to get myself killed, if that's what you're worried about. Hal was right; we aren't the kind of people who get killed. What happened to Hal was he got involved with a troubled, power-hungry client. He wasn't prepared. I am."

"Well," Betty said with a sigh of resignation. "I know you've made up your mind."

"At least now I have a couple fresh leads." I held her gaze, and then asked, "You wouldn't really want me to drop this investigation would you?"

CHAPTER 21.

Betty just stared across the table, not saying a word for a pulse-racing few seconds. Finally, she pursed her lips, then relaxed.

"No, Barnaby. I guess I don't want you to halt your investigation. Hal would have wanted you to carry on. He knew it was no suicide, and so do we."

I nodded my agreement.

"I can't tell you this pursuit won't produce a crop of gray hairs and another bout of sleepless nights, but I'll do anything I can to help."

Before I had a chance to reassure her, Betty went on to say, "But please be careful. If anything happened to you it would be like losing my own father all over again." Betty stopped, stretching her hand out, its palm toward me. "I know, I know," she said defensively, repeating words she'd heard a dozen or more times from me. "I won't go borrowing any pages from the book of gloom-and-doom. Just tell me how I can help."

"For right now, I'd like to hear all you can tell me."

The rest of the evening flew by in a wink. Betty filled me in on all she learned from Hal's investigation and confirmed, as I'd suspected, that Hal had not discovered the identity of the mystery man we now knew to be Tommy Morgan, nor did he have any knowledge of the baby boy Morgan claimed Lori had given birth to during her months of seclusion with Montcreif in the south of France. In turn I related what I'd learned from Tommy Morgan.

*****

I arrived at the office at the crack of dawn the next morning. In less than a full hour, my desk was strewn with file folders, memos, and papers of all sizes and shapes.

Hearing the door open, I looked up and rubbed my tired eyes.

"Good morning, Barnaby," Betty chirped. "Knowing you wouldn't have taken time for breakfast I stopped by McDonald's and picked up an Egg McMuffin." She looked at me like an indulgent parent. "But it seems that what you could really use is a good night's sleep."

Looking down at the mess on my desk I said, "That might help, but what I really need is a crystal ball to try and make some sense out of this mess."

Betty stepped over to the pantry, took out a small tray and a plate for the Egg McMuffin, then poured a tall, cold glass of milk and walked back to my desk. She stood for a moment by my desk, holding the tray.

I cleared a spot for the breakfast I didn't much feel like eating as she asked, "Did you call Lieutenant Biddle?"

"I was just getting around to it." Then shifting the focus I asked, "Where's Jedediah?"

Betty shot a glance at the clock on the wall behind my desk. "Only 8:45. He doesn't usually get in till 9:00 or so." She hesitated. "You are going to return Lieutenant Biddle's call soon, aren't you? He called twice yesterday."

"Of course I am. Detective Scott has most likely piqued his curiosity."

"Detective Scott?"

"The detective I encountered—"

"Oh, right," Betty cut in, a wide grin spreading across her face. "The one who apprehended you on Hollywood Boulevard."

I scowled. "I was hardly apprehended, just detained." She was teasing, but I couldn't let her faulty description hang in the air unchallenged.

I checked my watch. "Get hold of Jedediah, and ask him to get on in here pronto." I knew I must sound darn grouchy, but I'd been hoping to turn a fair amount of the workload over to Jedediah, head off to the Hollywood Precinct to enlist Biddle's expertise, and go through the evidence taken from the crime scene. I paused mid-thought. Surely the evidence the LAPD had extracted from the scene of Lori's death before ruling it a dang suicide was still available; if not at the precinct office, somewhere in their archives.

CHAPTER 22.

Betty had been unable to reach Jedediah. As usual, he didn't pick up his cell phone. But he finally managed to mosey on in about 9:45. He was carrying his briefcase, his hair neatly combed back away from his face, and he was clad in a navy suit rather than his usual blue blazer and slacks. "Got that motion filed," he said proudly as he shed his suit jacket and tossed it on the coat tree that stood in the corner of Betty's reception area. The jacket had not fallen to the floor but hung slightly askew on a hook of the mahogany coat tree.

All my well-chosen words flew out the window. This was no time for a lecture on punctuality. Obviously Jedediah had not been lazing about after a late night of carousing; he'd hit the courtroom bright and early.

Jedediah filled us in on his morning and the potential for closing the case in a "blink of an eye." Then, spotting my empty plate, he turned to Betty. "I didn't get a chance to eat before court. What do you have in that little pantry of yours?"

"Well, the usual. Fruit, milk—"

"Never mind," Jedediah said with a sigh. "I'll pop around to the deli." Without bothering to say another word he headed for the door.

"Hold it," I said. "Take a piece of fruit and a glass of milk and come on into my office."

I felt an objection crossing his expression, but he silently headed for the pantry, picked up an apple and a Dr Pepper, and followed me into my office.

I brought him up to speed on my plans to reopen the Lori London case and to put it to rest. The case was not new to Jedediah, but he seemed taken aback that I planned to work on it pretty much full time. Most likely he was puzzled that I was prepared to turn over the revenue-producing cases and go digging into a case that hadn't produced any new evidence in years.

At Jedediah's age I might not have understood this quest either. It was personal, and I felt the commitment to clear Lori's name. It was as necessary to my soul as sun in the morning, but I had no clear-cut rationale to offer on an intellectual plane, so I got on to the business at hand.

As I handed over my files, I filled Jedediah in on the jewel theft case for our steady client, California Meridian Insurance; the celebrity-stalking case; and three missing-persons cases I'd been working on with Lieutenant Biddle.

"I still have a couple of leads to follow up on the jewel theft, but the others I'll leave in your capable hands. If you need any help, just give a whistle," I said.

"Sure, but how about the Lori London case? Is there anything I can do?"

"Right now, I'd just like you to concentrate on our routine cases. I'll let you know when I need your help. The few leads I have I can handle myself."

Taking the files over to his desk, Jedediah placed them in one neat pile and said, "Mind if I jog on down to the deli?"

Meanwhile, I saw that Betty had busied herself with auditing the Hollywood gossip column of every one of the industry papers. She swept up, like a super mental vacuum cleaner, every pertinent bit of information from the daily press releases.

With a natural enjoyment of gossip, it was no chore for Betty to keep it all freshly arranged in her mind, ready for instant retrieval. Anything Betty didn't know about Hollywood rumors wasn't worth knowing.

"Barnaby, listen to this: 'Why the hush-hush on the Lori London set?'" she recited. "This was the lead item in 'Terry's Tinsel Town,' Terry O'Brien's column." Betty studied my expression as she continued. "'Closed set and rumors of a complete rewrite of the ending of Nigel Montcreif's novel. This is the first film to come out of Universal Enterprises in over a year. Is Tommy Morgan a genius or a lunatic?'"

Shuffling though the Hollywood rags, she found another article. "Oh boy," she said, "Amy Orchard's opening was blunt. 'Is the Legend of Lori London now to become a whodunit? Or will the secret new finish point a finger? And if so, at whom? I can't wait!'"

"Any more tidbits?" I asked, wondering how the secret filming had been leaked to the press so quickly.

"Well," Betty said, "here's a bit of editorial advice. It's directed to the new filmmaker Tommy Morgan: 'Let sleeping dogs lie. Because we like you, Tommy, we don't want to see you, because of your inexperience, self-destruct. We issue this timely warning. Be careful!'"

CHAPTER 23.

"Lieutenant Biddle?" Betty's voice followed me to my office door as it clicked shut.

I slipped into my desk chair, and hit the intercom. "Yes, I heard you. Give me about fifteen minutes and get him on the line."

I opened my middle desk drawer and took out an unused yellow legal pad and a sharp new pencil. Even thinking of putting pencil to paper was a glaring red flag that I was plumb out of new theories. I studied the pencil; as usual I tended to be long on studying, short on writing.

Giving my head a mental kick-start, I began sorting out the pieces of the puzzle.

(1) Nigel Montcreif, a top movie director, plucked Shirley Demstead, an unknown, out of Hollywood High, and through his guidance and Svengali-like influence, made her into the preeminent, world-renowned sex symbol of the era.

(2)   Their association soon became an intimate one. Lori moved into Montcreif's Venice home, where they lived together as man and mistress.

(3)   In time, as Lori's fame and success grew—and Montcreif's faded—their romance cooled. As Lori became indifferent to her aging benefactor, Montcreif's jealous rages swelled to major proportions.

The intercom blared. I wanted to ignore it, but instead pushed the button. "Lieutenant Biddle is on line one," came Betty's crisp tone.

I clicked off and picked up the phone.

*****

As I drove through the mid-afternoon traffic on my way to the 1358 Wilcox address of the Hollywood Precinct, I was still trying to put the pieces of the puzzle I had together. I wanted to talk with Morgan again today in person, but Biddle's call sent me in another direction.

Fortunately, a car was pulling out as I turned the corner from Sunset Boulevard to Wilcox and I secured a parking space directly across from the precinct.

I strode leisurely across the bronze stars embedded in the walkway leading into the Hollywood Precinct, never failing to note the Hollywood Police memorial plaque mounted on the brick wall to my left. The plaque with its original bronze star was dedicated in August of 1973; but unfortunately, the number of stars continued to grow. The inscription, "TO THOSE WHO STOOD THEIR GROUND WHEN IN HARM'S WAY," never failed to move me. I'd worked with many of the recipients of those stars; honest, dedicated officers who valued their duty above their lives.

I bowed my head in remembrance, then began to clear my mind for the work ahead, and bounded up the six shallow stairs. Even before I pulled the glass door open, I noted that there was no one at the desk sergeant's counter.

The banner across the back wall, just above the vending machine, read Welcome to Hollywood Station in English and Spanish. As I made my way to the detective area, I didn't run into a single soul, but as I turned left and stopped at the counter in front of the detective unit I saw a buzz of activity.

A young woman I'd not seen before sat at a desk behind the counter and gave me an officious, "May I help you?"

Before I could respond, Lieutenant Biddle's voice boomed out, "Come on in, Barnaby." He met me at the swinging gate between the counter and the wall. Then, turning to the officious young woman, he said, "Martha, this is Barnaby Jones, a private investigator and old friend of mine."

Once inside Biddle's office, I took one of the chairs in front of his desk and was about to get into my laundry list of needs from his area, when he said, "So you're not buying into the suicide verdict?"

Since Biddle was not around during Hal's initial investigation, I was sure that Detective Scott had reported our encounter, so we didn't waste our time on preliminaries.

"That's right, and I can use all the help you can give me." I crossed one leg over the other and leaned forward. "I realize this is a cold case, but it's time--"

Biddle, not yet seated behind his desk, gave an exaggerated sigh and said, "The Lori London case is no 'cold case,' Barnaby. It is a closed case, and has been for a good seventeen years."

CHAPTER 24.

"Well, John, the Lori London case might be closed in your books," I said, beginning to rise, "but she did *not* commit suicide. That conclusion is 100 percent wrong, and no matter how long it takes, I aim to prove it."

"Hold it," Biddle shot back as he took the chair beside me, gesturing for me to do likewise. I sank back down in the matching wood-framed chair, a style Betty called Danish modern. The chairs in front of Biddle's desk had been upholstered in a teal fabric, the same as his desk chair. "You're not alone in believing that Lori London was murdered. I'll do whatever I can to help you, but I can't spare any manpower."

"I didn't expect that, but if you could get a hold of the 'Murder Book'—"

"Since the Lori London case was closed as a suicide rather than a murder," Biddle cut in while raising his palm to ward off any counter I might offer, "the details were never logged into a 'Murder Book.' Of course, there was a Victim Case Book."

I knew the standard procedure. Whenever a body was discovered and before the cause of death had been determined, all the relevant facts, witness lists, and photos of the scene of death were logged into a Victim Case Binder. If the cause of death could not be determined and it appeared to be a case involving foul play, a four-inch band of orange tape was stretched across the top portion on the front of the blue binder and another on the bridge of the binder for easy identification by the Homicide Division. Cases that were considered solved remained in the precinct for four years and then were archived. They were either sent to one of the city's giant warehouses in their original written form—minus their blue binder—and placed in cartons, or stored on microfiche.

"So how long will it take to retrieve the detective's report?" I asked as Biddle looked off into empty air. When his answer was not immediate, my gaze roamed over the rows of blue binders on the bookshelves beside his desk, triggering my memory of the system for numbering the multitude of Victim Case Books.

I added, "The DR number would begin with 86-06." All Detective report binders began with the letters DR, followed by a two-digit number to indicate the year; the next two numbers indicated the precinct; and the last five the actual case number.

"Scott, the rookie detective you ran into on the Walk of Fame," Biddle said with a smile of amusement, "gave me a head's-up on your interest in solving the London case early yesterday. Apparently you piqued his interest, so he sought my take on the case. Wanted to know if I was convinced it was a suicide, or if I thought it might have been an accident, or murder."

"And you told him…?

"Barnaby, that case didn't happen on my watch. I'd have to know a lot more of the details to give an intelligent answer, but knowing your doggedness, I've already placed a request to unearth the files."

"So how long?" I asked again, all the while knowing it was likely to take a mighty long time.

"Probably a couple of weeks," Biddle said. "Unless you've found sufficient new evidence to reopen the case."

"Some, but not enough so far to pass the scrutiny of all the mucky mucks in charge."

"I'll let you know when the case file arrives."

"How about the Cold Case Team?"

"Unless you can bring me some concrete evidence why this case should be reopened, the team of cold case detectives has a full docket. The reinvestigation of the Black Dahlia, is sizzling on the front burner."

I was familiar with that case. There was no question that the young girl dubbed the Black Dahlia had been murdered; no chance of mistaking her severed body for a suicide.

"Didn't one of your former detectives solve that case?" I asked.

"He has some pretty convincing evidence that it was his own father. He also thinks his father, along with one of his buddies, committed a series of unsolved murders."

"But you don't buy it?"

"I didn't say that. The man you're talking about, Steve Hodel, was a detective at this precinct before my time, and he's nobody's fool. Quite impressive. I've had a fair amount of contact with him over the last couple of years, ever since he began his investigation. Originally, he set out to clear his father's name, but that's not the way it turned out."

"Didn't he just come out with a book?"

"Yeah. It's called *The Black Dahlia Avenger*." A good read. Turns out Hodel is one hell of a writer and darn convincing. He's stirred things up enough to get the attention of our Cold Case Team and get the investigation reopened."

As interesting as the Black Dahlia case was, it wasn't the one I was interested in pursuing. Since Biddle had taken the chair beside me rather than behind his desk, I had a clear view of the detective area. The Venetian blinds on Biddle's six-foot window were open, and I recognized Detective Scott, clad in a casual, plaid flannel shirt and jeans. He was talking to one of the other detectives at a desk just outside Biddle's office.

Biddle turned to follow my gaze and shook his head. "Afraid you're on your own on this one, Barnaby. I can't spare any of my detectives. Scott's interested and he's going to make one hell of a detective, but he's as green as they come—only been on the job a week—so he'll have no spare time. As well as learning the ropes on the job on *current* cases," Biddle emphasized the word current, "he's got a fair number of training classes to attend."

"I understand," I said, still eyeing the young detective.

"Barnaby," Biddle said as he rose from the chair beside mine, "Scott's plate is full."

I smiled. "I heard you the first time, John." I had too much respect for Biddle to go behind his back to solicit the help of any of his detectives, but if Scott came to me....

CHAPTER 25.

There was a stack of call slips by the phone on my desk when I came in from what might have been an entirely frustrating day of running down leads on the jewel-theft case. But on my last call of the day, I hit pay dirt. Without a smidgen of guilt, I could now hand the job over to Jedediah. He was bright and not afraid of hard work, so the mop-up should be a snap.

Riffling though the pink call slips, I came across one from Tommy Morgan. Good, he was next on my list. As I fingered through the rest of the messages, I set those involving our routine business aside for Jedediah. At the bottom of the pile was a message to call Detective Scott.

I pondered that one for a beat, then picked up the phone and dialed the number Betty had jotted down. After four rings an electronic voice said, "This is Detective Scott, please leave a message." I hung up without leaving a message. If it was important he'd call back.

Reaching for the message with Morgan's name on it, I dialed that number. What I reached was the switchboard of Universal Enterprises. A recording clicked on, but as I was about to hang up, a live voice stopped my receiver's downward movement.

"The switchboard is closed, sir." I had no idea how she knew I was a sir, since I hadn't uttered a blooming word, but when I mentioned my name and said that I was returning Mr. Morgan's call, the voice said, "Just a moment, please." After a couple minutes, she said, "I'm terribly sorry, Mr. Jones, I can't locate Mr. Morgan at the moment, but if you'll leave your number, I'll see that he gets it."

Again as I was about to abort the call, the voice said, "Oh, here he is now."

"Glad I caught you," Morgan said. "We've just shot the wrap-up scene on *The True Story Behind the Legend of Lori London*. Are you available for a private viewing?" Without as much as a breath, he continued, "Say, an hour or so?"

"Wrap up?" I asked. I hadn't been prepared for such a rapid conclusion.

"Yeah, now that the filming is no longer a well-kept secret, I wanted to get it in the can as soon as possible and get the theater copies rolling."

Preparing myself for a blow-by-blow scenario of the day's shoot, I slid my bottom desk drawer out, swung my legs to the side, and rested my feet on the opened drawer. As Morgan spoke, I checked the time.

"Well," Morgan repeated, "do you think you can join us in the next hour or so?"

It was 4:45, a darn poor time for driving though the Hollywood traffic, but I said, "I can make it, but I just hope you're not planning your premiere real soon."

"The sooner the better," Morgan stated.

Not in a pig's eye, I thought, but said, "At least give me a few weeks to run down a few leads."

There was a void as silence that filled the air.

"We still have a few connecting scenes to film. Then it'll take a couple weeks to generate the kind of publicity we need to create the colossal premiere this film deserves, and maybe one more to get the film copied, in the cans, and released to hit as many theaters as possible simultaneously. But, Barnaby, I don't intend to sit on this. I've already let too many pages spin off the calendars."

"I'll take what I can get. But Tommy, remember we're on the same team, and I need to run a few things by you. If we pool our knowledge, we might be able to cut the time frame, and if we can get a bit of concrete evidence, it might ward off possible lawsuits."

"Sure, sure," Morgan said impatiently. "When can I expect you?"

"'Bout forty-five minutes," I said.

When I was off the phone, I retrieved my suit jacket from the coat tree, straightened my tie, and asked Betty, "When do you expect Jedediah?"

Looking up from the keyboard of her word processor, Betty said, "I'm not sure. He told me he'd be out in the field for the best part of the day."

I handed Betty the messages I'd sorted out for him and said, "I'm taking off for Universal Enterprises. Give these to Jedediah when he returns." Then a thought flashed to another lead. I needed to get a move on. "See what you can find out about arranging a visit at Pelican Bay Prison."

Her face paled as she asked, "You're not thinking of actually going there to see Terry McCormack, are you?"

"Just as soon as it can be arranged."

CHAPTER 26.

I'd been dead tired before my brief chat with Tommy Morgan and should have been thinking about heading home in a couple hours to hit the hay at a reasonable hour, but my compelling curiosity and renewed sense of urgency sent the adrenaline flowing and propelled me on to this impromptu meeting at Universal Enterprises.

My mind buzzed with possibilities as I made my way through Hollywood's late-afternoon traffic. I pulled into the studio lot, leaving the acrid smells of vehicle fumes well behind. A glance at my dashboard clock announced I'd made the journey in record time—under half an hour.

Stopping in front of the kiosk, I gave my name; and as the guard picked up his clipboard and fingered his way through a list of names, I took note of the activity around the kiosk. The dailies—the cans of exposed films and the sum of the day's work—were being assembled under the watchful eye of the security guard, and they would remain under his watchful eye beside his kiosk while awaiting pickup by the lab.

"Yes, Mr. Jones, Mr. Morgan is expecting you," the guard said, directing me to a parking area that he explained was beside Morgan's office. As the large rococo gate swung open, I hoped the directions weren't as complicated as they appeared to be and was relieved when I encountered no problem following them. Morgan's bungalow office was located on a small island in the center of the parking area. His red Ferrari stood out like a beacon. Pulling in beside the Ferrari, it dawned on me that the letters M-O-R-G-U-E might have more significance than I'd originally imagined. Perhaps they weren't chosen merely to represent Morgan and Universal Enterprises, but might have been chosen with a double meaning in mind. The full impact could be literal. Rather than an acronym, Morgan may have intentionally spelled out the word morgue, the place Lori London had been taken, where he'd been unable to follow. Shoving open the car door, I dropped that line of thinking. Fact or fiction, that knowledge would get me no closer to clearing Lori's name.

Although I hadn't been anywhere near this location in years, I'd read that this was the last remaining historical film site—the launching pad of the two-reel comedies that had made 'Old Hollywood' rich and famous.

I took my time, leisurely making my way to Morgan's office. The past seemed like yesterday as my thoughts journeyed back to the days of the silent movies. Though a bit before my time, my parents adored taking me to see all of the reruns that came to our neighborhood theater. Gazing at the modern soundstage to my right, I recalled laughing until my sides literally ached as I'd been carried into the world created by the masters of the silent film era. The luxurious swimming pool and playground of the stars, long since filled with sand, served as the foundation for the structure. As I paused beside the soundstage, I felt the spirits of Mabel Norman, Fatty Arbuckle, Charlie Chaplin, and Chester Conklin, and imagined them surrounded by romping bathing beauties in daring Janzen swimsuits down to their knees. I'd nearly forgotten the absence of sound, since the storylines in those movies of yesteryear had been crystal clear. Perhaps I was left with that impression because I was taken only to the comedies, but I don't really think so. The vivid expressions and motions of these stars of old told the whole story.

The studio lot had been modernized. But while the new moniker of Universal Enterprises was lettered boldly above the entry to the soundstage, its original name, Metropolitan, was still legible in certain light. It bled through in ghostly persistence, demanding to be remembered.

As I mounted the two wooden stairs and stepped into Morgan's office, I heard voices from the next room. Following the sound, I walked past a small kitchenette and into a comfortably furnished living area. Three young men were huddled around Morgan beside a closed door that probably led into some kind of inner office, a bedroom, or perhaps a combination of the two. It was not posh but highly adequate.

Morgan met me in a state of excitement. "This is Andre, Mr. Jones," he said, "my film editor, who's doing a tremendous job for us." Then with a short intake of breath, he said, "Wait till you see what we've done."

The young man he introduced was slim, of medium height, with piercing blue eyes, his light brown hair pulled back in a ponytail. He appeared to be in his early to mid-twenties. He was civil, but barely. Perhaps just reserved, yet it was clear he had other things on his mind and was just marking time till he could get back to more important matters—hardly out of character for a serious young film editor.

Morgan began introducing the others in the room with haste. "And my camera crew, Chris, Jon, and Dean," Morgan said.

Dean was the first to extend his hand. He was tall, slim, with well-formed muscles bulging from his white T-shirt. His dark hair was cropped reasonably short for the Hollywood scene.

"Nice to meet you, Mr. Jones," Dean said, his friendly brown eyes meeting mine.

Jon, the stocky, sandy-haired cameraman with serious, dark eyes was next. His hair hung past his shoulders, blending right into the tinsel town image. Chris, the slight lad with a slim, angular, boyish face and weary, hazel eyes beneath bushy eyebrows, was the last to step up and extend his hand. His light-brown hair, like that of the film editor's, was rubber-banded back into a ponytail. When his eyes met mine, I felt as if he were taking my measure and I'd come up short.

I hadn't noticed the other person in the room, who had been sitting in a swivel chair facing Morgan and his crew, until Morgan said her name and she rose from the chair.

"Dawn is our leading lady," Morgan added. When the young actress placed her petite hand in mine, it was cool and lanolin soft. She was attired in the current style of a young working actress. She might have been dismissed as typical because of her tawny mane; well-worn, form-fitting jeans; loafers; and men's extra-large shirt with the tails belted around her slim waist in a square knot with a piece of ordinary rope. But when I began to search beyond the surface, I found subtle differences. Her face, now scrubbed free of the day's professional makeup, was fresh and clean. The clear, unadorned blue of her eyes smiled and telegraphed an inner beauty and intelligence.

After Morgan completed the introductions, he excused himself to have a short conference with his film editor and camera crew. Dawn's expressive, wide blue eyes followed Morgan until the door closed behind him. Her gaze telegraphed total adoration, but politely she returned her gaze to mine.

"Dawn Medford," I mused. "I don't recall ever seeing you on the screen."

"You haven't, Mr. Jones," Dawn replied. "This is my first job in a motion picture."

"And you're playing the leading role? Congratulations."

"Thank you. Oh, I know. It's such a responsibility. I'm scared. And I'm so grateful to Mr. Morgan for the faith he has in me."

This young girl had a striking resemblance to Lori London, so it was not totally surprising that Morgan had chosen her, and yet he was taking a big chance in casting an unknown in the lead role of the riveting blockbuster he was out to produce. It might be natural to assume the two were lovers, since that's the way things worked in Hollywood. And yet, looking into the depths of Dawn's expressive blue eyes and fresh young face, I found I could believe otherwise. Morgan didn't seem nearly as taken with Dawn as she did with him. The adoration I'd seen in her vivid blue eyes was reminiscent of the gazes Nancy Reagan was known to bestow on her husband, even after Alzheimer's had shattered their lives. No one would ever doubt that they were soul mates.

*****

When Morgan returned from his conference and his film editor and camera crew had departed, his spirits were soaring. He crossed immediately to the refrigerator in the bar area of his office, extracted a bottle of champagne, and turned to face me.

"Would you forego milk for this one time and join Miss Medford and me in a little celebration?"

I smiled. "Of course."

Morgan expertly popped the cork and the champagne flowed. "I'd like to thank you, Mr. Jones," he began almost shyly. "Barnaby, if I may."

"By all means," I said as we raised our glasses to include Dawn in the toast.

"And I wish to apologize for my abruptness and inhospitality at our first meeting."

"No need," I said. "You had cause. I barged in." I took a sip of champagne. "Now, I am interested in knowing how you changed the story resolution?"

"I'll cut straight to the bottom line. Brief and simple, leaving out all the frills," Morgan said. "At the Hollywood Heritage masquerade party, a man masked as the devil drugs Lori's drink. She drives home alone, and passes out in the garage at the Montcreif Estate with the motor running and spewing carbon monoxide. No one knows the identity of the man last seen with her in the devil costume, who has now disappeared."

Morgan stopped talking and looked up for approval.

I took another sip of champagne. "Is that it?"

"Yes, what do you think?"

"I never liked that blasted Hollywood Heritage party Montcreif created for the fictionalized night of Lori's death," I answered, "and hadn't expected you to keep it in your movie version." It was one whale of an understatement, but Morgan glossed right over my vehement objection to the use of the Heritage party.

"I don't intend to run with my original plan. I won't actually point the finger directly at Montcreif. Dawn," he nodded in her direction, "who's starring in her first major roll as Lori London, wasn't comfortable with my initial rewrite of Montcreif's ending."

"No," Dawn confirmed. "It could spell big trouble. Not for me, but for Tommy. I just don't see why he has to take that risk."

"At least my movie version leaves Lori London's murder a foregone conclusion. In audience appeal, that's a giant step up from suicide."

"And you're happy with that?"

"Not exactly, but I can live with a classic murder mystery. Besides, judging by all the attempts to sabotage the release of a version of Lori's death ending with murder, this film has a great chance of flushing out the truth."

"Won't the audience expect a resolution?"

"Sure," Morgan said, a wide smile showing off his pearly white teeth. "That in itself is in my denouement."

"Come again? I'm not following."

"The penultimate scene will show how Lori's murder was set-up. From there we'll pan in to Gregory Shepard for the final scene...."

Raising a brow, I repeated, "Gregory Shepard?"

We considered Dick Van Dyke, Harrison Ford, and a few other big stars for the finale`. Shepard was actually our second choice. I'd have given my firstborn child to get Dick Van Dyke. It would have been a perfect tie-in with his *Diagnosis Murder*, but he's out of the country. We're thrilled to have Shepard. I know he can handle the dynamite ending we have in mind."

I knew Gregory Shepard was a superstar and had won an Academy Award a couple of years back. I wanted to ask Morgan what in tarnation he had to do with the film, but knew he'd get around to it, so waited him out.

"Can't wait for you to see what we shot these last few days."

I cleared my throat, "And your big finale`?"

"Oh yeah. Shepard will announce a plea to the audience, asking them to sign on as amateur detectives in solving this eighteen-year-old murder. I forget just how we scripted this part, but it ties in with an offer of a hundred-thousand-dollar reward for any concrete evidence leading to the capture of the murderer. And one million dollars to whoever actually tracks down the killer of Lori London."

As I mulled this over, I nursed more than a vague sense of disappointment at Morgan's choice of the trumped-up story ending and just what kind of havoc this sort of challenge to the general public might bring about. "It's your movie, Tommy, but I don't think this costume-party version will wash. I know it was in the novel Nigel Montcreif fabricated. I also realize that shooting something like a Hollywood Heritage-type party in a posh setting, with Lori London mingling with guests masked as Hollywood stars the likes of Charlie Chaplin, Gloria Swanson, Clark Gable, Marilyn Monroe, and an entire array of the motion-picture greats, might add excitement, color, and a true theatrical bent—but I don't like it. There's been a barrelful of newspaper articles telling of Lori's true whereabouts before her death. You mess around with the known facts and the public won't buy your movie as anything but fiction."

I didn't need to mention that Lori was alone for the greater part of the evening at the Hilltop Café in Santa Monica, not at a costume ball, prior to being found in her white Cadillac in the garage of Montcreif's Venice Estate. And as far as the audience challenge, that could be like opening Pandora's box. I had no idea how many wannabe vigilantes might be in the audiences.

Before Morgan had an opportunity to respond, our attention was grabbed by the high-pitched wailing sounds of a fire engine close by. Morgan shot to the window in time to see two more arriving. The deep-throated engines and the wail of sirens made their presence impossible to ignore.

"Hey, that's us," he announced, and ran for the door. Close on his heels, I was hit with the acrid smell of smoke the second Morgan threw the door open. Smoke billowed beside the guard's kiosk at the studio gate. As we sprinted toward the kiosk, I could taste the gritty flavor of charcoal, and my eyes burned as firemen with CO_2 extinguishers sprayed the flames—the flames engulfing the entire stack of film cans.

"I called 911," the security guard called out to Morgan. "You weren't picking up your phones and I wasn't able to leave my post to give you a head's-up."

"That's today's stuff burning!" Morgan howled in dismay. "Who the hell would do a thing like this?"

A fireman picked up one of the film cans with gloved hands. As he opened the can, the ruined contents spilled out onto the ground.

I stood, silent and thoughtful, then stated the obvious. "Someone who doesn't want this picture made, at least not with the ending you've filmed. Maybe not with any ending that indicates anything other than a clear-cut case of suicide, as spelled out in Montcreif's novel."

CHAPTER 27.

After the firemen and arson squad left, Morgan looked as if he'd aged a decade. Too devastated to talk about the evening's trauma or carry on any semblance of sensible conversation, he headed to his office to mourn his loss.

Dawn Medford, her vivid blue eyes filled with tears, stood just outside the door. She wrapped an arm around his waist and was about to close the door behind them, when I called out, "Mind if I look around?" I received a mumbled response before the door closed which I took for a yes and set off for the soundstage.

Earlier, before the arson detectives arrived, I'd gathered up a sufficient sample of ashes among the ravaged tin cans beside the guard shack and placed them in one of the plastic evidence bags that I always kept handy in my inside coat pocket. Everything else worthwhile in that area had been gathered up and carted away by the arson detectives from the Hollywood Precinct. I hadn't known a single one of them, but intended to follow up the next day.

I began a purposeful stroll through the night-shrouded lot and into the deserted studio. As I traveled along one of the studio's shadowy streets, a weathered papier-mâché dinosaur, probably a relic of some science-fiction epic, came into view. I stepped back in startled surprise.

I halted for a second or two, wondering if I also hadn't heard something. I cautiously stepped forward but I found nothing other than the ordinary soundstage paraphernalia, so retraced my steps, and then tried the door to another soundstage. It swung open.

Inside the empty soundstage, my footsteps made ghostly echoes as I walked toward center stage. I looked up and around, my gaze sweeping the deserted catwalk grid and underscoring my solitude. Still I saw nothing, but felt a presence. Some instinct told me I was not alone.

A noise from behind whipped me around in time to see an enormous arc light coming straight for my head. The monster arc light, the type known in the trade as the "brute," now dislodged from the catwalk, swung precariously, suspended by its own cable. Then the cable snapped, sending the light careening toward me.

I hit the deck. The light, picking up speed, passed above and barely missed me, then crashed to the floor. It set off a shower of glass and sparks. From overhead there came the sound of pounding feet.

Quickly rising, my .38-caliber Smith & Wesson in hand, I saw no target but moved toward the wall ladder.

I slipped the pistol into my waistband, climbed to the catwalk, and tread quietly toward the location in which I'd heard the running footsteps.

I raced toward the open roof-access hatch, and pulled myself up. The roof was deserted. I moved cautiously toward the sloping edge and looked down in time to see a shadowy figure descend the last rungs of the outside ladder and run toward a parked car.

I started to follow, changed my mind, drew my gun, and took direct aim at a back tire, but was a bit too late. Burning rubber, the car disappeared, leaving a trail of acrid smoke. I was winded and more than a mite frustrated in the cold night air.

CHAPTER 28.

Tommy Morgan paced the floor of the modest reception area of his studio office, his gut tied in knots, and talking under his breath. He'd been at it ever since Barney and the film crew departed. He'd paused only to pour himself a drink.

Dawn sat huddled on the sofa, wondering if he even knew she was there. What she did know was that until the Lori London film was completed, in the cans, and distributed nationwide, she might as well be made of cellophane. But, far from discouraged, she had the tenacity to wait. Tommy would one day get over his obsession with the murdered actress. She'd been excited when he cast her in the role of the woman he still called his soul mate, but it was time he moved on. She needed him to notice her—really notice her.

She would never settle for being a mere shadow of Lori London for the man she had grown to love over these past few months. Far from being spoiled by the size of his inheritance, Tommy Morgan was the kindest, most sensitive man she'd ever known. His handsome good looks and intelligence were a bonus and she was willing to wait. He was a man worth the wait, but only if he was able to move past this eighteen-year obsession and notice her for herself, Dawn Medford.

Pulling the afghan up to her neck, she ran a hand though her hair. She must look a sight: no makeup, tear-stained cheeks, and most likely red-rimmed eyes. But what did it matter? Tommy didn't even look her way; she might as well be invisible.

She rose from the sofa and padded over to his side. "Tommy, I think I'll turn in. It seems you could use some time on your own," she said, painting an upbeat smile on her face.

"Sure, kid," he said as he turned and gave her a halfhearted hug.

"I can be back first thing in the morning," Dawn said. "I haven't forgotten a single line. We can begin reshooting—"

"No need to come to the studio tomorrow morning. Not sure just where to start. I'll give you a call." Tommy gave her a smile that didn't quite reach his eyes. "Sorry to be such rotten company. Take the morning off, catch up on whatever personal business you have, but keep your cell phone on. That bast—Sorry. No arsonist is going to shut us down. We've got a story that must be told and we're going to tell it. This is a real setback, but not the end. If anything, I'm even more determined to see that the true story is told." He paused, took hold of Dawn's arms at the elbows, and looked straight into her eyes. "Baby, I'm going to rewrite the ending. Can you be flexible?"

Dawn nodded, her heart beating so wildly she couldn't trust herself to speak. If only she'd had a chance to tell Tommy about the note of warning she'd found on her dressing-room table just before coming to his studio office this afternoon. But it would have to wait. Tommy had enough on his mind; she wouldn't add any further worry to his troubled mind.

Standing on tiptoes, she kissed his cheek, said good night, and headed for the door.

She opened the door. The business card on the end table caught her attention. It read *Barnaby Jones Investigations*. She glanced back at Tommy, who was pouring himself another drink, and pocketed the card.

CHAPTER 29.

On my drive home I made a mental note to fill Morgan in on the studio drama first thing in the morning. I pressed the button on my garage-door opener and drove straight in, acutely aware of the silence. I shifted the car into park, turned off ignition, slid out of the car, and mounted the two concrete steps from the garage to the kitchen of my suburban home. Flipping on the light, I strode directly to my bedroom, slipped off my suit jacket, and heaved an exhausted sigh. Boy was I glad to be back in my own quiet home after the eventful evening at Universal Enterprises. Whoever had been in the studio and behind that well-orchestrated accident meant to get me out of the way permanently. It was no more an accident than the destruction of the film was. If Montcreif somehow was alive and behind tonight's vandalism, he had either an accomplice or a hired hand. A man in his nineties would not have the agility for tonight's shenanigans up on the catwalk.

I whipped through my nighttime routines and slipped into bed knowing I was bound to nod right off to sleep. I'd had a particularly trying week and needed a good six or seven hours of sleep to get back up to par. And sure enough, the minute my drowsy head hit the pillow I was out like a candle with no remaining wick. But after a blink—two hours would be closer to the truth—I found myself wide awake. Reaching out to my bedside clock, I flipped on the light and saw that it was only 2:45 a.m. Too darn early to crawl out of bed.

After another hour or so of tossing and turning, I gave in. There would be no sleep for these tired old bones until I could clear my mind. No point in lying in bed worrying. Best to get up and put it to rest. There were too many dang-gum areas to pursue to remain idle. The familiar refrain, "Don't lie there and stew. Get up and do," rang through my head as I swung my long legs over the side of the bed and pulled on a robe, the vivid blue one that Betty claimed just jumped out at her because it reminded her of the sparkle in these tired blue eyes of mine. I smiled as I tied the sash around my waist. That girl did have a way with words and a fair amount of blarney. But where were my slippers? I looked under the bed then padded across the carpet and finally found them on the closet floor. Sliding my size thirteens into the slippers, I went in search of a pad of paper and pencil, flipped on the hall light, and turned up the heat on the wall thermostat; then continued down the hallway to the kitchen. After finding a pencil and well-used yellow pad in the cluttered drawer to the left of the sink, I tossed them on the kitchen counter and set about filling a mug from the "Instant Boiling Water" gizmo that Jedediah had installed this past Christmas, as a gift.

As I closed the refrigerator door and was carrying the hot mug and lemon to the counter, the phone shrilled. Glancing up at the clock, I wondered who'd be calling at this hour. It must be important, so I leaned over and whisked the receiver off the hook.

"Barnaby, Tommy Morgan here."

"Yes," I said. No point telling him it wasn't even five a.m.

With no preamble, he said, "You were right."

Right about what? I wondered, but was sure he was about to tell me.

"I thought about it all night. I don't know who is trying to sabotage my film. No, dammit, I do. I just can't prove it."

I listened, knowing he'd get to the point sooner or later.

"Maybe it was providence that our masquerade party ending went up in smoke. You were right on when you said I should stay true to what the public already knows about Lori's whereabouts on the night of her murder." His voice rose as he enunciated the word murder. "And I plan to lay it on the line that Montcreif was the murderer."

"Now, Tommy, hold on. I never said you should go that far. What I said was that Lori's final night should be at the Hilltop Café, but actually accusing Montcreif could still land you in a heap of trouble, with the potential of a big fat lawsuit."

"I don't give a damn, and Dawn has agreed to go along with the new ending."

Again Morgan had my mind spinning. I'd left him less than seven hours ago. "Are you telling me you've already rewritten the new ending?"

"Not on paper. But I've outlined what we need to do and I know just how it will play out. The actual script writing is a no-brainer. I could even do it myself, but I plan to give it to the writer I've got under contract. But this time, he won't come up with any cockamamie ideas of his own. *The True Story Behind the Legend of Lori London* will be played my way on this final shoot."

"It's your movie, and you're the one who will take the heat, so I won't offer my advice. It sure would do my heart good to see Lori's name cleared. I just wish we had a single chicken scratch of evidence. Lori was religious in her own way and that suicide label has always stuck in my craw. But—"

I heard Morgan's baritone laugh on the other end of the line. "I was waiting for the B-U-T."

"Can we work together?" I asked.

"Sure. As you said, we're on the same team."

Before outlining my needs, I filled Morgan in on the events of the night before and alerted him to expect detectives on the studio premises as soon as I reported the incident.

"I'd like to get a few things from you and from that PI firm you had on retainer."

"Whatever you want," Morgan said amiably.

I slid the barstool out, mounted it, picked up my pencil and yellow pad, and wrote as I ticked off what I needed, beginning with the name and address of the literary agent from which he'd purchased the movie rights.

"Barnaby, we're not going to get in a pissing contest over sticking to the damn contract, are we?" Without leaving space for a response, he said, "I'm not negotiating; I'm producing and directing this film the way it should be. I don't give a tinker's damn about what Montcreif wants or wanted."

"Hold on, young fella," I interjected. "I told you it's your movie; I'm not telling you how to end it. But it sure won't hurt either of us to find out as much as we can about this Montcreif trust and who runs it now."

"Okay, but I sure hope this doesn't come back to bite me in the butt," Morgan said. "The agent's name is Tanya Guttenberg." He took a couple of seconds, and I could hear a drawer slam shut and the sound of something like Rolodex cards being shuffled. He gave me the address and phone number, then asked, "What else?"

I continued with the laundry list of information I needed from him and his former PI firm. My list included information on the house where Lori died. Was it still in the Montcreif trust or had it been sold? If sold, to whom? I also wanted to know if the whereabouts of Lori's 1986 white Cadillac were known, and if Morgan's former PI firm might be able to assist me in picking up the thread. I needed to know what had happened to Lori and Montcreif's son.

Noting Morgan's dwindling interest, I left him with just those major concerns I intended to pursue. Morgan had to be every bit as sleep-deprived as I was, so I said good-bye and we promised to keep in touch.

As I set the receiver back in the cradle, I slipped a slice of bread into the toaster and took a sip of my now-lukewarm water and lemon. I glanced over my list as the toast popped up. Buttering the toast, I put my mind to sorting out the few priorities I hadn't listed while on the phone with Morgan. I took a bite of toast and a sip of warm water, then wrote:

—check out ash samples

—Biddle on last night's arson

—Find a way to get into Pelican Bay to talk with Terry McCormack

—Who he dealt with from the Montcreif trust

—Montcreif's motive behind the financing of McCormack's campaign

Ripping off the top page from the yellow pad, I tossed the pencil and pad back in the kitchen drawer, finished my toast and tepid water, rinsed the plate and mug and left them in the sink to drain, and headed for the shower.

CHAPTER 30.

I opened my office door around a quarter to nine to the gurgle of the percolating Mr. Coffee machine and the hearty aroma of strong Colombian java. Apparently my seven a.m. wake-up bark had fired up the troops.

"Good morning, Barnaby," Betty chirped as she took something out from the small refrigerator in the pantry. Jedediah was already at his desk with case files spread across the surface of his work table like a tablecloth. He appeared freshly scrubbed and raring to go, but with a slightly quizzical tilt to his head as he looked up and greeted me.

I seldom held what you'd call a formal staff meeting, but I had a half-dozen loose ends, along with our routine case load that had to be kept on track.

As I shrugged out of my sports coat, Betty walked into my office with her notepad and an uncharacteristic frown.

"Can't be that bad," I said, trying to lighten her mood.

"Well, just let me tell you. You have no idea what I've been up against. Trying to arrange that visit to Pelican Bay is no easier than arranging to take the next Space Shuttle to the moon. I'm getting no clear answers about how you—"

"Security pretty tight?" I said, realizing that had to be one whale of an understatement considering all the controversy I'd read about. Pelican Bay was the premier maximum-security prison in the state of California. Super tough on the inmates and equally tough on the guards and staff. And yet I was bound and determined to find a way to find out what McCormack knew. I wanted to get any information I could that might prove Nigel Montcreif had not died at sea in 1987. If he'd faked that misadventure at sea, it would be a step up in placing him at Lori's death scene and not at sea the previous year.

"More than tight, Barnaby," Betty said with an unmistakable tone of exasperation. "I've spent half a day going in circles and talking to machines. I even broke down and asked J. R. to pull up whatever information he could find on that Web he's always logged on to." She picked up an inch-high stack of printouts on Pelican Bay. "I know more about that correctional facility than I ever wanted to know, just not how you can possibly get in to talk to an inmate—even a prisoner who might want to talk to you!"

I scowled. It couldn't be that impossible. "I know it's in Northern California, but just where?"

Betty glanced down at her notes. "Two hundred seventy-five acres in the northwest corner of California. It's designed to house our state's most serious criminal offenders. About 2,550 inmates at various levels of security; some of the worst never see the light of day, and staff outnumbers—"

"Betty, I appreciate all the work you've put into this, but I don't need a rundown of the place, just the location. What's it near?"

Betty shrugged her shoulders. "It's in a place called Crescent City, wherever that is." She started shuffling through her stack of papers. "I think there's a map in here somewhere."

"Never mind. Let's take it one step at a time," I said. "Just find out how I can set up an appointment."

"Haven't you been listening? That's what I've been trying to do. I have the phone number, but haven't been able to talk to a single live human. I just got shuffled from one electronic voice to the next. I have no idea how anyone gets in without breaking the law." Most likely observing what must have been a look of total exasperation on my face, Betty went on. "Just hear me out, Barnaby. I've spent a lot of time on this, and what I did find out is that visiting days are only on Saturdays and Sundays and some major holidays, between the hours of 9:00 a.m. and 3:00 p.m."

"Well, that's more like it," I said as I slipped into my desk chair. "I was beginning—"

"Hold it," Betty said, "I'm not through." Again, she referred to her notes. "You need to have an appointment at least twenty-four hours in advance and can stay no more than two hours."

"Piece of cake. I sure don't need more time than that," I said, beginning to relax.

Betty tossed the papers on my desk in an uncharacteristic flare of temper. "Barnaby, will you please let me finish. In order to be granted a visit, the prisoner has to fill out a request form." She stood glaring at me, her hands on her hips.

That piece of news burst my bubble in a heartbeat. I leaned forward, resting my elbows on my desk, "Well, that'll be tough." I paused, trying to crank out a bit of logic. "There's got to be some way around that." I paused again; the gray cells were dulled from lack of sleep. A few scenarios buzzed through my head. An attorney would need a way to talk to his client if he were planning an appeal. I aborted that line of thought, realizing that it was going nowhere. Obviously, the prisoner would want to talk to his attorney, so he'd fill out the paperwork. Then my mind traveled to the prosecutor; he'd have to have a way....

"Barnaby," Betty raised her voice, bringing me back to the here and now.

"Sorry, my brain was moseying down the road of possibilities, but let's forget about that for now. I'll think it through and see what I can come up with. But now it's time we have a little powwow on how we'll get through the next few weeks."

Betty and Jedediah pulled up chairs beside my desk, but before we had a chance to begin our brief meeting, the phone rang.

Betty picked it up and looked at Jedediah. "It's Emily," Betty said, covering the mouthpiece. "Would you like me to tell her you'll call her back?"

"Sure," Jedediah said, his youthful face turning scarlet. It was only natural for a young man his age to be interested in the young ladies, so I wasn't sure why he always blushed when one of his girlfriends called when I was around. He seemed to change girlfriends as often as he changed his shirt, but he sure wasn't shy about telling me about some hot date if he had to take off early or got to work a bit late. Maybe he just didn't like being caught with one of the ladies barging into his workday when I was within earshot.

Betty hung up the phone and we quickly got down to business. When we finished our update, my two associates immediately returned to their own desks and were quickly engrossed with their own priorities.

I retrieved the evidence bag containing the ashes I'd collected the previous night from inside my suit jacket pocket and took it into my lab. Slipping into my lab coat, I began the preparation for determining the specific combustion initiator.

Betty and Jedediah had left hours earlier, and by the time I slipped off my lab coat, scooped the ash sample back into the plastic envelope, and returned to my office, the only trace of light outside my office was artificial. I must have taken more time in the lab than I thought.

Time to call it a day. I'd call Biddle first thing Monday morning and compare my lab results with those of the arson squad.

Looking around my now-deserted office, I decided to give myself a much-needed day off. Although, I'd like to go full steam ahead, I knew my brain was stuck in a circular path. To remedy this, I needed time to unwind—time to review all I now knew about the death of Lori London and figure out my next step. I had to unclutter my busy mind and get some uninterrupted time, and I knew there was only one way to get it. No point in taking anything home other than my fishing pole, which was in the supply cabinet in the lab. I took the pole and my tackle box out, planning for a relaxing day of fishing. Tomorrow I planned to fish for those wiggly little critters and give my fishing for leads a one-day vacation. I headed for the supply cupboard, confident that a few hours on the lake was just what I needed to unclog and renew the ol' thinking machine.

Pole and tackle box in one hand, I flipped off my desk light and the wall switch with the other and headed into the reception area.

Setting the pole and tackle box on Betty's orderly desk, I pulled my sports coat from the mahogany coat tree, slipped it on, and was about to pick up my gear and turn off the lights in the outer office, when the phone began to ring.

CHAPTER 31.

I stood staring at the ringing phone, wondering who'd be calling my office on a Saturday evening. Reluctantly, my curiosity taking control over my better judgment, I picked up the receiver.

"Barnaby Jones Investigations."

"Mr. Jones?" a soft, hesitant voice asked.

"Yes," I said, trying to place the female voice.

"This is Dawn Medford," she said, then needlessly added, "I met you last night in Tommy Morgan's office. I'm the one who's playing the part of Lori London."

"Hello, Miss Medford. How can I help you?"

"Well, Mr. Jones, I meant to call you first thing this morning, but Tommy called the cast and crew together to go over plans for completing the film." She broke off, leaving a long stretch of silence.

I didn't fill it.

After a bit, she said, "Mr. Jones, I know it's late, and it's the weekend, but I'd really like to talk to you as soon as you can find the time." Her voice was shaky and lacked the effervescent self-confidence she'd displayed when we first met.

I looked at my wristwatch. It was nearly eight and I hadn't eaten since breakfast. I didn't ask the young actress what she wanted to see me about, sensing she wasn't comfortable discussing whatever it was over the phone. "Are you at the studio, Miss Medford?"

"Please, call me Dawn," she said, then answered my question. "No, I'm at my apartment. It's only a few blocks from the studio."

"Well, Dawn, I'm hungry as a bear out of tourist season, so how about meeting me for a bite to eat while you tell me what's on your mind."

"Are you sure this isn't too much to ask of you on a weekend?"

"Are you familiar with the Formosa Café?"

"Oh, sure. It's that red building on Santa Monica Boulevard. Tommy takes the cast there a lot since it's so close to the studio."

"Can you meet me there in about half-hour?"

After returning the phone to the cradle, I looked down at my fishing pole and tackle box, and headed for the door. I wondered what Dawn Medford had on her mind and how it tied into the Lori London film, all the time knowing that somehow it must be related. But why hadn't she at least given me a hint? Perhaps she truly had taken on Lori's characteristics

******

I'd taken a few minutes to freshen up at the office and thought I'd arrived before Dawn, but found she'd already been seated at a table off to the side.

Dawn's face appeared pale and drawn. Even in the dimly lit café, I could see she was more than a little rattled. I approached the table and noticed her expressive blue eyes were pooled with tears and her long lashes were damp. She looked like such a vulnerable young kid, I felt like giving her a fatherly hug but resisted.

"Good evening, Dawn," I said. "Sorry I wasn't here when you arrived."

"Oh, that's all right. I just live a few blocks from here. I'm just glad you could see me tonight."

Before I could respond, a waiter appeared, asking if we'd like anything to drink.

"Perrier," Dawn said, looking toward me.

"I'll have the same," I said. I'd already had my quota of milk for the day.

When the waiter departed, I asked, "Would you like to tell me what's on your mind?"

She looked down and fumbled around in her handbag. In a moment or so she pulled out a folded piece of paper and handed it to me.

"Mr. Jones—"

"Barnaby," I corrected.

Dawn blushed and said, "Thank you, Barnaby. I haven't told Tommy about this. Before last night he was the first person I wanted to tell, but after the fire I didn't have the heart to bring him anymore grief."

I unfolded the paper and looked up to see Dawn's anxious eyes.

On an unlined piece of notebook paper, letters had been cut out of colored newsprint, most likely from the Sunday comic strips. The letters were all capitals and looked as if the sender had used a stencil, as there were no random sizes. The note read:

YOU WERE CAST AS LORI LONDON

BECAUSE OF YOUR LOOKS.

A TRAGIC SUICIDE IS ONE THAT CAN

MAKE YOU A STAR.

PORTRAYING HER DEATH AS ANYTHING

BUT SUICIDE

MAY RESULT IN YOUR OWN EARLY

DEATH.

There was no need to ask Dawn if she'd been careful about fingerprints. By the way I'd seen her fumbling around in her handbag, it was obvious fingerprints had been the last thing on her mind. Still, I picked up a napkin and smoothed out the colorful warning. No point in adding another set of prints.

"When did you receive this?" I asked.

"Yesterday, just before I went into Tommy's office and met you. I was going to show it to Tommy right away, but wanted to wait till we were alone. I thought it was probably one of those sick jokes. But after the fire last night—"

"You began to take it more seriously," I suggested. "When and where was this delivered?" I nodded in the direction of the note, which I spread on the tabletop.

"It was on my dressing room table about 4:30, after we viewed the last scene."

"Who has access to your dressing room?"

"Well, I guess just about anyone on the lot," Dawn said, "since I never lock the door. I mean I never did before."

"Do you have any suspicions about who might have done this?" Again I indicated the technicolor note. Someone had gone to a lot of trouble cutting out all those individual small letters.

Dawn shook her head.

"How strict is the security on the lot?"

"It's real tight. My sister stopped by last week so she could take me to lunch, but they wouldn't let her drive in till I came out to the guard's kiosk and put her name on the list."

"Then your guess would be the note was written by someone in the cast or on the crew."

"Now, I wouldn't want to say that."

"No one stands out as being somewhat out of tune with Tommy Morgan's vision for this movie?"

"Well, not exactly."

Dawn twisted her napkin, her eyes not meeting mine.

"Dawn, you must be totally candid with me if you expect me to help you."

"I know," she said. "I just don't want to start any trouble."

"I don't want to frighten you any more than you already are, but I'm not taking this warning as some sort of joke. Nobody goes to all this trouble for a joke. It had to have taken more than an hour to cut out all those letters.

"Now help me out a little. Nothing you tell me will go any further other than this old information bank." I tapped my head.

Dawn's mouth turned up in a stoic smile. "Well, we're all working very hard to make this a memorable movie...."

Dawn continued to tell me of all the hard work everyone was putting in and how difficult it had been, when I felt I had to cut in. "What you were going to tell me about was if you noticed anyone who seemed unhappy about the way the film was headed."

"Oh, sure. I guess I'm just a little nervous about saying anything that could be taken wrong."

"Dawn, please just give me your perception. That's the only way I'll find out whose behind this note."

CHAPTER 32.

"I'm sorry, Barnaby. I'm not trying to be difficult."

"I'm sure you're not," I said. "You were probably brought up a lot like me and learned from the time you were a tadpole not to say anything about a person unless you could say something nice. But sometimes in life, we run up against someone who doesn't play by the rules."

Dawn gave me a bright smile, showing perfectly straight white teeth. The tension seemed to have melted from her body, and a smile reflected in the blue of her eyes. "It may just be my imagination but I've been noticing the way Andre—" She looked up, as if she wanted to make sure I could place the young man before continuing.

"Yes," I said. "We met last night. Not what I'd call a real friendly type."

The waiter arrived, temporarily halting our conversation. I already knew what I wanted, but Dawn hadn't even looked at the menu. I was about to ask the waiter to give us a few minutes when Dawn looked up at him and said, "I'd like the Caesar salad."

"Yes, Miss Medford. You'd like that as your entrée?"

She nodded, then added, "No bread."

I needn't have worried; it was obvious Dawn had been here many times before.

Dawn picked up just where we left off. "Tommy thinks Andre is brilliant, and I suppose he is very good at his job. But it's his attitude that bothers me. I guess you could say it's more of a feeling than anything specific. He nods and seems on track when he's with Tommy, but as soon as Tommy turns his back he seems to show his true colors."

"Can you give me an example?"

"As I said, it's nothing specific, but I'm pretty good at reading body language. I guess all actors are. Out of Tommy's sight, Andre's tells me he thinks Tommy is way off track, and the expression on his face seems to mirror his disapproval."

"Body language and facial expression can be a fairly good barometer of what someone's thinking. Are there any signs that he won't be editing the film the way Morgan sees it?"

"Well, no. We'd gone through the rushes of Friday's shoot and they were terrific. I'm probably wrong, but he sort of gives me the creeps. Those eyes of his are cold and seem to look right through you."

"How about the others?"

"I don't know the entire cast, since some of their scenes are shot separately. The one I've gotten to know best is Charles Stafford. He plays the part of Nigel Montcreif and he's marvelous. He's strikingly good looking." She paused, and with a mischievous grin, she said, "If Montcreif were that good looking, I could see how Lori fell for him. But I've seen pictures of Montcreif, and he's nothing to write home about. Anyway, Charles is wonderful; he's warm and funny, and yet when he's in the role of Nigel Montcreif, he comes across like a mean old bastard." Dawn's skin turned a blush red from the base of her throat to her temples. "Sorry. You must think I'm terribly vulgar. Honestly, I hardly ever swear. I'm afraid that was Lori London talking."

I chuckled. "Yes, she did pick up some rather colorful language during her journey through Tinseltown. And I'm afraid Montcreif was responsible for much of her unladylike verbiage." I paused, then asked, "How about the crew that was on the lot last night?"

"Other than Andre, there were only the three guys on the camera crew, and the guards."

"Any questionable body language?"

Dawn's brow knit in a mock frown above dancing eyes. "You wouldn't be making fun of me, now would you, Barnaby?"

I held my hands up in surrender. "Not at all. I buy into those body-language readings. I also detected a bit of what you were describing. Last night when he was introduced, he neither extended a hand nor said a single word. He merely nodded his head, but I've noticed that sometimes these young film editors get so into the job at hand that they barely tolerate an interruption of any kind."

"That's Andre. But Ben, the good-looking cameraman with the short dark hair, is great. He's polite as they come and isn't into that obnoxious ogling. Jon's okay, too, but a bit of a flirt. He's the one with the long blond hair and seems to think he's God's gift." She paused to see that I was tracking. "Then there's Chris. He's a bit strange but seems to get the job done."

"Is he the other fellow with the ponytail?"

"Yes, Chris and Andre wear their hair back in ponytails, but Chris was left out when the good looks were passed out, and I think he knows it. Beneath those busy brows, his eyes are so deep-set it's hard to read what's on his mind."

"How about the guards?"

Dawn let me know she had only a passing acquaintance with most of them, but told me what she could.

"So do you have any idea if any of the people we've discussed could have been responsible for this missive?" I asked, indicating the warning note that was folded on the napkin beside my plate.

"No, I don't. Do you think whoever left this would actually—"

"Have murder on his mind?" I finished her thought. "Dawn, I don't rightly know. But we can't take this lightly. We'll be checking out everyone who was on the lot at the time of the fire, and since that warning arrived a couple hours before the fire, we'll be widening the time frame."

"Didn't you and the police talk to everyone last night?" she asked.

"Just a handful. But we'll follow through with everyone who passed through the gate for the entire day."

"Barnaby." Dawn's voice was tentative as she asked, "You know Tommy has no intention of filming a suicide."

I nodded. "That's exactly why you must not keep this from him." Leaving no pause for an objection, I said, "We'll stop by my office and make a copy for him. I doubt that I'll get any good prints, but I want to give it my best shot."

CHAPTER 33.

Monday morning rolled around none too soon. On Sunday, I'd caught up on some personal business, working till almost three a.m. When I fell into bed, my brain refused to shut down. It continued working overtime, and I only dozed for the first few hours, falling into a dead slumber somewhere around six or so. I'd planned to roll into the office by eight, but missed that mark by over an hour.

After greeting Betty and Jedediah, I poured myself a glass of milk and headed for my desk.

I was reaching for the phone to call Lieutenant Biddle, when I saw the new crop of pink call slips on my desk.

Shuffling through the call slips, I saw Tommy Morgan had called the office, and so had Detective Scott. I went no further. Picking up the phone I dialed the detective's number, was transferred to Robbery, and after a brief delay Scott came on the line.

"This is Barnaby Jones," I said, waiting for him to take it from there.

He told me of his interest in the case and how he'd already filled in a lot of holes in his knowledge of the Lori London death scene. He spoke with such enthusiasm that I found if difficult to cut in, but felt obliged to lay out the obstacles for him.

"I appreciate your interest, Detective, but Lieutenant Biddle made it clear that you had no time to assist."

"It wouldn't be on the LAPD's time, it would be on my own. My curiosity is piqued, and I'm raring to dig in."

"And you've got spare time on your hands?" I asked, somewhat amused by the young detective's eagerness.

"Well," Scott said, "I don't require much sleep and—"

"Hold it. I could use some law-enforcement help, but you'll have to clear it through Lieutenant Biddle. He seems to think you have a pretty full plate. In fact, he told me it was plumb full."

"I'll touch base with the lieutenant right away," Scott said. We wrapped up our conversation a moment or two later.

Before severing the connection, I asked if he'd mind transferring me to Lieutenant Biddle's office.

"Sure," he responded.

To make sure there was no misunderstanding, I said, "I'm not going to discuss your possible involvement on the case with Lieutenant Biddle. That's up to you."

When my call was transferred, I remained true to my word, not even mentioning Scott's name.

*****

An hour or so after our phone conversation, I met Biddle in his office. He was in uniform as he ushered me into his office. He lost no time in bringing me up-to-date on the investigation into the arson at Universal Enterprise. Their lab's result mirrored mine. The fire was done by an amateur. The film cans were doused in kerosene and ignited with a wooden matchstick.

I filled Biddle in on my encounter with the monster "brute" light after the detectives had taken off.

"Did you report this right away?" Biddle asked.

"No, I was too dang tired." And before Biddle had a chance to cut me off I continued, "The assailant sped off in a dark-colored coupe with the headlights off. Wasn't able to get the license number," I said. "And it was too dark to even get a make on the car." Again, before he could ask, I added, "It was dark, and I didn't get a good enough look at the guy to give a description worth a nickel in a dime store," then added, "Betty faxed a report on the incident to your precinct first thing this morning." Shifting focus, I asked, "You have any leads on the identity of the arsonist?"

"Other than the fact that we're not dealing with a professional, we haven't got much, but our arson unit is working on it," Biddle responded. "The guard at the studio gate that night swears no outsider could have gotten by him. The only ones on the lot for the entire day either worked at the studio or their names were on his security clearance list. We're checking out all the visitors as well as those who work on the premises." He paused and said with a smile in his voice as well as a twinkle in his eye, "According to the guard, you were the last one to be admitted on the premises before the fire broke out."

Not bothering to comment, I said, "Are you leaning toward an inside job?" It was a rhetorical question. It would have been hard for anyone to slip past the guard. Not room enough for more than one car to drive though the gates, but there was a lot of activity around his kiosk when I pulled up.

I told Biddle most of what I knew, which wasn't much. I had my suspicions, but nothing I could wrap my arms around. When we'd just about emptied our box load of suppositions, I got around to asking another question high on my list of priorities. "John, what do you know about arranging a visit to an inmate serving a life sentence at Pelican Bay? Betty tells me she just keeps running in circles, and then ends up against a series of bureaucratic walls; or to be more precise, she says she gets caught up in a sea of electronic voices, apparently never any live voices available."

"Budget cuts. In the current economic climate, public relations for the California penal system are considered non-essentials and would be the first to go. Ergo, the push-button electronics replace the human touch." Biddle hesitated, then asked, "Why on earth would you want to go up there?" Before I could respond, his brows squeezed together, creating a multitude of shallow creases across his forehead, and he asked, "Do you have any idea where that is?"

"Not before I looked it up this morning. It's about 400 miles North of San Francisco—nearly up to the Oregon border." Not wanting to waste time on geography, I explained the possible relationship between McCormack and either Nigel Montcreif or whoever was running his trust. It was a good decade or so after Montcreif was reported missing at sea, so who might that be?

Biddle leaned forward, elbows supported on the narrow chair arms, while his chin rested on folded hands.

After a brief silence, he shook his head. "Entrance into Pelican Bay is no piece of cake, but it can be done. But hitting pay dirt with McCormack is a real long shot. Hard enough to track living, breathing perpetrators without chasing after ghosts."

I filled Biddle in on the recent information I'd obtained from Tommy Morgan. "Things are beginning to sizzle," I said. "If Lori London wasn't murdered, why was Morgan's new take on how she died destroyed? And if not sabotaged by the murderer, then by whom?"

"Hold on, Barnaby," Biddle chided. "Wasn't Nigel Montcreif in his seventies at the time of Lori London's death?

I nodded. "And before you remind me, I know about how old he'd be now. If last night's events are connected, and I believe they are, I do realize that it was no ninety-year-old man climbing around on that catwalk. But if Montcreif is alive he has the means to hire it done, or maybe…." I didn't bother to finish. "I've got to find out who's running the Montcreif trust—Estate—or whatever it's called.

"Now back to entering Pelican Bay."

"I'm not up to speed on that. I can find out, but I don't have to tell you that Pelican Bay houses only the most serious criminal offenders, so their security is more than stringent. What I do know is when you're cleared for a visitation, you better be carrying proper ID. And dress simply. They don't allow blue clothing of any kind—no blue shirts or pants."

"Betty said she was sent on a merry chase with electronic voices and was only able to come up with general information. The part I had the most trouble swallowing is that it's up to the prisoner to fill out a form to allow for visitation. And since I'm responsible for his apprehension…."

"You don't think it's likely he'll initiate the paperwork?" Biddle filled in.

"Not unless he's real hungry for conversation with someone on the outside," I confirmed. "Being the man who ended my son's life, he'd have to be pretty dense to think I wanted to bestow some kind of favor. But there's got to be some way around protecting criminals from—"

"Prisoners' rights activists have had an enormous impact," Biddle cut in. "There have been more coalitions formed over the treatment of the prison population at Pelican Bay than in the entire prison system. That's one notorious 'supermax' prison, with the most violent predatory offenders in our state's 160,000-inmate prison system. A real bad-ass place to be a prisoner, a law officer, or even a visitor. Be prepared for anything, including a body-cavity search."

I flinched.

"Don't wear anything with any metal, not even a belt buckle."

"Now you're pulling my leg."

"Afraid not, my friend. I've heard more horror stories than I can count on all my fingers and toes. One of the most humiliating I've heard of was of a defense attorney whose leg had been blown off in the Korean War. When he went for an authorized visit, the guards made him remove his prosthesis before he was allowed to meet with his client." Biddle held a palm out. "God's honest truth."

"What a shame," I said, "but I guess that's for everyone's safety. Bizarre as it seems, who knows what someone might attempt to carry inside a wooden leg?"

By the end of our chat, Biddle again let me know he couldn't spare any manpower, but conceded that Detective Scott had spoken to him and was so keyed up and willing to use his own free time that he'd tell him it was okay. He then emphasized that it must be on Scott's own time—not the LAPD's.

I headed back to my office. I'd take time to get a bite to eat and set up an appointment with Tanya Guttenberg, the literary agent who handled the sale of the movie rights to Nigel Montcreif's novel to Tommy Morgan. I wanted to find out more about this provision not to change the ending.

Who was there to enforce that clause if not Montcreif or a rightful heir?

CHAPTER 34.

Tommy Morgan had given me an earful about his initial encounter with Tanya Guttenberg. His description was comical and somewhat clichéd. I couldn't imagine a living soul that would fit Morgan's hackneyed description.

As I parked in front of the suburban address Morgan had given me for Tanya Guttenberg, I noticed that her home was similar to my own in many respects but was in somewhat disrepair. The white paint of the low picket fence was peeling and worn through in many spots and the lawn looked as if it hadn't been mowed in months. The flowerbeds had been taken over by weeds, and the dirt around them was dried and brittle.

When I pushed the gate open, I saw that the hinges were rusty and were attached to the gate with a single remaining screw. I wondered what I might find inside as I mounted the three wooden stairs. They creaked and buckled slightly under my weight. Even before I made it across the warped wooden porch to the front door, my nose was assailed by the stench of something most unpleasant. It reminded me of visits to the old drunk tank at the city jail. The odor was reminiscent of the mixture of urine and stale tobacco.

Still a few feet from the closed door and not looking forward to what lay beyond, I noticed the doorbell hanging from a single wire, so I knocked loudly on the door.

The door slowly creaked open.

"Come on in. I've been waiting for you," a small old gargoyle of a woman greeted me. "Probably all my life," she added with gusto and a wink of her creepy eyelid.

"Tanya Guttenberg?" I asked rhetorically. It could be none other. She was as Morgan had described her. In appearance she was totally unattractive; she had a large bulbous nose, thick glasses, thinning hair, and a cigarette dangling between her fingers.

"Of course it's me," Tanya said. "You must be teasing. I remember you." Her gaze was piercing and flirtatious. "We met at the premier of *Rude Awakening,* as if you don't remember."

"Of course," I lied. I didn't actually recall ever meeting her before this moment. Tanya's was a face I was unlikely to forget. More than age had taken its toll on her parchment-textured features.

My recollection of attending that premier with Hal and a former girlfriend was clear. Hal never tuned down an invitation from Lori and had not allowed his unease around Nigel Montcreif to deter him from attending what Lori lauded as her big comeback film, even though she'd been missing from the silver screen for just a tad over eighteen months.

"Barnaby Jones," Tanya chortled as she swung the door wide open. "Welcome, stranger. I always knew you'd look me up, but you sure took your own sweet time." She seemed oblivious to the fact that her voice was grating and had an abrasive tone.

"Hello, Tanya," I said cautiously, as I waded my way through her herd of countless felines in the dimly lit living room of her dilapidated home.

"'Hello, Tanya' indeed," she scoffed. "What an odd reception, after all we could have been to each other. How's your love life, sweetheart?"

"No complaints." I grinned, now remembering Tanya as a young woman. Though not as hard on the eyes at that time, she had never been what you might describe as attractive. But as I recalled, she'd possessed wit and humor. I had indeed met her at the premier she'd tried to remind me of, but I know I hadn't seen her since. I recollected that she'd unabashedly dropped a few lures at that time, which I'd ignored, but which put me amusingly on guard.

"Well, I have," Tanya announced. "You may not get out of here alive. Oh Barnaby, you beautiful man. I could get lost in those baby-blue eyes of yours. I could positively eat you up."

I reluctantly followed Tanya through the house, winding my way around her cats. When we reached the kitchen, she pulled two chairs from the round table in the small dining area, indicating that's where we'd sit.

"How would you like a cup of tea?"

"Sounds great," I jumped at the change of subject.

"Good," she warbled as she moved into the kitchen and opened the cupboard above the counter. "I've got some new stuff. East India Special. It's mixed with ground rhino horns, guaranteed to retool you. Wait till you taste it."

Tanya's bustling with the teapot gave me the opening I needed to change subjects.

"I presume you heard about what happened to the Lori London film over at Universal Enterprises."

"No, what?" Tanya lied. I was sure of it.

"Somebody tried to sabotage the film."

"Really?"

I wonder why she overplayed her lack of concern. "I think it was because Morgan changed the ending."

"Oh," Tanya said as she selected two tea mugs and set them on the kitchen table. "That was naughty."

"Sabotaging the film?"

"No, changing the ending. It violates the contract." She gave me a scrutinizing gaze, then continued, "I ought to know. I wrote it. I locked up all Nigel Montcreif's creative works, three novels, his unproduced movie scripts, and some short stories. The one abiding and controlling tenet of the agreement with the estate was 'no changes.' His works, if ever done, were to be exactly as he wrote them, not subject to 'improvement' by any genius-come-lately." She locked my gaze to hers as if she needed to be sure I was taking it all in. "His words were to be sacrosanct, if you know what that means."

"I understand what you're saying." I said as I eased two of Tanya's climbing cats off my lap. The house was overrun by cats of all colors and description. "My question is who might have taken it upon himself or herself to police your agreement?"

The teakettle had built up enough pressure and was beginning to scream.

Tanya shrugged off my question. "Who knows? Could have been some nut. There are a lot of nuts around."

The teakettle's scream died as she lifted it from the stove and filled my cup.

"Try this, Barnaby. It will do you good and help you, too. It'll give you back ideas you never thought you'd have again."

She sipped her tea, favoring me with a wicked, insinuating gleam in her eye, and lit another cigarette from the one smoldering in the ashtray.

But before I escaped, I got some answers to several questions.

Tanya represented the executor of the trust for all of Montcreif's literary works, and while she said she was not at liberty to tell me to whom she reported, she confirmed that the Venice Beach estate where Lori died was still part of the estate.

CHAPTER 35.

When I left Tanya Guttenberg, I took a long, circuitous route and thoughtful drive to the address Tanya had written for me. I drove past Hollywood High and the swarms of nubile young future stars, schoolbooks in hand or in backpacks, clothes and hairstyles in keeping with the trends.

I continued down Hollywood Boulevard, past pornographic marquees and an 'art house' playing an old Lori London picture. As a black-and-white pulled alongside my car at the light, the two young cops aboard and I exchanged a wordless grin and nod.

My cruising was not without purpose. I drove west to the Sunset Strip, on to Beverly Hills, Bel Air, to the beach, and past the pier to Venice. On the Venice Speedway, I recognized the house: the one pictured in clippings preserved in the Lori London file; the one captioned, "Where Lori died."

I parked in front of what had been known as the Montcreif Estate, which was located in the rather exclusive area of Venice. The

1920s-era beach mansion was still in good repair but apparently vacant, since the windows were shuttered. Sliding from behind the wheel of the Lincoln, I took a good look around. Although the house was somewhat secluded, I thought it best to try my luck at entering through the back of the house. The tall gate was locked, but I saw that it was not at all complicated, so I reached inside my jacket pocket and chose one of my favorite and most-used picks. The lock snapped open in seconds. I swung the gate open just wide enough for me to slip through. The lawn area around the pool was as well manicured as the one in front of the house, and the pool was filled and clear, making it apparent that the gardening and pool had not been neglected. I'd never been here, but Hal had. He'd only been here once for the wrap party following the private premier of *Destiny*, the movie that made Lori a star. After that party, he told me, "Dad, I adore Lori, but those people just aren't my kind of folks. I sure hope she isn't in over her head." His description of the estate pretty much matched what I now saw—minus the herds of drunk or drugged-out partygoers he said were in plentiful supply.

As I made my way around the low hedges to the back door, I prayed Montcreif hadn't invested in one of those high-tech security systems. I wasn't up to speed on breaking into that level of sophistication. The lock on the back door seemed as uncomplicated as they came, but I took a closer look and felt around the door to see if I could detect any type of wiring that might set off an ear-shattering blast, or a silent one wired to law enforcement. I found none and had no trouble picking the lock. Still, I stood for a breathless moment, making sure I hadn't set any alarms off. Nothing happened, so I pushed the door open and stepped into the house. I moved silently through the kitchen.

Still hearing no sound, I flipped on the light. To my left was a door I assumed led to the garage, where Lori's body had been discovered. But before viewing that area, I wanted to check out the house. More confident now that I was totally alone, I strode through the kitchen and dining area into the living room. I moved around the dusty, sheet-covered furniture until I came across something that stopped me dead in my tracks. On the wall above the fireplace I was arrested by the stunning impact of a life-sized nude painting of Lori. Morgan had a similar painting in his Lori London shrine, but this one showed a far less innocent young woman. This was the one Montcreif had photographed and leaked to the tabloids. He claimed to have loved Lori, but this kind of exploitation showed no love. It proved that Montcreif's true love was power and money. He wanted Lori and had also used her in a very unloving way. His exploitation of her may have attracted moviegoers, but it seemed that there was no level too low for Nigel Montcreif to stoop to boost box-office sales.

Disgusted, I made my way back through the kitchen to the door leading to the garage. There was a small peep window with beveled glass in the door, affording a view of the garage interior from the kitchen.

Surprisingly, this door was unlocked. I opened the door and felt for the light switch, then flipped it on. The first thing that captured my attention was some sort of automobile beneath a dusty tarpaulin. Below the dark blue cover, I saw the bottom half of two large whitewall tires.

My heart beat wildly against my rib cage as I bolted to the car and ripped off the tarp. Dust particles billowed from the cover and filled my lungs as well as the air around me. It temporarily obscured my view and sent me into a spasm of dry coughs, followed by a series of three rather loud sneezes.

Almost too good to be true. I found myself staring at Lori London's legendary white Cadillac, the one pictured and labeled 'the place where Lori London died.' I tried the car door but as expected it was locked. Luckily it wasn't like one of today's nearly impenetrable varieties. I returned to the closet I'd seen in the entry and retrieved a wire coat hanger.

In less time than it had taken me to recover from the recent dust cloud, I had the car open and slid inside. The plush, white leather interior was in mint condition without a visible speck of dust.

Visions of Lori's lifeless body slumped over the steering wheel invaded my mind, paralyzing me for a full moment or two. Finally, I steeled myself and was able to hold those thoughts at bay and return to the job at hand. I looked and discovered to no great surprise that there were no car keys in the ignition. I then inspected every inch of the interior. There were no keys under either car seat, in the glove compartment, or anywhere in the car.

I always left my keys on the kitchen sink if not on the nifty key holder that my daughter-in-law tacked up for me. I wondered if any such gimmick existed at this grand old estate. Reentering the kitchen, I saw there was no key rack on the wall above the counter where it might have been expected, so I randomly opened one kitchen drawer after another. No luck. I didn't fancy attempting any type of hot-wiring, and I'd just about given up when I took one last scrutinizing gaze around the kitchen. That's when I noticed I'd left the back door ajar, so, retracing my steps, I pushed it closed. Something jingled. I followed the sound. My heart began to tap out a wild tattoo. In a small compartment on the inside of the kitchen door, I found a key rack. Among the clusters of keys, I spotted one slender gold key on a ring that bore the Cadillac emblem. I discovered good fortune was indeed smiling on me today and rapidly returned to the garage.

Again slipping inside the car, I wondered how long the Cadillac had been housed in this location. Had it been here before Hal had been murdered? Had he returned to check it out, as he intended? Abruptly, I halted my introspection. What was important now was that the investigation proceed.

I turned the key in the ignition. Nothing happened. I checked the gas gage. It indicated empty, so I withdrew the key and slipped it in my pocket as I pushed the car door open wide and slid out, leaving the door ajar.

I strode to the front of the Cadillac and fumbled for the hood release. Finding it in a blink, I raised the hood, and set the bar so it wouldn't come crashing down on my noggin. The engine appeared to have been steam-cleaned. I was vaguely familiar with the setup. These older cars, before the computer age, were a lot easier to understand. I saw nothing that seemed out of order and wondered what might have been done before Lori's death, and what, if anything, had been done since.

Taking my tools from my jacket pocket, I rolled on a pair of latex gloves and leaned back into the car, steadying myself on one bent knee, and then proceeded to remove the ignition, which I would have managed in a swish of a horse's tail, but I noticed that the wiring wasn't quite right. I pondered a beat but not so long as to throw me off track. I'd remembered to bring my pocket-sized camera and slipped it out of my inside coat pocket. I wanted to check out the ignition switch but didn't want to destroy any evidence in the process. I took a number of pictures from every angle, then fumbled for a piece of paper, took out my pen, and wrote down the sequence of colored wires attached to the ten posts on the steering column. I wrote, "Red wire with green strip from connecter one to connector ten, blue strip from connector...." I continued with each wire connected to each of the ten posts, then disconnected the ignition and placed it in one of my larger evidence bags. I relocked and closed the door before carefully rearranging the cover as I found it, minus several ounces of dust.

That done, I saw that there was an electrical garage-lock system controlled by three buttons, one marked *open,* one marked *close,* and the third marked *lock.*

I tried to activate the garage door, but found there was no power. I looked around inside the garage for the fuse box and found none. After rechecking to make sure I hadn't overlooked it, I went back through the kitchen to the rear of the house. I looked in both directions and finally spotted the metal doors of what looked like a fuse box and felt as agile as a young colt as I jumped off the low rail-less porch. The master fuse box appeared to have been painted more recently than the rest of the house trim, but not too recently. Opening the metal door, I saw that only one switch had been turned off or had blown out. I flipped it and the switch stayed where I placed it, indicating that it had been flipped off rather than blown out.

Back in the garage I tried all three buttons. When I hit *open* and nothing happened, I tried the one labeled *lock* and heard a grinding sound, then retried the *open*. The large garage door creaked open slowly when I depressed the *open* button, and closed with the same creaking slowness as I depressed *close*. After trying the third, which was labeled *lock*, I heard the lock tumble back into place. Satisfied that all were in working order, I was about to turn out the light in the garage when my attention was drawn to the oil-stained concrete floor. It appeared that attempts to scrub the cement clean had been unsuccessful. Surprisingly, the stains were not confined to under the car, as might be expected. I added one more conundrum to my mental list.

Leaving the house as I found it, I spotted and picked up a business card from the kitchen counter. It read Coast Realty, 16422 Venice Boulevard, and gave a phone number.

Pocketing the card, I reset the backdoor lock and departed.

I sat in the car for a few moments after I slipped in, and stared sightlessly toward the garage. This was where Lori London's lifeless body was found. I couldn't get the picture of Lori slumped over the steering wheel of her white Cadillac parked in this very garage out of my mind. I flashed back to the newspaper accounts heralding the death of Lori London in her married lover's garage. The article stated that when Lori was found, the ignition had not been turned off, the car was out of gas, and her blood reflected traces of alcohol. The coroner's verdict had been suicide or accidental death due to carbon-monoxide poisoning. Unless Hal was mistaken and the bartender at the Hilltop Café flat-out lied, Lori was drinking nothing stronger than tonic water and lemon.

CHAPTER 36.

It was just past seven o'clock, the night air veiled in winter darkness, while the city fought back with artificial illumination. Streetlights and neon signs had been set aglow for more than two hours when I swung into the underground parking of my office building. Betty's parking slot was empty, as was Jedediah's, but I was too keyed up to call it a day.

My mind was recapping all I'd learned and how far I had to go when the elevator stopped at the sixth floor. Key in hand, I halted abruptly as I noticed a light through the stippled-glass window of my office door. Withdrawing my gun, I stood to the side of the door window and inserted the key. The door swung open, but I stayed put for a beat, then ventured forward, my gun at the ready.

"Mr. Jones," I heard from inside the reception area. "It's Detective Scott."

I relaxed, placed my gun back in my holster, and swung the door open wide.

Before I could ask, Scott explained, "Betty said it was okay for me to wait here."

"Yes," I said. "I just wasn't expecting anyone since—"

"I know," Scott said, rising from the chair where he'd been waiting, "but I'm off duty and I've run down some of the information you needed."

"Which is?" I asked, somewhat perplexed. We hadn't spoken since Biddle gave his okay. I gestured for Scott to be seated and took the chair beside him.

"Getting into Pelican Bay. It's mighty tough, but not impossible. Since it contains the 'SHU,' and the authorities truly don't want people exposed to how barbaric it seems to be, security is air-tight."

"SHU?" I parroted.

"Sorry, I've just come up to speed myself. That's the acronym for Secure Housing Units for the most dangerous prisoners. There was a big lawsuit not too long ago by a prisoners' rights group that exposed horrible abuses. It included holding a prisoner down in a scalding bath until his skin sloughed off, terrible beatings, neglect of the seriously ill and mentally ill, and all sorts of other things that would make your skin crawl."

I winced and pushed both palms forward; I'd heard enough. Every time I'd mentioned Pelican Bay, I was given an earful of alleged abuses. The information Jedediah had pulled up on the computer was enough to curl your hair.

"Terry McCormack, the man I need to see, is as rotten as they come, in my book, but it's unlikely he'd be in the SHU. Since he's a politician right down to his rotten core, I wouldn't be at all surprised if he has landed a cushy job as prison trustee."

"Don't know about that. I haven't heard of anything too cushy in that joint," Scott said. "Now here's what you've got to do...."

By the time Scott came to the end of his litany regarding the number of steps required to obtain admittance into Pelican Bay, it seemed that McCormack had more darn rights than the honest folks.

"My associate Jedediah Jones has his law degree, and I suppose he could write a letter, but what about this locator number you mentioned?"

"You mean the CDC number. It's a code beginning with two letters to indicate the specific prison of incarceration, followed by the five-digit prisoner ID. But don't worry, I'll take care of it," Scott offered, and, with an amused smile, he added, "I understand the California Department of Corrections actually has real people on the other end of the line. That'll be a terrific change."

"This could take a long time," I said, not wanting to wait any longer than I had to. "It seems to me that law enforcement might be able to cut through some of that red tape."

"Well, this is all new to me, but you're probably right. Let me run it by Lieutenant Biddle. I sort of bypassed getting him involved, but—"

"I don't want you sticking your neck out on my account. I'll have a go at Biddle, first thing tomorrow morning. Although he's never gone to Pelican Bay, I'm sure he could find a way to pull some strings and cut the time frame."

CHAPTER 37.

After walking Detective Scott to the door, I returned to my lab and picked up the envelope containing the ignition switch I'd taken from Lori London's white Cadillac. I plunked myself down on the tall stool, rolled on a pair of latex gloves, and placed the ignition on my lab table. I had a theory, but it was far from fleshed out. As I began to ponder, I pulled the gloves off and picked up the paper with the diagram of the ignition and the wiring. It didn't look right, but I'd need an expert to confirm my belief. I'd call the local Cadillac dealership and ask for a schematic of their ignition wiring.

I was now bushed but not quite ready to call it a day, so I slipped back into the gloves, and, fiddling with the ignition switch, I pondered over the litany of questions that needed answering. Questions such as: Why is someone intent on preventing the new ending on the Lori London story, the one suggesting she was murdered? Who is that someone? Why had the Montcreif trust financed Terry McCormack's political campaign? Was the person behind that decision Nigel

Montcreif? Could McCormack have dealt with him after his so-called death at sea? If not Montcreif himself, who? What had happened to the son of Lori London and Nigel Montcreif?

My thoughts were abruptly curtailed by the shrill of the telephone. Glancing at my watch, I noted that it was now eight fifteen. It must be Betty or Jedediah. I smiled, knowing no one else would expect me to be here at this hour. But I was wrong.

The phone call was from Tanya Guttenberg. The abrasive, guttural tones of Nigel Montcreif's literary agent filled the air. "Hello, lover," she began. "I have some information for you, but it is for sale and it won't be cheap."

How much? I wanted to know, but I asked, "What makes you think I'm buying?"

"Oh you'll be buying all right, but while it will be expensive, we might be able to work out a deal. Part cash and the rest in trade." She guffawed so loudly I felt my stomach do a cartwheel. "Come over tomorrow at noon and we'll discuss it over a cup of tea," Tanya said.

******

The next morning, I arrived in the office at nine o'clock sharp. "Morning," I said, my sweeping gaze taking in Betty and Jedediah. They returned my greeting, and Jedediah went back to his computer, while Betty handed me a call slip and said, "Detective Scott called just as I was unlocking the office door. He says he has some good news."

Betty eyed me with a hint of rebuke in her eyes. "Burning the midnight oil again?"

"Yes, but I'm bright-eyed and ready to begin again," I said. I reached for the glass of milk she held out for me.

I had a fair bit of work to plow through before my appointment with Tanya, so I got right to it.

Returning Detective Scott's call was first on my mental agenda.

"Detective Scott," a voice met my ear before I was aware the phone had time to ring. Scott must have picked it up on the first ring.

"Came in early today," Scott said, "and talked to some of the detectives in Homicide with a lot more time under their belts. You were right; law enforcement can set up an appointment without having to go through all the bullshit. Seems the criminals aren't protected from the law. I spoke to Jim Armor, who's been in Homicide for five years or so and has made two trips to Pelican Bay. Says it's not for the faint of heart. I'm pretty sure Lieutenant Biddle could get us in, but when I stopped in to see him, I discovered he'd gone off to some sort of training meeting today—left about ten minutes ago."

"Thanks. I'll give him a jingle first thing in the morning," I said

My next call was to Coast Cadillac. After being transferred around, I reached a man called Bill Schaefer, the quick-service manager. He pretty much confirmed my suspicion about the wiring being off but said he'd pull out a schematic that someone in my office could pick up today. I'd pick it up myself on the way to Tanya Guttenberg's.

CHAPTER 38.

As I pulled into the driveway of Tanya Guttenberg's dilapidated house at precisely noon, I steeled myself for the onslaught of stench from the cat litter, breath-wrenching decay, and Tanya's inevitable and unbearably pathetic attempts at seduction.

This time I was prepared and barely noticed the signs of neglect as I made my way to the front door. I knocked loudly on the frame of the torn screen door, which stood half open and attached by a single hinge. The house was eerily silent. I heard no approaching footfalls and rechecked the time on my wristwatch. One minute after twelve o'clock, the time Tanya wanted me to meet with her. I rested the screen against the house for support and was about to knock again when I heard the screech of the tea kettle. "Tanya," I cried out. No answer. I knocked again, this time on the door rather than the frame of the wobbly screen. From the pressure of my knock, Tanya's door slowly swung open, and the teakettle's whistle rose to a scream—almost an alarm.

I called out again and entered the living room. Wading through a houseful of hungry, meowing cats, I continued through to the kitchen. Tanya was nowhere in view and the teapot was still wailing, so I turned it off.

Again, I called out Tanya's name as I proceeded down the narrow hallway toward the bedrooms. Still no answer. The first door stood ajar, so I nudged it open with my foot.

I stepped inside and found myself staring at Tanya, who was sprawled grotesquely on the faded quilt of her bed. There was a wool scarf wrapped around her neck. She'd been garroted with what appeared to be one of her own knitted scarves. Two cats were on the bed beside her, one licking her face. I pulled the cats away and closed the door, leaving them on the outside. Although Tanya was obviously quite dead, I attempted to take her pulse. There was none, but I could still feel a near-normal amount of body heat. She hadn't been dead long.

I can't say I ever got accustomed to the sight of a lifeless body or that I felt nothing, or that I ever would. I was moved by the circumstances of this unfortunate old woman's death, but my many years of exposure to the seamy side of life had prepared me to take this development stone-faced.

I took a handkerchief from my pocket, picked up the phone, and dialed the Hollywood Precinct.

While waiting, I casually perused the bedroom, and withdrawing one of my plastic evidence bags from my pocket, I placed it on the knob of the top and only drawer of the night table and pulled it open. Into the phone, I said, "Put me through to Homicide." Waiting again, I saw that there was no sign of ransacking but spotted a small, black address book, picked it up and turned a few pages, then pocketed it.

"Hello … yes … better dispatch a unit to 1759 Franklin to check out a body … Who? … My name is Jones, as in Barnaby."

In response to the detective's question, I said, "No, an ambulance will not be necessary; just notify the M.E."

Taking a compassionate last look at Tanya's crumpled body, I started out to my car. As I passed the kitchen sideboard I spotted a half-empty can of cat food and stopped to spoon the remains out for the hungry cats. With Tanya's black book inside my jacket pocket, I left the sorrowful scene behind me.

CHAPTER 39.

I leaned back in my desk chair again, running the death of Tanya Guttenberg through my head. Her death had been no random act. What had she planned to tell me? It couldn't be anything insignificant if she felt I'd be willing to pay her. And preventing her from departing with whatever that was had caused her murder.

Paging through Tanya's little black book for the umpteenth time, I began making a series of brief notes. I went from cover to cover, but finally came to the point where I could use some assistance. I asked Betty to come into my office, and together we pulled phone numbers and names of places out of Tanya's book and began acquiring meaningful scraps of information. "How do you feel about spending the day at the library doing a bit of research while I spend some time with Sunset Cadillac's technical expert going over the ignition wiring?" I asked.

"Sure. It'll be a nice change," Betty said, picking up my laundry list of unknowns. "Anything else you want me to look into while I'm there?"

"Anything you can find out about the Montcreif family in France, and try to confirm the existence of that son Morgan told me Lori had planned to track down. Find out where he might be today. He'd be around twenty-three or twenty-four by now."

Betty was slipping into her coat when Jedediah poked his head up from the computer screen. "Hey, you don't have to go to the library; I can look up most of that family stuff for you on the Web."

"Web, schmeb," I said. "Betty, you run along to the library, and Jedediah, see what you can find on that dang computer. But print it out. I don't want to be hunched over your shoulder staring at that flickering screen."

Betty traversed the office to the copy machine and made a copy of my list of questions looking for answers and handed it to Jedediah.

Turning to Betty, I said, "Also get whatever you can on Tommy Morgan."

Betty stopped mid-stride and with a raised brow asked, "Morgan? I thought he was one of the good guys."

"I think he is, but I'd still like as much background as you can dig up. Follow up your library search with the usual sources."

"You question whether Tommy Morgan's on the level?" Betty asked.

"You know I question everything," I said.

An hour later I was sitting across from Bill Schaefer, the service manager for Coast Cadillac. The schematic he supplied for me the day before had been a great help, but it didn't tell me what would happen if the ignition had been wired as I found it.

I pulled out my drawing indicating how the wires had been connected when I removed the ignition.

"Well," Schaefer said, "you could still start the car, but until that wire," he pointed to the red one with the green strip, "was removed, the ignition would keep running until it ran out of gas."

I pondered his words. "So if a woman was behind the wheel, she wouldn't know how to stop it?" I questioned aloud.

"Most men wouldn't have a clue as to the cause, but they'd probably start ripping wires loose until the engine came to a stop." I nodded my head. "And you're correct in assuming most ladies would not think of that—would probably leave the car running and go for help." Schaefer gazed up at the ceiling, then added, "Well, some of today's females are a lot more with it on mechanics, electronics, and all sorts of things that used to be relegated to the male domain."

"Well, the lady I have in mind was not from that new school." I paused, trying to work out the theory that had been trying to find a place to land, and asked, "How about the door locks, could they have been rigged to remain locked?"

Schaefer rubbed the sides of his temples in deep concentration. "It's possible, I guess."

I waited, not wanting to interrupt his train of thought.

Nodding his head, Schaefer said, "Sure, it's possible. But if that had been the case in the scenario you gave me, the police would have had to break into the car."

I shook my head. "Another theory falling apart," I said with a smile; but still, the idea of an ignition that could not be disengaged was intriguing.

CHAPTER 40.

Before stopping at the office, I headed straight to the Hollywood Precinct, but not quite early enough to find a convenient parking spot. I parked my Lincoln around the corner from the precinct off Wilcox.

As I bounded up the five wide stairs into the precinct, the memorial to the detectives who had given their lives in the line of duty did not escape my notice.

When I reached the counter outside the detective's area, Martha, whom I met on my previous visit, pushed her intercom button and said, "Lieutenant Biddle, Mr. Jones is here." Turning back to me, she said, "Go right in."

Biddle's uniforms always looked as if they'd come straight from the cleaners. Today was no exception. His thinning hair was a bit more evident this morning, probably due to the still-damp strands plastered close to his scalp.

After exchanging a brief greeting, Biddle gestured me to the chair in front of his desk and asked, "I was sure I'd see you sometime today, Barnaby. But what brings you in so bright and early?"

"It's early, but not sure about how bright." The day was overcast as I drove in this morning, but that's not what I was talking about.

"I suppose you're here to find out what we know about the Tanya Guttenberg murder case."

"Among other things."

"Can't tell you much about the Guttenberg woman yet, but I've got a team of detectives on it. No fresh fingerprints, other than the ones you left on the teakettle," he said with a tilt of his head. "And as far as fibers are concerned, forget it. Considering the condition of that rundown house she called her home, it is nearly impossible to determine what's what." He paused, then said, "Did you realize that woman had thirty-four cats in that house?"

"There was a whole caboodle of them," I said, then quickly changed directions to get on with my own agenda. "John, I don't know who killed Tanya Guttenberg, but I'm pretty sure it's tied in with the fire at Universal Enterprises and Morgan's Lori London film with an ending that spells out M-U-R-D-E-R."

"How so?"

"Did you know that Guttenberg was Nigel Montcreif's literary agent?" Biddle nodded. "What you might not know is that there was a clause in the contract Tommy Morgan signed when he purchased the rights to the book; a clause that prevents any changes to the story line."

"So you think Morgan could be involved in the Guttenberg murder?"

I shook my head. "It's possible, but I don't think so. While Morgan might have wanted the literary agent's contract to disappear, I don't think he would have killed her."

"Or had her killed," Biddle added, then said what we both knew to be true. "He had a motive, and he certainly had the means."

I nodded. "But my gut tells me it wasn't Morgan. That scenario would also lead us to believe that the fire at Universal Enterprises and Guttenberg's murder were not connected, which means we are looking for two criminals: an arsonist and a murderer. And it's a coincidence that both would have something to do with the Lori London film." I paused. "I don't buy it."

Biddle looked thoughtful. "I've considered the Lori London connection. And being of like minds, I don't like coincidence any more than you do, so we'll check it out." Biddle glanced over at the clock on his desk and said, "You came in before I had my first cup of coffee. Are you ready for a cup, or do you prefer your usual?"

When I indicated that I'd prefer the usual, he stepped out of his office and returned with a cup of coffee and a glass of milk.

Biddle moved his in-box to clear a place for the small tray on his desk and slid into the chair beside mine. I got straight to the point. "I've come to ask a favor and to give you some new information."

"I like the part about new information." Biddle smiled, took a short sip of his scalding coffee, and put it back down. "But I assume you'd rather get right to the favor."

I felt my mouth turn up in a silly grin. "Sure enough. Detective Scott looked into the rigmarole of getting into Pelican Bay as a private investigator, but it wasn't too enticing. I thought maybe you might be able to pull a few strings."

"Well, since your last visit, I did look into it, and I think I can ease the path."

Biddle rose and walked around to his side of the L-shaped desk and reached for the phone. I saw that he just happened to have the phone number for Pelican Bay written on a Rolodex card beside the phone. He gave me a knowing smile as he dialed the number.

"This is Lieutenant Biddle, LAPD. I'd like to speak to Warden Pierce." Biddle picked up his coffee, which had apparently cooled, judging by the amount he took in a single gulp.

"Yes, Warden. This is Lieutenant John Biddle at the Hollywood Precinct of the LAPD. We have a few loose ends on an old case, and we'd like to talk to one of your prisoners, a Terry McCormack, serving a life sentence for murder in the first degree...."

I sipped my milk as I listened to Biddle's side of the conversation.

Biddle covered the mouthpiece of the phone and asked, "How does Tuesday at 10:00 a.m. sound?"

I nodded, a bit taken back by the speed of the appointment. "Yes, Tuesday suits me fine," I said.

Biddle hung up and sat down in his desk chair opposite me.

"I owe you," I said.

Biddle nodded and said, "You may be on the track to solving the ongoing mystery over the cause of Lori London's death. Coincidences don't suit me one bit, and as you pointed out there is someone who doesn't want to see Tommy Morgan's take on Lori London's death hit the theaters with the potential of turning Montcreif's nonfiction book into pure fiction."

I smiled, seeing Biddle was beginning to see the light, a theory that began to unravel as he continued to vocalize his take on the events of the past week.

"While Guttenberg's representing Montcreif's book is a connection," Biddle said, "it doesn't point in the same direction. Her contract prevents the changing of the story line, so I'd say her agenda was similar to that of the person behind the fire at Universal Enterprises. Morgan doesn't know the identity of the arsonist, but he does know that he could have a hell of a lawsuit over the contract he signed when he releases his version of—what's it called?"

"*The True Story Behind the Legend of Lori London*," I filled in, waiting to see where he was going, although I had a pretty good idea.

"Right. That would create a darn good motive for wanting Guttenberg out of the way. So in my book, we could indeed be looking for a murderer and an arsonist."

"Can't say that isn't one of the paths I'm following, John. But it doesn't feel right. Morgan doesn't seem all that worried about lawsuits. In fact, he's hoping the release of his movie will smoke Montcreif out in the open."

"More power to you if you can prove Lori London's death wasn't a suicide or an accident. As I told you before, even though it's in the books as a solved case, you're far from alone in the belief that it was a case of murder. If it had been an open-and-shut case, it wouldn't resurface every few years. But in my opinion attempting to resurrect Nigel Montcreif's ghost is a wild hare."

I leaned forward, but before I could speak, Biddle said, "But I know you're not about to let it go, and I haven't found you out in left field too often."

Again I nodded. "I always feel a lot better when I have your blessing. And listening to your side of the conversation, I assume you told the warden the detective you'd be sending is Detective Scott."

Biddle leaned to one side of his desk chair, his elbow on the arm of the chair and his chin resting between thumb and index finger. "You're a crafty old fox," Biddle said, "but I meant what I said about Scott having a full plate. I'll arrange for him to accompany you to Pelican Bay on his own time, for this one assignment, but remember:

he's assigned to Robbery, and we have no shortage of current cases."
Then leaning back in his chair he said, "Now it's payback time. What
is this new information you have for me?"

CHAPTER 41.

For the past few weeks, there never seemed enough time during the weekdays, so I'd called a Saturday morning meeting. This was far from the usual for the offices of the Barnaby Jones Investigative Agency. While not unusual for me to show up on a Saturday, it was for my associates. I sort of feel like a loafer when I take off two days in a row, unless I'm out fishing. But today, not only were Betty and Jedediah on hand, but Detective Scott had dropped in as well. It was Scott's day off from the *LAPD*. Clad in a pair of beige chinos, loafers, and a casual red crewneck sweater stretching across his barrel chest, he was eager to lend a hand.

As I shrugged out of my windbreaker, I noticed that Jedediah had appeared in his usual casual attire, worn when he was not expected in court or on official business. With his well-worn blue jeans and UCLA sweatshirt, he looked like a kid. He didn't like to be reminded of his youthful appearance but he was bound to appreciate it in the years to come.

This morning, it seemed that Jedediah and Detective Scott were of like minds in their food choices. Both had trooped in with a box of Krispy Kreme doughnuts, while Betty, clad in white wool slacks and a bright royal-blue sweater rather than her usual office attire, prepared a bowl of high- fiber cereal for the two of us.

I introduced Jedediah to Detective Scott.

Jedediah popped in at the speed of a colt bucking at the saddle the first time 'round. "Call me J. R.," he said, reaching for the coffee Betty had poured for the three of them.

As I picked up my glass of milk and cereal, I said, "Detective Scott and I will work from my office." I wondered just what this day might surface.

Scott put a couple of doughnuts on the plate Betty had given him and picked up his coffee, preparing to follow me, when my resistance faded. There were a lot of doughnuts and they sure looked good. "How about picking up one for me?" I asked. By the end of the day I was pretty sure Betty's willpower would wane and she'd also indulge in a doughnut or two.

Scott grinned and put another two doughnuts on his plate, then followed me into my office, while Jedediah and Betty set to work in the reception area.

******

An hour or so later, after bringing Scott up-to-date on the activities of the past couple days, I pulled out Tanya's little black book.

"I picked this up from Tanya Guttenberg's bedside table the other day," I said. At Scott's raised brow, I continued, "There isn't much in there that would be of interest to the investigation."

"And you took it because....?"

I waited a long beat, then said, "There's information that might lead to who's behind or is now running the Montcreif trust, and so far I haven't been able to get law enforcement to give a hoot."

Scott gave his broad shoulders a shrug, and looked down at the pages I was leafing through. I pushed the pad of notes I'd taken when I'd first gone through this little black book toward Scott.

After about an hour we'd gone as far as we could with the current known facts. I caught Scott's gaze and said, "Let's meet with Betty and Jedediah out in the reception area. I want to take a look at that map on the wall behind Betty's desk."

As Scott followed me back to the reception area, I asked, "Betty, do you speak French?"

"En peu, Monsieur," she replied.

"Impressive," I said, "but what the heck does it mean?"

Giving me a smug little smile, she said, "A little."

Jedediah interrupted with, "Listen up. I was able to get into the archives of the little resort town of Cavalier-Sur-Mer." He paused. "That's the town you found from your library research," he said, catching Betty's eye. "Anyway, Cavalier-Sur-Mer is just down the coast from St. Tropez. When I broke into their archives, I came up with the old deeds and tax records that establish beyond doubt that a certain

Monsieur Montcreif owned a villa there in the 1980s. Checking the name on all other existing records, Betty and I, with commendable tenacity," he boasted, "have discovered that the baby boy you wanted to know about was born to a Monsieur Nigel and Madam Germaine Montcreif in the winter of 1978."

"Records after that time are incomplete due to some kind of civil uprising," Betty chimed in. "However, I did find an unconfirmed report that Montcreif was reported lost off a yacht in the Mediterranean in the spring of 1987."

"Unconfirmed?" I said, thinking aloud. "In this country, I thought his death at sea was a matter of record. Maybe the French aren't so willing to accept a mysterious death at sea.

"So, where are we?" I continued. "Montcreif had a wife in France all the while he was living here with Lori." Perching on the corner of Betty's desk, I continued, "Well, it seems that old saying 'Even a broken clock is right twice a day' holds true in this case. The tabloids hit it on the head."

Betty pulled the book of Hollywood biographies off the shelf and took center stage sharing the information she'd absorbed from her two days in the library stacks and here in the office. "From July of 1977 to February of 1978, Lori London made no pictures. She traveled and vacationed in the south of France."

Seven months? Long enough, if discreet, to have a baby without the whole world knowing about it. I held out my hand and Betty turned the book over to me. Next to Lori there was a large picture of Montcreif. Without a second thought, I tore out the page.

On closer inspection, I noticed the ring on Montcreif's finger. It had some kind of a crest on it, one I'd seen before, and not very doggone long ago. But where?

CHAPTER 42.

"Betty," I called out as I was leading Scott back to the lab to explain my theory on how the ignition might have been rigged so that it couldn't be disengaged. "Find out if Crescent City has an airport, and if not, where the nearest one is. Then book a flight for Detective Scott and me."

"Craig," the detective reminded me for the third time.

"Sorry," I said with an expression I hoped showed my sincerity.

"Also make arrangements for us to pick up a car at the airport. We need to arrive at the prison before 10:00 a.m. on Tuesday."

"Will do," Betty said, as I pulled the ignition switch out of the plastic envelope and handed Craig the schematic that I'd obtained from the Cadillac dealership.

"So why wouldn't she have just left the car running and gone into—" He stopped mid-sentence, apparently remembering the newspaper blurbs he'd read. "Wasn't she found passed out with a high alcohol content in her blood stream?"

"That's the theory, but it's all wrong. Lori hadn't been drinking for several weeks, and according to the bartender at the Hilltop Café, Lori spent the evening drinking nothing stronger than tonic and lemon."

"Yeah, I heard that version, but it was discredited in the Detective's Report."

Momentarily stunned, I asked, "You've seen the DR book?"

Scott nodded. "Arrived late yesterday afternoon. Biddle was out on a case, so I took the liberty of browsing through it. I burned some serious midnight oil at the station last night and think I copied down most of what we'll need." Scott strode back to the chair where he'd dumped his jacket on the way in, and pulled some folded papers from the inside pocket.

I stared at Scott, somewhat incredulous. "And when did you plan to let me in on this bombshell?" I was annoyed and pretty sure my voice reflected it.

A full-scale blush spread across Scott's ruddy complexion, and he held a hand out in front of him as if to shield himself from the temper I seemed to be losing. "I wasn't holding back, I swear," Scott said, handing over the folded sheets. I took the paper, but didn't let up on my steely glare. "Last night I made a copy of all the notes I thought might be important and planned to hand it over to you first thing."

"But somehow it slipped your mind?" I said with more than a hint of sarcasm.

"Not exactly," Scott stammered. "Well, maybe. While you were bringing me up to speed on the more recent events, I guess

I sort of got sidetracked." Then swiftly turning defensive and somewhat indignant, Scott said, "This is ancient history compared to what we've been discussing today. I've got a complete list of the witnesses."

"Witnesses?" I said with what might have been described as a blank expression, because that's how I felt.

"Well, not on-the-scene witnesses, but people who'd been at the Hilltop Café that night, along with a number of people who supposedly knew Ms. London and knew of the problems she was having with that Montcreif character. There were quite a few people from Montcreif's studio who claimed suicide was not out of the realm—"

"Enough," I said. "Sorry I overreacted. I've been waiting for the pages from that DR book to be unearthed for a coon's age and hadn't expected to be left in the dark when it finally surfaced."

I saw that Scott was about to give me another apology, and waved it off. But I smiled inwardly as I tossed the copy he'd given me on my desk, and finished explaining my thoughts on just how Lori's death had been set up to look like a suicide.

Scott had hit the nail on the proverbial head when he'd judged the here-and-now top priority, but I still wanted to go over everything. That old case file with the list of witnesses and what they said then, versus what they might say today, might lead somewhere.

"How about the photos of the crime scene?" I asked.

Scott looked at me for a second or two before it seemed to dawn on him I'd switched back to the DR book. "Yeah, there were pictures of the death scene, but you'll have to come to the precinct to see them."

Nodding, I made a mental note that the detective had switched my wording from crime to death, making me wonder just where he stood in this investigation.

"Tell me, Craig, what is your take on the true cause of Lori London's death?"

At that precise moment, Betty exploded into my office. She appeared far from the calm, cool, collected assistant I'd come to rely on.

"Barnaby," she said, "you're not going to believe how impossible it is to get you two into Crescent City in the morning. Best I can do is 5:33 p.m."

I smiled, "Can't be that tough. Don't they have an airport?"

"Yes," she stated, her hands on her hips. "They *do* have an airport." I was waiting for the but, and she gave it to me good. "I'm sure it would be a lot easier to get you into Fort Knox."

"Well that's not exactly what we had in mind." I halted the satire when I caught her fiery glare. I'd seldom seen my daughter-in-law in this heightened state, so I held my tongue until she had a chance to say her piece.

"Okay, gentlemen, I'll give you your choices for making your 10:00 a.m. appointment at the Pelican Bay Prison. But first let me give you the logistics. There is an airport in Crescent City, but there are no direct flights from Los Angeles. United Express is the only airline that flies into Crescent City. So you can choose a flight from LAX to either San Francisco or Sacramento on Monday."

I wanted to stop her right there, but sank back in my desk chair and just listened. Betty was on a roll, as Jedediah might say.

"Then," holding up one finger, she said, "number one, you can fly to San Francisco, spend the night, and take a flight out at 6:20 the next morning. But you'll have to change planes in Sacramento. That flight makes one other stop and gets you in to Crescent City at 9:38 a.m. It's a ten- or fifteen-minute drive to the prison, so you'll have to put your skates on."

I felt a scowl forming on my forehead and did my best to keep cool.

"But that doesn't make a lot of sense. Number two," she said, raising a second finger, "I book you a flight to Sacramento and a room near the airport, and you take that same flight you would have changed to from San Francisco at 8:10 a.m., which still gets you to Crescent City at 9:38 a.m. and you still have to hustle." Betty stared down at my hands, which were making circles on the desktop. "Did you lose something, Barnaby?"

"Only my temper. There's got to be a better way."

"I haven't finished," Betty said. "Number three," and the third finger rose, "you fly into Crescent City via San Francisco and arrive at 5:33 Monday night and stay overnight there. You can then get as early a start as you like the next morning."

"Oh, that should be a real delight," I said.

"Actually, under other circumstances, I bet it would. I talked with the administrative assistant at their Chamber of Commerce. Crescent City is located in a beautiful part of the country, right on the coast and surrounded by redwoods."

So far Scott had remained silent, but he chose the slight lull in the conversation to add his two cents. "I guess we're a bit tainted by all we've heard about the prison and the conditions there. I'm sure you're right about the city, Betty, but I have another idea."

"Shoot," she said, spreading her hands outwards. "I can use all the help I can get, but I've got to warn you: I've spent the better part of the day running into steel doors."

"How about booking us on an early flight to San Francisco or Sacramento?" He paused. "Which is closer?"

"Well, I just happen to have that information." She picked up one of Jedediah's computer printouts and said with one of those tongue-in-cheek sort of expressions, "San Francisco. It's only 361 miles. Sacramento is 378, so San Francisco is a whole, uh … seventeen miles closer."

Scott held his hands up in mock surrender.

Resigned, I said, "So what kind of accommodations are in Crescent City?"

CHAPTER 43.

I was alone in my lab after the others had taken off for the day. I had just set up my spectrophotometer when the phone rang. It was Tommy Morgan.

"Barnaby, have you seen tomorrow's headlines in the *Times?*"

Tomorrow's? It took me a few seconds before it dawned on me that Morgan meant the early Sunday edition, which would have already hit the newsstands. "No, I've put in a pretty full day at the office and—"

"Tanya Gutenberg's murder is smeared all across the front page."

"I sort of figured reporters would have a field day with that one. It wasn't likely they'd bury it in the California section." I couldn't fathom what had him so riled up. The murder details had not hit him by surprise. We'd gone over every grisly details the day before when I'd spoken to him by phone after my visit with Biddle. The grotesque circumstances of Tanya's murder, along with the macabre setting, were bound to be grist for any journalist's mill.

"Are you at the studio or at home?" I asked.

"At the studio. Where else?" Morgan replied. "This publicity on Guttenberg's death is throwing a real monkey wrench in our plans."

"How so?" I asked.

I heard Morgan heave a sigh. "For one thing, it's taking the spotlight off Lori London."

"Mind if I drop by in about a half hour?" I asked.

******

When I arrived at Universal Enterprises, the security was tight. There was a guard in the kiosk as usual, but there were also two guards with walkie-talkies beyond the gates. When I rolled up in front of the sound studio and parked my car, I saw one guard in front of the studio's double doors and the other on the porch of Morgan's office.

Entering studio 1B, I spotted Morgan. He was viewing a film, most likely a section he'd salvaged from the fire in hopes he wouldn't have to reshoot it all.

In one close-up scene, as the camera scanned the crowd, a splash of red light flashed from the lens. "Damnation," Morgan roared. "Whoever that is has ruined the entire shot. The A.D. should have gotten rid of that cockamamie ring."

"Wait, let's see that again," I said.

They backed up the film and ran it again, freezing the frame on the section of the film containing the flicker of red from a large ring as the reflected light from the lens panned across it. The person wearing the ring was not visible; only a partial glimpse of hand could be seen.

I took the page I'd torn out of the Hollywood biographies book. I studied it, comparing it with the frame on the screen. "Tommy, I'd like to see that frame blown up."

******

Early Monday morning, Morgan arrived at my office while I was still in my dark room.

"Hang on," I called. "I'll be right out." I'd managed to produce an 8 x 10 and a maxi-blow-up of the ring captured on the frame of the film.

Walking out of the dark room, I told Morgan, "The ring looks a lot like the one in my picture," I said, holding up the larger blow-up beside the picture I'd shown him before. "If only the camera had caught the ring straight on, we might have picked up enough detail to be certain."

I crossed the floor to my desk and clicked on the intercom. "Betty, see if you can find the French heraldry book. I believe it's on the second from the top shelf."

"Be right there." She disconnected and was in my office in a flash. She slid the ladder over to the spot I'd indicated and nimbly climbed up to retrieve the book. It was an impressive book, leather bound, embossed, and gilt-lettered. Morgan stepped over to take the heavy book from her and laid it on my desk.

I opened it to a bookmarked page. There beside a picture of Nigel Montcreif was a picture of the Montcreif coat of arms. It seemed to match the signet ring in the picture I'd torn from the book, but since we had no straight-on shots, I couldn't be certain. The three of us studied the evidence wordlessly. The ring in the picture could be this very ring or half a dozen others pictured in the book. The colors were right, but the actual crest was not visible,

After a beat, I looked from one to the other with a faintly amused smile, before my gaze rested on Morgan. "If this is in fact the Montcreif crest, there may indeed be a phantom in your opera. If only we could be certain. I'd already poured over each film frame and there were no more glimpses of this unique ring."

Morgan shook his head. "If it was Montcreif, the guy's got to be ninety years old. How could it be?"

Following a brief silence, Betty said tentatively, "Health food?"

We both looked at her. "Yeah," I added, "and clean living."

CHAPTER 44.

Betty dropped Detective Scott and me off directly in front of the United Airlines departure area at 11:30 a.m. Neither Scott nor I relished the idea of twiddling our thumbs at the airport for nearly two hours, but we'd agreed on the earlier flight rather than risk arriving a minute too late for the only remaining flight to Crescent City for the day. We both came equipped with plenty of reading material. I brought along the last few issues of my forensic periodicals to keep myself up-to-date on the latest technology. I was particularly interested in the data on the most recent breakthroughs in DNA fingerprinting, while Scott had a slew of material from his LAPD training sessions. It had been a tough sell to get Lieutenant Biddle to allow Scott the day and a half it required to get to and from Pelican Bay, but in the end Scott had convinced the lieutenant that he'd use every bit of his free time on his LAPD studies.

Scott and I had only carry-on luggage, so we strode straight to the departure area, showed our credentials, and slipped directly through security without a hitch—not an easy task since 9/11. Airport security had been stringent, and, while somewhat of a hassle, most of the inconvenience of confiscated manicure scissors, nail files, and the like were to be endured. Even the embarrassing ordeals of having to remove shoes or be subjected to a body scan when something as innocuous as the metal in a belt or the under-wiring in a bra set off the buzzer must be tolerated. Today, Scott and I bypassed those bothersome indignities.

It seemed Scott had made good use of our idle hours on the plane and in the airports, but I had trouble concentrating on much of anything other than the upcoming meeting with Terry McCormack. Which of his many faces would he show? Would he refuse to talk to me, or would he be the ultimate politician? Since I was the man who had put him behind bars for the cold-blooded murder of my son, it wouldn't be out of the realm of possibility for him to give me the cold shoulder. But the more I thought about it, the more I didn't think he'd take that road. Before his trial he'd written me two letters of apology, explaining he was under a tremendous strain, and as he looked back over those days it was hard for him to believe he'd even thought of shooting Hal. He also wrote again after his life sentence began, begging my forgiveness. I never responded. I looked down at my forensic journal, but the words just drifted past in an unconscious blur.

Finally, the last leg of our trip came to an end. As we made our way to United Express Skyway's flight 6190 and boarded the small turbo-prop plane, we noticed the flight that could hold up to fifty passengers was less than half full. Betty had booked us aisle seats across from each other to accommodate our long legs. The flight to Crescent City departed at 4:06 as scheduled. My mind was mulling over several possible scenarios for tomorrow's meeting, but as we began our descent, I slid over to the unoccupied window seat to enjoy the view. It was breathtaking. Crescent City was on the coast, and I could already see the abundance of Redwood and fir trees described in the material Jedediah had pulled up from his computer. The airport appeared to be a narrow strip of land with only a couple of outbuildings. I noticed that we were descending at a rapid rate in the direction of the ocean, when an unnerving thought skittered through my head. If the pilot of this contraption didn't throw back the throttle pretty darn quick, we could be spitting out ocean water. I glanced over at Detective Scott and wondered if his white-knuckled grip on the seat in front of him meant that his mind was trotting along the same path as mine. Then I heard the roar of the throttle and the plane eased down on the landing strip, bounced once, rolled, and shuttered to a stop.

Scott and I went straight to the small car-rental counter in the tiny airport, since neither of us had checked any baggage. I showed my driver's license, signed all the papers for our pre-arranged car, and was given the keys to a white Ford Taurus. I asked directions to the Crescent Bay Hotel.

"You won't need any map," the attendant said. "Just follow that road." He gestured toward the highway running beside the airport.

"It'll take you no more than ten minutes. It's a nice, reputable hotel; been in business for about thirty-five years."

Tossing our bags in the back seat of the Taurus, I pulled out of the parking lot and onto Highway 101. We drove past a quaint marina and on through a small, rural downtown area. There were no high-rises, just single- or two-story structures in the architectural style of the '70s.

The man at the Hertz counter was right. We needed no map to find the Crescent Beach Hotel. It was right off the highway, alongside the ocean. As I turned into the parking lot, loose gravel pelted the car. I pulled up in front of the office of the twenty-five or thirty-room hotel. It was what we might call a motel in the Los Angeles area. The sun was setting behind the hotel as we crunched our way across the graveled lot to the manager's office, the peaceful sound of the surf temporarily distracting me from the morbid internal monologue that had been pounding through my head for the better part of the day.

Opening the office door, I heard the tinkle of a bell and looked up to see a tiny set of silver bells attached to the door frame.

"Be right with you," a pleasant voice echoed from somewhere beyond the redwood counter. In seconds, a plump, smiling young woman bounced into the room. She came out from a doorway behind the counter, most likely her living quarters. She had a round face with deep dimples, a halo of light brown hair, and a lyrical voice. "Welcome," she said. "My name is Molly, and you must be

Mr. Barnaby Jones and Detective Craig Scott." She looked first at me and then at Scott.

"You got that right," I said. "How did you know which one of us was the detective?" I asked, smiling with amusement.

Her face flushed, then she quickly recovered. "Just a wild guess," she countered, catching my amusement. "I have two nice rooms for you gentlemen. We're not fancy, but the rooms are clean and comfortable, and they're right on the ocean. Wonderful views from your rooms, and the sound of the sea will just lull you to sleep."

Scott hadn't said much all day; perhaps we'd both been in our own private worlds of contemplation, but he spoke out now. "Before we get lulled to sleep, maybe you can suggest where we might grab a bite to eat."

She smiled again, brushing back her hair. "I sure can. Since you're only staying one night, I think you should try the *Beachcomber Restaurant*. It's just down the road about an eighth of a mile. It's a nice walk, just north on 101. It's not on the ocean, but you can see the ocean from there. It's one of my favorites. It's a family-type restaurant; near as you can get to a home-cooked meal."

Scott thanked her then asked, "How far is Pelican Bay Prison from here?"

"Only about ten or fifteen minutes."

"In what direction?" Scott asked.

She pointed north.

"I didn't see any sign of it from the road."

"No, it's pretty well enclosed, surrounded by a lot of big redwoods. About the only time we're aware of it is at night. You can see the ambient light from that direction."

"Do we follow 101?"

Molly shook her head. "No, you take Lake Earl. It will lead you straight into the prison, but it's sure not any place I'd like to visit."

"I understand it's had its share of problems and has had a fair amount of activist groups demanding better treatment for the prisoners," I said.

Molly looked me straight in the eye, her defensive tone a direct contrast to her earlier congeniality. "They've had a lot of bad press, but that prison houses the most dangerous criminals in the entire state, and the guards are constantly at risk. They have to protect themselves. I know quite a few, and not a one of them seems to lack compassion."

"I understand," Scott and I said in unison, just like Frick and Frack.

She laughed, her deep dimples giving her a jolly demeanor. "Oh, I almost forgot. What time is your appointment at the prison?"

"Ten o'clock," Scott said. I held my tongue to avoid looking like some kind of comedy team.

"Good," she said. "That will give you plenty of time for breakfast. And I'd recommend the Northwoods Restaurant. It's about a half-mile drive north on 101, right next door to the Best Western."

Molly handed us our keys and said, "Enjoy your stay."

******

Detective Scott and I decided to get unpacked, shower, and head for the Beachcomber Restaurant around 6:30 p.m. The evening was cool with a light breeze coming from the direction of the ocean as we trod along the shoulder of Highway 101. The restaurant was about half full and had rich, dark wood paneling and a nautical decor. We were greeted at the door by a tall, rather thin young woman who had her hair in a ponytail. She gave us a wide smile and seated us at one of the tables by the large window, which would have given us a clear view of the ocean if it had not been enveloped in darkness. I ordered the chicken-fried steak and a glass of milk, while Scott ordered pasta and a beer.

As the waitress left our table, I turned to Scott. "Detective," I said, "you've been mighty quiet today. What's been on your mind?"

"Nothing much gets by you, does it?"

"Not much," I agreed.

"Guess, I've been running all the aspects of this case through my head and wondering what our next step might be if McCormack confirms that Nigel Montcreif was alive at the time of his campaign."

"As I said before, the purpose of this trip is to find out why the Montcreif trust financed McCormack's campaign. What could the Frenchman or the power behind that trust possibly get out of the arrangement? I also need to find out who McCormack dealt with. His dealing directly with Montcreif is unlikely but not impossible. Knowing the contact will at least give us a starting point."

"Yeah, I understand all that. I'm also aware it would prove Montcreif didn't die at sea in 1987. And I know that's important to you."

"But you think that's irrelevant?" I questioned, again wondering why Scott had signed on for this extra duty detail with me if he wasn't sold on the fact that Lori was a victim of murder and not a suicide.

"No, not at all," Scott responded at lightning speed. "I'll be damned if I'm not beginning to feel like a damn rookie all over again." Scott's eyebrows rose like two crochet hoops as his ruddy face took on a rosy glow. "Sorry."

"Welcome to the club," I said with a chuckle. "I don't have to remind you, the longer a case goes unsolved the tougher and more twisted it becomes." Scott knew the drill; a fresh murder case took precedent over a cold one. And just as in the case of Tanya Guttenberg's murder, what is on the front page the day following a murder gets buried deep in the Metro section a few days later, and in another week it would be colder than yesterday's hot biscuits.

I picked up the tall tumbler of water and took a long, refreshing drink. "We need to cover all the possibilities and convoluted twists and turns of the past as well as the present. It's clear the murder of Tanya Gutenberg, the arson at Universal Enterprises, as well as my near accident are all part of one well-orchestrated conspiracy to keep the true story of Lori's death from coming to light. And who but the person responsible for Lori's murder would want this investigation shut down?"

When the waitress who served our dinners quickly retreated and we again had some privacy, I added, "I plan to cover all the bases and attack this case from the past and the present. And I sure do appreciate your assistance, but if you don't mind, I'd like to clear my head. How do you actually view this case. Do you believe Lori London's death to have been the suicide it's presumed to be?"

"Of course not. I wouldn't be here if I believed that," Scott shot back with a fair amount of indignation. I noticed with interest the change in expression on the young detective's features as he pulled his emotions in check and visibly relaxed. "My interest was first piqued the night I ran into you on the Walk of Fame. At that time I had no idea if Lori London's death was a suicide, a murder, or a tragic accident, but we've learned enough at this point to know it was no suicide or accident."

The next moment, Scott again became tense and clasped his pudgy fingers on the edge of the table. "Barnaby, I've got to be straight with you about my motivation for working this case with you on my own time."

CHAPTER 45.

"Come again?" I asked.

Scott looked down at his plate and began pushing his remaining pasta from one side to the other. "Everything I've told you regarding my interest in this case is the truth. It's just not the whole truth."

"And the whole truth is?"

"I'm what you might call a wannabe writer. I've been writing short stories since I was a kid and—

Amused, I said, "So you 'wannabe' the next Joseph Wambaugh?"

"From your mouth to God's ear," Scott smiled, the tension easing from his bulky frame.

"And you're going to all this trouble to be the writer of the true Lori London story?"

"No. Well, maybe. That wasn't my goal when I began. My goal was to pack as much experience as I could into as short a time frame as possible." Scott tipped up his beer and gulped down the last drop. "But the more I get into this case the more intriguing it gets. Would it bother you if I did choose to write my first novel on this case?"

"Not at all, but you'd better get saddled up and ready to go by the time we get our proof before some other wannabe writer beats you to it. Even with the scant concrete facts we've pieced together so far, Tommy Morgan's celluloid version will soon hit the theaters. The only thing he'll be missing is proof-positive. If Montcreif is still alive today, you'll need to have a pretty good idea where he's been for the past seventeen or eighteen years.

"By the way, have you had any luck selling your short stories?" I asked.

"A little, but I've got to tell you, I've had my fair share of rejections."

"I understand it's a tough business. Seems to me I heard that *Gone With the Wind* received something like sixty-four rejections."

Scott nodded his head and abruptly shifted back to the case at hand. "There's one question I have to ask you."

"Only one?"

"Well, only one for the moment. You don't think Nigel Montcreif is the one who murdered the Gutenberg woman, do you?" Scott quickly added, "While he might have been the one to set the plan in motion, he'd have to be too damn old to do it himself."

I repressed my laughter and said, "Not unless you buy into Betty's theory about health food. But seriously, I believe Montcreif is pulling the strings, but it would have to be someone on his payroll playing the role of our phantom."

Scott nodded, scratched a note down on the paper napkin, and said, "Makes sense."

"So once you've written this 'Great American novel'; are you following in the footsteps of Wambaugh and resigning from the force?"

"Not on your life," Scott said. "I have two passions: writing and police work. I don't want to give up either."

CHAPTER 46.

I spent a restless night at the Crescent Beach Hotel. Even the sound of the sea, which would ordinarily lull me right to sleep, failed to halt my mind from slipping back to the day I learned of my son's senseless murder. Though mellowed by time, I couldn't erase the past. But ready to relegate the past to the past, I had no real problem with the upcoming meeting with Terry McCormack. What I did have a problem with was finding the words to begin our dialogue. In Jedediah's vernacular, I knew I had to play it cool. If I put McCormack on the defensive, he'd shut down, and this trip could turn into the dead end Lieutenant Biddle hinted it might be. I couldn't allow that. I continued to role-play in my tired old brain until I finally drifted off to sleep around 3:00 in the morning.

Feeling groggy when my 7:00 a.m. wake-up call came in, I took a speedy shower, re-packed my carry-on bag, and opened the door just as Scott was about to knock.

"Full speed ahead to the Northwoods Restaurant," I said, handing the car keys over to the detective. "Had a lousy night, and I'm hankering for a cup of strong black coffee."

Scott's mouth spread into a wide grin. "What, no milk?"

"I'll take that, too," I said, noticing Scott's red-rimmed pupils. "Appears that you also burned a little midnight oil."

"I did indeed," Scott responded, looking smug as he slipped behind the wheel.

******

Feeling a whole lot more like myself after a hearty breakfast, I was ready to play the role of navigator, using the map Molly had drawn out for us when we checked out of the hotel.

Lake Earl Road took us through a light-residential area and past open fields and a forest of redwood and fir trees. Although Molly had said the prison was ten or fifteen minutes from the restaurant, we saw no sign of it until we were almost there. A forest of trees kept it from view until we reached a stop light at the gates.

There were clearly written directions posted from this point on, so I put the map in the glove compartment and read the signs as we followed the prison pathway to the visitors' area.

We passed an unmanned guard station and I began to read aloud, "No blue clothing, no firearms, no pointed—" I hadn't a chance to catch the rest before we turned left onto the path to our destination. We followed the east perimeter. "So far, no problem." I said. "I expected there to would high-level security."

"There is no lack of security," Scott said. "With the current state deficit, manning of the entry gate was one of the first cuts. But we've been under camera surveillance since we crossed the entry. We make a single suspicious move and an armed vehicle will be on us in a flash."

I craned my neck trying to see if I could spot any cameras. "Could be a bit nerve-wracking," I said, an obvious understatement.

"Relax, Barnaby, we're cool. All our paperwork is in order, and from what I understand, the guards refrain from interrogation-style questioning unless there's due cause. They just approach suspicious-looking incoming vehicles to find out what kind of business they have here, or to assist with directions."

I peered out the passenger-side window, noticing the double fences lining the entire perimeter. "Hate to get caught up in one of those dang things."

Scott grinned. "You would indeed. The inside coiled fence is electric. You could get that thick white hair of yours curled posthaste into an instant Afro."

"You're not going to catch me within a Missouri mile of that high voltage," I said as I directed my attention to the wood-sided building. It was a medium-brown structure with a tall blue watchtower, directly to the right. A sign clearly designated Visitors Parking a few yards from the buildings.

"This must be the place," Scott said as he pulled into a space not far from the tower. I started to walk toward the visitors' building, when Scott reminded me, "Hold it, I've got to check my gun."

I strode in beside Scott and waited as he showed his credentials and unholstered his Beretta. I still missed my old .22 caliber, but there was no point taking issue with Biddle's expert advice. Now, taking a good long look at Scott's 9mm, my own .38-caliber Smith & Wesson didn't seem as much like overkill as I first suspected. The gun of choice for today's detectives was the 9mm Beretta with the four-inch chrome barrels, but I didn't need all that firepower and still preferred my blue steel. I had no need for anything so darn flashy.

After exchanging a few words, the guard handed Scott a small silver key. "Place your gun in one of those lockers," he said, gesturing toward a wall of lockers, "and take the key with you. You can pick up your gun on the way out."

After depositing Scott's Beretta, we proceeded directly to the brown visitors' building and through the doors. The first thing that caught my eye was an expanded list of guidelines on the back wall. A repeat of the no firearms, as if anyone could get this far carrying. A more detailed and stringent dress code was also posted. Not just no blue clothing, but no denim, no see-through fabrics, no low necklines, no skirts more than three inches above the bottom of the knee.... These guidelines appeared to be the same ones that Jedediah had printed out from the Pelican Bay Web site.

We stepped up to the counter and showed our credentials to one of the guards. He verified that we had an appointment and a valid CDC approval on file. The California Department of Corrections left nothing to chance; absolutely no loose ends.

We were handed plastic clip-on badges and were buzzed through by the tower to the "sally port." A gate opened into what the guard assigned to us referred to as a coiled cage. As we stepped in the cage, the gate closed behind us. Once we were inside, the door in front of us opened and we stepped out.

Outside, we followed the guard straight down the path, past the lethal electric fence, across the crosswalk, and through the glass doors.

Inside the next building was central control. We were led to a short hallway. To the right and left of the entrance were two small desks manned by an officer who sat in front of a video monitor. We checked the signs above the desks on either side of the room. The letter A was above the desk to our left and the letter B to our right. Our escort led us to the desk to our right, for Prison Yard B, where Terry McCormack was housed

After looking over our credentials and visitor approvals again, a guard asked Scott, "Would you like to meet with the prisoner in the visitors' room or in the outside patio?"

"In the visitors' room," Scott said, looking to me for approval, although, being law enforcement, he was now the top dog in our duet.

I nodded, glad the appointment had been made for a weekday rather than the normal Saturday, Sunday, or special holiday visitors' hours. I realized the red tape had been cut to a minimum but remained thorough.

Inside the visiting area, my attention was drawn to the high podium centered close to the back wall. Several uniformed guards observed the prisoners and guests from the raised platform surrounding the podium, and there were several uniformed guards, clad in dark green pants and tan shirts, milling about.

Scott and I had been briefed and knew better than to ask for privacy. In this maximum-security setting, there was no such thing as privacy. Guards were everywhere, and we learned there was nowhere free from camera surveillance, a fact that I had no objection to whatsoever. The high-powered cameras were sensitive enough to pick up the small print from a newspaper. It made me realize the necessity of the high-tech security, and I wondered how the reported cases regarding notes being passed between visitor and prisoner or prisoner to prisoner were even possible.

Another guard accompanied us to visitor room B. Just outside the room was a walled patio with razor wire around the top. There were a number of tables and chairs in the large room and an abundance of vending machines on the prison side of the wall. The only thing different from your run-of-the-mill visitors' area or employees' lounge was the abundant presence of prison guards.

As we waited for Terry McCormack to be brought to us, Scott leaned toward me and said, "Doesn't this make you think of Aldous Huxley's *Brave New World* or George Orwell's *1984*?"

I scanned the room. There weren't many prisoners or visitors around, but enough that I said, "Well, right about now I'm not opposed to having 'Big Brother' watching over us."

Detective Scott and I rose as Terry McCormack was led to our table. He may have lost a bit of weight but looked pretty darn good for a man serving a life sentence for murder. His blue long-sleeved shirt and pants appeared fresh from the laundry, and his dark brown hair was neatly groomed, showing little gray.

The man who murdered my son stopped about five feet in front of our table. His dark brown eyes locked on mine and stayed locked for what seemed a very long time.

CHAPTER 47.

Scott pulled out one of the chairs and said, "Hello, Mr. McCormack. I'm Detective Scott. I realize you weren't expecting Mr. Jones, but we have a few loose ends on a case totally unrelated to yours."

Terry McCormack gave his typical politician's smile. "No problem," he said as he pulled a chair up to the table. Then addressing Scott as if I weren't there, he said, "I'm glad that Mr. Jones came. Not a day goes by that I don't live with the heavy burden of regret over having been the cause of his son's death. It never should have happened, and never would have if I'd been in my right mind."

"Mr. McCormack," I said, not wanting to hear anymore or give him a chance to ask for my forgiveness, because I had none to give, "as Detective Scott said, we are here on an entirely different matter."

"Call me Terry, please," McCormack said.

I cleared my throat and said. "All right, Terry it is." I noticed his eye straying over to one of the vending machines.

Scott also noticed, and said, "Before we get started, would you like something to drink?"

"I'd love a scotch on the rocks," McCormack said, getting a rise out of neither of us. He immediately dropped his failed attempt at humor and said, "A Diet Pepsi would sure hit the spot."

"How about you, Barnaby?" Scott asked, then answered his own question, "A carton of milk?"

"No. If you don't mind, I'll have a cup of coffee for a change. Cream, no sugar."

Scott took off across the room. Immediately, one of the guards was at his side, accompanying him to the vending machines. Scott was most likely seeing what additional data he might get about McCormack, grist for the wannabe writer's mill.

Although I wanted Scott to be privy to whatever might be gleaned from Terry McCormack's involvement with the Montcreif trust, I didn't care to give McCormack a chance to engage me in conversation from his own agenda, so I filled in the silence by asking McCormack what he knew about the death of Lori London.

"Not much. I just know she seemed to have everything going for her when she committed suicide ages ago. I understand she was even nominated for an Academy Award that same year. Damn shame. She was 'drop-dead' gorgeous," McCormack offered.

I corrected neither his perceptions nor his unfortunate choice of metaphor.

"Are you just making conversation or are you dredging up a cold case?" McCormack asked. "Like following up on those suspicions that her death was a murder and not a suicide?"

"Something like that," I responded.

Scott arrived with our drinks, and I was spared making small talk with this slick politician. I'd only brought up the past to keep him occupied until we were no longer alone.

As Scott pulled out a chair and McCormack reached out for the soda, I began, "I understand that one of the backers of your campaign for Congress was the Montcreif trust."

McCormack's forehead crinkled into deep groves. "My campaign? Why do you want to know about that?"

"It may be relevant to another case we're investigating," Scott broke in.

"But I don't see how—"

"Terry," I said, "what we want to know is who you dealt with from the Montcreif trust and why they were interested in financing your candidacy."

McCormack sat back, his chin resting on his steepled fingers. "The reason is sort of convoluted."

"Let's start with the who," I interjected. "The person who approached you regarding the backing."

I opened the packet of creamer as McCormack gazed up to the ceiling. After a moment of contemplation, he met my gaze. "My main contact was a man named Laurence Legend. And, as you know, I was being blackmailed." His eyes remained riveted on mine, looking for some kind of reaction. I gave none, just emptied the creamer into my Styrofoam cup. "So having this guy drop in from out of nowhere seemed like a real godsend. I was in need of an influx of cash to keep the campaign going without draining my entire cash flow."

"What were you expected to give in return?" Scott asked, inadvertently turning the conversation away from my goal, which was to find out if the man could have been Montcreif or someone very close to him.

"That's the part that is a bit strange," McCormack said. "Legend wasn't so interested in my winning the congressional seat as making sure that my active participation in spearheading the legalization and federal funding for the brain stem cell research did not take a back seat."

"Brain stem cell research?" Scott and I echoed.

"I know," McCormack said, taking a swig from his can of soda. "Legend's proposal seemed to come right out of left field to me, too. At first it seemed too good to be true, and I've learned that most things that seem too good to be true are usually just that. But this was for real." Then, shifting focus, McCormack set down his soda and said, "If you're up to speed on the more recent medical advances, you must be aware of the 'Pandora's box' that was opened when the use of human fetal tissue for treatment of spinal cord injury and a host of other conditions was first introduced a few years back."

I raised a palm up to McCormack, "Hold on, I'm having trouble following this. I'm getting lost in this a tangle of brambles and coming up with a lot more questions than answers. Like why—"

"Before you go on, Barnaby, hear me out. I know it's confusing, so let me take it one step at a time. I know you didn't come to hear about my problems, but I've got to tell you a little to have this make any sense. My younger brother, Tom, has been a quadriplegic since a bad dive while on the USC swim team, about ten years ago. The brain stem cell research gave us the first real hope for spinal cord-injury recovery. Christopher Reeve, the guy who played Superman before he was thrown from his horse, had the same sort of injury and had been backing this research to the hilt...."

As McCormack continued his spiel, going into the fact that brain stem cells were invisible to a transplant recipient's immune system and therefore do not trigger rejection, I tuned out. This conversation had veered way off track. I didn't want to offend the man, at least not until I got what I'd come here for, so I willed myself to appear attentive until he wound down.

"Legend was aware I was backing a couple of lobbyists who were fighting for funding, and he said he wanted to make sure I didn't withdraw my own support, so he was willing to back me to the hilt financially."

"Back your lobbying efforts or your political campaign?" I asked.

"Both. It was a real win-win situation, and it came at a time when I needed it most."

"And what did Legend get out of it?" Scott asked. "Did he have a loved one with spinal cord injury?"

McCormack shook his head. "No, not spinal cord, but he told me his wife, Germaine, had Parkinson's, another condition where it seems brain stem cell therapy is the only hope. Stem cells can replace damaged or diseased organs, making it a ray of hope for all sorts or diseases. Alzheimer's, cancer, and so on."

I wondered if Scott had picked up on the so-called Mr. Legend's wife's name. Germaine had been the name of Montcreif's wife in France. I felt a flush of anticipation and wanted to get straight to specifics, but I bided my time as I picked up my coffee and took a small sip. It was still pretty dang hot, with only powdered cream to cool it down.

McCormack turned his attention back to me. "As you know, I never had a chance to follow through on that mission. And I blame no one but myself," he said contritely, maybe hoping to gain a few points, but I had none to give. "But despite George W.'s decision to allow federal funding for limited human embryonic stem cell research a couple years ago, we've lost good stem cell scientists, such as Roger Pederson, who deflected to Britain due to frustration over the U.S.'s restricted stance on the research. The project is now being conducted under his leadership, but still a long way off before the human trials can begin with significant numbers."

I'd held my tongue for about as long as I could and asked, "What can you tell me about this Mr. Legend? Such as how old was he?"

Seeming a bit taken aback by my switching tracks, McCormack looked thoughtful for more than a beat then said, "An older gentleman. Maybe in his mid-eighties."

"And how was he connected with the Montcreif trust?"

"Said he'd been the executor since Montcreif's death at sea sometime in the late '80s."

"Did he say who he represented as executor?"

"No. I didn't ask and he didn't say. But I see where you're headed."

"Terry," I said, "how would you describe this Laurence Legend?"

"Let's see," McCormack rubbed his left temple. "He was around six foot, with thinning gray hair, a Salvador Dali-type mustache, and now that I think about it, it seems he had a slight tremor." He gave a short laugh. "Funny, I never thought about that tremor until I started to describe him. Maybe he was the one with Parkinson's."

It was clear McCormack had never given Legend's tremor a single thought before this moment. I wasn't surprised, since it appeared McCormack had always been a fairly self-absorbed man.

I pulled out my picture of the Montcreif crest. But before I got any further, a guard approached the table. I held out the picture to him, then showed it to McCormack as the guard walked away. "Have you ever seen this crest before?" I asked.

CHAPTER 48.

McCormack took the glasses out of his shirt pocket and scrutinized the picture of the Montcreif crest. "Sure, at least I think so. If I'm not mistaken, the man with the Montcreif trust, Laurence Legend, wore a ring just like that, or awfully close. If the light caught it just right, it was not an item that would go unnoticed."

I slipped the picture back in my pocket. We'd hit pay dirt. "Thanks, Terry, that's very helpful. Do you happen to know where this Mr. Legend lived at the time?"

"No, that never came up. We usually met at my campaign headquarters, and he came to a couple of parties at the house."

I turned to Scott. "Anything else, Detective?"

"Now hold on a minute, Barnaby. It appears I gave you what you were looking for even though I'm not sure what it's all about. I want to tell you again how many times I wish I'd turned that gun on myself and not Hal. He was a real decent fellow and—"

"You're right on that account. But he's gone and you're still here."

"Yeah, I'm here living in luxury." McCormack snarled, his politician's veneer slipping several notches as he said, "I'm in a cell with a window a whole three by four inches to view the outside world; I sleep on the bottom bunk with a snoring roommate who tosses and turns for the best part of nearly every night. I also have a stainless-steel table in the center of our room with one—not two, but one stool, and a push-button stainless-steel sink and john. All the comforts of home."

Scott looked at me for a reaction as we rose from the table and signaled for the guard.

After a beat, I said, "Well, Terry, I wish I could feel for you, but you're alive and my son is dead."

I turned away as a guard approached the table and led McCormack out of the visitors' room. I felt drained on one level, but triumphant on another.

Scott said, "How do you feel? I can't imagine how tough it was for you having to face the man that murdered your son."

I nodded. "I'm ordinarily not a vengeful man, but I'm not about to let McCormack flimflam me into feeling sorry for him. As things stand, his life sentence won't even be the full twenty-five years, with his cushy library clerk job, which I understand he charmed his way into before he served the first full year of his term."

"I know what you mean. When it comes to murder, that day-for-day rule sucks. I just hope they have enough lockdowns on his workdays to keep him from adding up workdays too damn fast."

I'd been troubled over that loophole myself. Any prisoner would welcome time out of his cell, and since McCormack had wangled his way into a library clerk job with access to a world of law books, it hardly seemed fair that each day he spends in the library gives him one less day to serve on his sentence.

As the guard guided us to the sally port, I said, "Well, I won't be around to see that day, so let's put thoughts of Terry McCormack behind us, like I've been doing for the past few years. It's now time to plan our strategy for tracking down Montcreif, if he's still alive, and his probable heir. We gained not just one insight but two."

"Got it," Scott said. His mouth turning up in a satisfied grin, he added, "Number one, we have good reason to suspect that Montcreif is alive, or was three or four years ago; and number two, if McCormack was correct, and I suspect he is, that Parkinson's-like tremor gives us a new lead. How about if I check into hospital records?"

"Check away, Detective. I'm following up with Morgan and his crew—working out how to implement the wiring to create a faulty ignition. Schaefer, the guy I worked with at Cadillac service, said he'd give us a hand. Betty and Jedediah are checking into leads on Montcreif's son. So far they haven't come up with anything on Nigel Montcreif III since he entered a boarding school in England at age five. Seems to have fallen off the map since he turned six, so we can only assume he's going by another name. I'm guessing he's in the U.S. but—"

"You're thinking he might be doing his dad's dirty work?" Scott conjectured.

"Well, Craig, whichever hat you put on, LAPD detective or wannabe writer, it seems our plot continues to thicken. So as soon as we can mosey on out of here with your gun back in its holster, let's head straight for the airport."

CHAPTER 49.

Detective Scott was as talkative as a magpie during our grueling periods of downtime switching planes and airlines on our return from Crescent City. He hadn't missed a beat, his thoughts paralleling my own. We'd booted around the coincidence of a Germaine Legend and a Germaine Montcreif connected with the Montcreif trust. Neither of us bought into coincidences, and certainly not that one. The fact that Montcreif's wife had supposedly committed suicide about sixteen or seventeen years ago made it more than merely unlikely that she was the one with Parkinson's disease. The irony of the name Montcreif selected had not gone unnoticed,

"Isn't it just too cute?" Scott mused. "The author of *The Legend of Lori London* choosing to dub himself Laurence Legend." Scott stopped mid-stride. "Didn't you say the PI firm Morgan had on retainer discovered another of Montcreif's girlfriends was reported to have committed suicide?"

"Yes, before Lori's time." Seems the coincidences were adding up.

Having no baggage to collect, we headed straight to the arrival door. About three yards inside the exit door we found a very distraught Betty.

"Barnaby," she cried out. "We've been trying to reach you since early this morning."

I was hoping she wouldn't bring up the idea of a cell phone again. I had no intention of carrying one of those dang things around and listening to it shrill at inopportune times, but I guess I should have left Scott's number with her.

"We checked out early to grab a bite to eat before making the trip to the prison," Scott offered, seemingly oblivious to Betty's unusual demeanor.

I got straight to the point, "What is it, Betty?"

"Someone broke into the office last night. It's a real nightmare."

I took Betty by the elbow and asked, "Where did you park?" Since 9/11 the security at the airport had been too tight to allow cars to wait for plane arrivals, so I imagined she'd parked in one of the structures across the street.

"I didn't park. J. R. is circling the perimeter."

Jedediah pulled up, and I opened the back door for Betty. I motioned Scott into the passenger seat since his legs were even longer than mine, but I wasn't about to try and wind my six-foot-four frame into the back seat like a sardine in too tight a can, so I turned my attention to Jedediah. "Hold on," I said, "let me take the wheel."

He shifted the Lincoln into park. "Be my guest; this boat is a real drag," he said as he slid from behind the wheel.

As I took my place behind the wheel, I countered with, "Just about any real automobile would seem like a bus compared to that flashy Mustang of yours."

"Barnaby," Betty said, with eyes that I imagined to be steely by the sound of her tone, "if you two are through with your banter, I'd like to tell you what's been going on at the home front."

"Sorry," I said, "just let me maneuver through this wall of vehicles, and I'm all ears."

Betty described the condition of the office when she walked in at 9:00 a.m. Then, before I had a chance to ask, she said, "I didn't touch a thing. I went next door to Gary Bradley's office to call the police." Bradley was a CPA who'd been in the building almost as long as I had.

"Was Lieutenant Biddle informed?" I asked.

"Of course." Exasperation again spiced her tone. "I didn't go to school just to eat my lunch."

I grinned. "Of course you didn't."

"If you two are through sparring, I'd like to add my own two cents," Jedediah said, not pausing for any response. He'd held his cool for about as long as he was able. "They trashed my computer, but not before printing this out." He reached over the seat to hand me a piece of letter-sized paper.

While keeping one eye on the road as we drove down the Hollywood Freeway in the carpool lane, I glanced at the paper. In large, bold, red letters, in a style best suited for a haunted house or a Halloween invitation, the message read:

'Stop stirring things up that were meant to

remain buried.

Lori London was a disturbed young woman.

She committed suicide.

Let her body rest in peace.'

"This isn't the original, is it?"

"No, Uncle, it's one of a couple of copies" Jedediah said indulgently. He seldom called me Uncle unless he had a point to make and he was trying to let me know he was on top of things.

"And you think this came off your computer?"

"No, it came from my printer." He leaned over the seat, pointing out the thin black line on the right-hand side of the page. "I need a new ink cartridge," he added.

I remembered the same thin black lines on the information he'd pulled up on the Montcreif heritage Web site. "Guess it's a good thing you procrastinated on fixin' that little problem."

"The library shelves were ransacked, but all I know for sure that's missing is that big book on French heraldry."

"How about my lab?"

"No equipment damage," Betty said.

"But?"

"But whoever it was rummaged through all the drawers."

"Anything missing?

"Just one thing that might be of significance."

"Well, darn it, Betty, spit it out."

"The ignition you were fooling around with from Lori's Cadillac."

CHAPTER 50.

The next couple of weeks flew by with little new evidence. Scott had been unable to unearth any kind of hospital records for a Laurence Legend. Failing a hit with the Legend name McCormack had supplied, Scott had run down scores of Parkinson's victims in the appropriate age groups in Hollywood, Beverly Hills, Brentwood, Bel Air, Westwood, and other nearby areas, as far as Malibu and Venice. But so far he'd come up empty.

After the break-in at my offices, Lieutenant Biddle had changed his tune. He couldn't help but get involved on the fringe of the investigation, but he'd been up to his neck in "bureaucratic red tape" for the past few days.

Betty had gone for the day and I was caught up in a myriad of speculation, so I hadn't been aware of anyone coming into the reception area until I heard Biddle call out my name.

"Back here in the lab." I was fiddling with another ignition switch when he made his way to my lab table. I noticed he was in plain clothes today: a gray suit, white shirt and tie, and well-polished black brogue shoes.

"What's up?" he asked as he peered around me, his voice husky, his tone suspicious.

"Just the man I want to see," I said, walking away from the table. "I'm going to have a cold glass of milk. How about you?" Biddle followed me out to the reception area while I strode straight to the pantry. "There's still some hot coffee, but I'm not sure how fresh it is."

"It's got to be fresher than what I've been drinking for the better part of the day."

As I took care of Biddle's coffee and my milk, I said, "I have an idea I'd like to sell you."

"Not sure I'm in any position to buy," Biddle said as we walked back into my office. I pulled my desk chair out beside the one in front of my desk for easy conversation.

"Well, first things first." I said. "We'll start with what we both agree is official police business."

We ran through the progress, or more precisely the lack of progress, on the open cases we shared. Nothing new on the arson at Universal Enterprises, the phantom that sent the brute light careening toward my head, the threatening note delivered to Dawn's dressing room, Tanya Guttenberg's murder, or the break-in at my offices. A big fat zero. Finally we got around to the crux of my investigation.

"Barnaby, you've made me a believer. But I don't have to tell you how hard the downsizing has hit law enforcement. I simply have no manpower to spare. My detectives are on overload as it is, with fresh cases that keep cropping up." He took a sip of the strong black liquid, holding my gaze as he said, "I don't have to remind you that while Detective Scott's assigned to Robbery and on the LAPD payroll, the only assistance you can expect from him is strictly on his own time."

I nodded, "Understood. I know you'd lend a hand if you could."

"You understand I am buying into your murder theory on this Lori London case. I'd be a damn fool not to with what you've managed to dig up, but, unfortunately, there's not a scrap of concrete evidence to clearly point a finger at the murderer or to officially reopen the case." Before I could comment, Biddle went on. "And I still think tracking the whereabouts of Nigel Montcreif is a long shot and not one I'm willing to buy into. Frankly, I think you're chasing your tail."

"John, I respect your opinions, but in this case I think we're viewing the evidence from different sides of the table. I have more than the hard facts, and, on this particular case, personal knowledge is far from strapping on blinders. It's given me a leg up." I paused, just long enough to take a breath, knowing it best to continue and ward off the possible retort I felt coming my way. "Let's just agree to disagree." I smiled.

I noticed that Biddle had drained his coffee, and asked, "More?"

He held out his cup. "Now what was it you had in mind to try and sell me?"

CHAPTER 51.

"Hear me out," I said and detailed the plan. "How's that for a gripping penultimate scene?"

"Penultimate? I've heard the word but can't put it in context," Biddle said.

"Sorry. It's just another way of describing the next-to-last scene."

Biddle stared off, his focus somewhere over my left shoulder. "I don't like it," he said, "It could be dangerous. How about just shooting the scene as if the ignition switch were rigged? After all, it's a movie, so this young actress can just fake it. The audience would never know the ignition was in working order." Despite his thinning hair, Biddle was an attractive man. But as his eyes narrowed, a frown settled on his well-defined features, making him look a good ten years older. I was about to respond when he posed a somewhat rhetorical question. "Wasn't the ignition switch taken during your recent break-in?"

As I walked back to the pantry, scavenging around for a snack, I said, raising my voice, "Yes. The one I borrowed from Lori's Cadillac was in turn borrowed from my lab, never to be returned. But that specific ignition is unimportant. What prevented the car from shutting down wasn't that particular ignition; it was the way it was wired. Any '86 Cadillac Deville ignition can be wired so it can't be turned off." I didn't bother reminding him that he'd been privy to the schematics I'd obtained from the Cadillac dealer showing the proper wiring, versus the pattern shown in my photos and drawing. "We want this scene to be authentic, down to the smallest detail. The cameras will swoop in for a close-up of Dawn, the actress playing Lori London, showing her frantically attempting to disengage the ignition switch. That can't be faked. Tommy Morgan pantomimed that kind of action for me the other day and proved that without tension from the switch, it looked as phony as a cheap carousel pony. Morgan has dubbed this a reality film, and he wants everything authentic. He didn't even plan to tell Dawn prior to the filming that the ignition switch can't be turned off. That way, he said, he'll have a realistic shot of the terror, one that Lori may have felt on the night of her death. That is, if she'd been conscious. The part about not telling the actress, I didn't cotton to, and I told him he didn't have the right to put Dawn through that kind of trauma. Fortunately, he came to his senses, but it took more than a Hollywood moment."

Biddle scowled his disapproval as I placed a bowl of almonds, another of jelly beans, and a bunch of grapes on a small plate on the desktop in front of us, then lowered myself back into my desk chair.

Backing up a bit, Biddle asked, "I know you're not implying Ms. London drove the car in while she was unconscious, so are you saying someone else drove her there? I'm surfacing this since we're pretty sure London was the driver. It's in the Detective's Report."

"I've read the DR books, and I know about there being no prints other than Lori's on the steering wheel, or any obvious smudges where prints might have been rubbed off. But if you were the one in charge of investigating that case today, you'd be checking for the presence of fibers that might indicate Lori was not alone and that her killer could have worn gloves or wiped the steering wheel clean, then placed Lori's fingers on the wheel." I realized that DNA testing wasn't in such wide use or such a big part of detective work in '86 as it is now. I selected a few jelly beans—the red ones and black ones were my favorites. "If I remember correctly, it was about '86 when the first big murder case was solved through 'genetic fingerprinting' in England." I knew the case well; my only uncertainty was the timing. England's landmark Narborough murder enquiry had brought the revolutionary scientific discovery to light. The technique of 'genetic fingerprinting' brought into play to solve this murder spree may well have been to forensic science what fingerprinting had been in the nineteenth century.

"About that time," Biddle said. "A former LAPD officer, the one who wrote *The Onion Fields*, went to England and ran down all the facts on that case and wrote a pretty darn good book about it."

"Joseph Wambaugh," I said. "I also read that book several years ago but can't recall the title." I smiled inwardly, thinking of Detective Scott out collecting as much grist as he could for his own writer's mill.

"Me either," Biddle mumbled, his mouth chock full of almonds.

"I've been doing a fair share of reading on the new breakthroughs in DNA profiling, and I just bet if we had a single snip of Lori's hair, we'd be able to prove she'd been drugged, and by what."

Biddle sighed. "Now, that's a bit far-fetched."

"Not at all," I insisted, knowing darn well I didn't have nearly enough evidence to get an order to exhume Lori's body, for all the good that might do. I was working on the premise that she'd been drugged, but it hadn't brought me any closer to proving who the murderer was. "Just read in last month's journal where the analysis of a single lock of hair proved the victim had been poisoned. The DNA even pin-pointed the specific type of poison."

Biddle crunched down on a few more almonds. Either ignoring my last statement or lost in his own conjectures, he picked up from where we left off before getting sidetracked into the world of DNA. "So you believe the killer drugged London, drove her into the garage, closed the garage door, and let the carbon monoxide poisoning finish the job?" Biddle looked thoughtful and closed his eyes. Even though this wasn't the first time I'd drawn the picture, when his eyes shot open, I was sure he got it. "If the killer had waited for her by those steep stairs leading from the Hilltop Café to the beach and carried her to the car, it could explain the lack of sand in her sandals. That single unexplainable piece of evidence was the factor that stuck in everyone's craw and kept the case open for a while."

"That's one of my theories," I said. "Morgan is turning that particular theory into a scene in his film.

"The thing I find hard to swallow is that Ms. London could have walked out of the bar under her own steam, then passed out before she got to the car. According to the reports, the bartender claimed he didn't actually see her leave, but he claimed he would have noticed if she'd talked with anyone other than the man she'd met in the secluded booth, and the young man he said hit on her."

"Let me paint you a clearer picture," I said. "The man in the booth was Nigel Montcrcif—" I held up a hand to ward off a rebuttal. "I know Montcreif claimed to have been mid-Atlantic on his yacht and had a boatload of witnesses to back him up—well-paid ones would be my guess. But let's chuck that aside for now and see how you like this version. Morgan knows that Montcreif and Lori met earlier in the week while Morgan was in Thailand on business, because Lori was calling him every night. He talked to her after she and Montcreif met, and, according to Morgan, she was elated, telling him that everything was working out even better than she'd ever dreamed. She reported that Montcreif had told her he was returning to his wife in France and wished her well."

"Did Montcreif know about London's relationship with Tommy Morgan?"

I shook my head as I stretched out my legs and rested them on the edge of the trash can I'd pulled out earlier to discard the grape stems. "Lori was nobody's fool. In this Tinseltown of rumors, she and Morgan made a point of never being seen together. By the time they knew they were meant to be together, Morgan said that even at parties they both attended, they avoided even casual conversation, always keeping their distance while in public view.

"Lori also told Morgan that when Montcreif asked the identity of the new man in her life, she told him it was a secret but he'd be the first to know and he'd be invited to their wedding as soon as they worked out the details. Apparently, Montcreif didn't press, but we figure that's when he began planning her demise. I was darn sure Montcreif never intended to let Lori go. Even if he'd tired of her, he'd never have let any other man take her from him. He'd handle her disaffection permanently."

"And this great romance was a big secret because London was afraid of Montcreif?"

"That and the fact that Morgan was married and had too much at stake in some gigantic business venture in Thailand to risk sending his wife on the warpath," I said. "John, it's not just Morgan vouching for Lori's state of mind at the time of her death. My son, Hal, talked with her during that same week Morgan was in Thailand and Montcreif was supposed to be on his yacht. He told me he'd never known her to sound so happy; said her spirits were soaring. She was no candidate for suicide."

"I got that, Barnaby," Biddle said. "But how about finishing that picture you were painting of the night London died."

I did. The replay rattled though my head like a record with a big scratch. "When Lori took her tonic and lemon over to the booth to meet the man—that man no one has been able to describe other than that he wore an overcoat…." I stopped, making sure I had Biddle's full attention. "Now, John, how many American men living in Southern California do you know who wear an overcoat?"

Biddle shrugged. "Can't think of a one, but there were a few times this winter that I wouldn't have turned one down."

"So my guess is it was the Frenchman, Nigel Montcreif, who joined Lori in the booth. He led her to believe he was granting her his blessing, maybe even offered to give the bride away. Other than Morgan, he was the only man who had a prominent place in Lori's life. As we know, it was dark in their secluded booth, and it wouldn't take a magician to distract Lori long enough to slip something into her tonic. The bartender didn't keep his eye on her all the time. She might even have gone to the ladies' room to powder her nose. Flash to the next scene," I said, moving right along. "Lori gives Montcreif a hug, ecstatic that he isn't trying to coerce her into staying with him and that she's free to go on with the life she's planned with Morgan. And knowing Lori the way I did, if Montcreif told her he was returning to his wife, she'd have been happy for him.

"The next scene," I continued, reaching for another handful of jelly beans, "is with the guy who comes on to her, just like it's detailed in your DR books. Around midnight, she decides to leave but is feeling a bit woozy, so she leaves quietly and heads down the stairs leading to the beach; but Montcreif is waiting for her. I'm a little foggy on just how drugged she might have been at this point, so either she made it down the stairs on her own or Montcreif assisted her. Lori could have been surprised to see him, but this master of alibis probably had a good story to hand her. From the dissipated condition Lori drew of Montcreif when Morgan spoke to her, I don't think he'd have been up to carrying her down the stairs, but carrying Lori's petite body from the stairs to her car would be no big feat for a man Montcreif's size, particularly since this was no crime of passion. It was premeditated to the last detail, with an alibi for his whereabouts already in place." I glanced down at my desktop, offered some grapes to Biddle, and took a few myself, knowing I'd already overdosed on jelly beans. "You know how the rest plays out," I said.

"It's all plausible, and you could be absolutely on target, but how do you expect to prove it, and how do you explain this new rash of crimes? You told me yourself this Frenchman has to be in his nineties by now."

I went over my theory again, not sure whether he was buying or not.

When Biddle returned from a quick trip to the restroom, I was clearing our snacks from my desk. "Now, if you'll agree to be on hand with a few well-selected men on the night Morgan films the garage scene, we just might hit pay dirt." I paused. "And if it's not a problem, I'd like Detective Scott to be one of them."

"Still don't like it, but I know you're like a Missouri mule and won't give me a moment's peace until you wrap up this case. So tell me, what do you expect to happen on the Montcreif garage set?"

"Maybe not a thing. But my guess is whoever has been trying to sabotage this film won't be too far afield."

"So you agree with the detectives on the case that the person or persons responsible for this mini-crime wave is most likely connected with the studio?"

Nodding, I said, "The security is darn tight and the security guard is adamant that no unauthorized visitors could have slipped past him. I tend to agree. It would be possible for someone with the proper equipment to get over the fence somewhere on the back lot, but the gates aren't wide enough for more than one vehicle at a time. And the creep that tried to stop my clock with that brute light made his escape by car." Biddle and I had already gone over my brief glimpse of the unlicensed car my assailant jumped into to make his escape; a car I couldn't describe past the fact that it had been a dark-colored coupe. It wasn't in view for more than a flash, and I wasn't able to catch the make. The guard at the entry hadn't either. He said he'd been busy with clean-up after the fire, and hadn't been seen the exiting vehicle until it passed the kiosk, since the headlights were off."

"You really feel someone will make a move while the film is being shot?"

"Since the only ones privy to the new movie ending are Morgan and myself, and now you and Scott, my guess would be that our man...," I hesitated, "... and I'm sure it was a man. It was no woman I saw up on that catwalk ... anyway, my theory is that our guy won't be able to resist a first-hand view of the ending we're staging at the

Montcreif garage. And even if I'm wrong about our recent mishaps being an inside job, which I doubt, there's no secret about Morgan's plan for a blockbuster ending that is light years away from the one Montcreif concocted in his novel. Besides, his general plan has been leaked in all the gossip columns."

"Maybe Morgan has hired an inside gossip as well as one bent on sabotage," Biddle commented without amusement.

"There's bound to be another attempt to destroy the film. If not right after the shoot, sometime before the film is duplicated for distribution and released in the theaters."

"Back up," Biddle said. "Lori London is not a fictional star, so has Morgan considered the legal ramifications involved in shooting your idea on how she was murdered, without a single ounce of proof?"

"Just think of all the TV dramas, movies, and even documentaries on JFK's assassination. As far as I know there's a whole trainload of speculation, and no two alike. JFK was a public figure and so was Lori," I said, hauling myself to my feet and crossing over to my lab counter. "Besides, I think I have more than an ounce of proof." I lifted the ignition I'd been fiddling with when Biddle came in, as well as the photos I'd taken of the wiring of the ignition I'd taken from Lori's Cadillac.

To jog Biddle's memory, I spread the pictures in front of him.

"While these photos are detailed enough to show that the ignition was tampered with—" Biddle stopped short, interrupting himself to ask, "Isn't it going to a hell of a lot of trouble for a movie moment? As I hear it, having a film crew on standby can get pretty damn expensive. Also having the actress, sitting in the car with the motor running long enough to be filmed in a closed garage, could be dangerous."

"Morgan's covered all the angles. The camera crews will be set up outside the Montcreif Estate when Dawn pulls into the driveway and opens the garage door. She'll be out of the car while the camera crew sets up inside the garage...."

Before I got a lot further, Biddle jumped in and asked, "They're actually filming at the Montcreif Estate?"

"Sure enough. But don't worry; it's all on the up-and-up."

"Barnaby, I've been trained to worry," Biddle said. "With that Guttenberg woman gone, who'd you scrounge up to grant permission for access to the Montcreif Estate?"

"Well, after I left Montcreif's place...." Giving Biddle a steady gaze, I continued, leaving no space for him to take issue with my unofficial visit to the estate. "I followed up with Coast Realty." I could tell from the expression on Biddle's face that he wasn't tracking, so I added, "I got the number of the realtor from the business card; the one I told you I found on the dining room table."

"You didn't tell me the house was on the market."

"It wasn't exactly."

"Meaning?"

"Let me give you the abbreviated version," I said.

"Abbreviated, meaning not the whole story?" A stormy frown shot across Biddle's forehead."

"No," I said, my mouth widening into a grin. "You know me better than that. You wouldn't accept less than the whole story, and I have no intention of flimflamming you. By abbreviated, I mean I'm not going to tell you how to build the barn when all you want to know is what's inside."

Amusement lit Biddle's eyes. "Good enough."

My abbreviated version turned out to be more like building the barn, but it covered the fact that Coast Realty had an exclusive listing for the Montcreif Estate and all the furnishings, but had not been given the go-ahead to show the property. Morgan was able to bypass a heap of red tape and had worked out a deal to purchase the property and everything in it, keeping his name out of the negotiations.

"Morgan asked for an appointment with the person who was running the Montcreif trust, but Kathy Porter, the real estate broker at Coast Realty, said it wasn't possible. She wouldn't even reveal the name of the person she is representing."

"I thought you said Morgan wanted his own identity to remain anonymous?"

"That's right, he did," I said. "We talked about sending Jedediah. He was to be the attorney representing Dawn Medford. We had an entire scenario worked out in the unlikely event the meeting could be arranged. No such luck. Montcreif or his representative is under deep cover. The real estate broker said all of her dealings with the executor have been by phone or by mail. She admitted she had a name, or at least the name the executor goes by. She could hardly conduct business without it but informed us she was not at liberty to divulge it."

"And Lori London's Cadillac—was that part of the furnishings included in Morgan's deal?"

"Well ... there was nothing in the contract that spelled it out. It neither specifically included nor excluded the car."

CHAPTER 52.

I found Tommy Morgan wearing a path in the carpet of the emergency room waiting area at Hollywood Presbyterian Hospital. He seemed deep in concentration and hadn't looked in my direction, so I headed straight to him. "Tommy, I came as soon as I got your message. How is she?" I asked.

Morgan looked at me, his face full of anguish. "Barnaby, it's all my fault. I've been so damned focused on this movie I haven't given Dawn the time of day other than to drive her harder and harder. For the past week I kept her going over her new lines till two or three o'clock in the goddamned morning. She was scared to death that something was going to happen before we completed the film, but did I listen to her? Hell no, I just kept pushing. I'm afraid I'd let myself turn into something like that bastard Montcreif. If I'd given her an ounce of support she never would have done such a thing."

During this long dissertation, Morgan continued his pacing, making it difficult for me to make eye contact. "Tommy, could we take a seat over there?" I pointed to the attached chairs on the far side of the waiting area, by the window.

"Oh sure," he said, finally meeting my eyes. "Sorry. I guess I'm wound up pretty tight. I appreciate your meeting me here. I just never figured Dawn as the type to try a dumb stunt like this."

I couldn't figure Dawn downing a bottle of pills either. "What kind of pills did you say she'd taken?"

"I don't know. There was a bottle of Valium on the floor by the coffee table in my studio apartment. I'd left her there while I ran over to Jack in the Box. Nothing else was open." He shook his head and got back on track. "The doctor said it was either Valium or some other type of tranquilizer or sleeping pill. They are in there pumping her stomach right now. After that, the doctor said he'd have the toxicology report and could be more definite."

"About how long will that take?" I asked.

"The doc said they'd have it in about an hour. Two at the most."

"Do you have that Valium container?"

Morgan's eyes widened. "Oh shit. The doctor asked me the same question. I know I should have brought it. I just wasn't thinking when I found Lori—I mean Dawn on that couch, her arm hanging limply to the floor. I picked up the pills and read the label as I tried to rouse her, then just tossed it on the coffee table or maybe back on the floor. I don't really know. Her breathing was so shallow I was afraid she'd die. Since we were so close, I drove her straight over here—was afraid to wait for any ambulance. I called on the way over here and they met us at the car, lifted her on a stretcher, and started to intubate her right away." Morgan looked down at the carpet for a second or two, then continued. "She looked so damn pale and vulnerable with that tube stuck down her throat."

I didn't know the girl well, but I knew enough about human nature to doubt that she was the sort of young woman who would even contemplate suicide. It was totally out of character. Just in the brief time I'd been in her presence I knew she was infatuated with Tommy Morgan and would do nothing to jeopardize his pet project. "Are you aware of Dawn taking sleeping pills?"

"Hell no," Morgan roared. "But that's not necessarily something I'd know about."

"Did you notice if the bottle had her name on it?"

"I think so. Oh hell, I don't know."

"I understand," I said, not wanting to rattle Morgan any more than he already was. "Just one more question. Did you notice a glass near Dawn?" Morgan stared uncomprehendingly. "Something she might have used for liquid to down the pills."

Morgan took a few seconds, then answered, "I'm not sure whether there was a glass or not, but she'd been drinking a Diet 7-Up, and I did notice the can on the floor beside the couch. It was on its side and had spilled on the carpet. I set the can on the coffee table but didn't take the time to do anything about the stain." Morgan took out his cell phone and, even though their use was prohibited in the hospital, he punched in a string of numbers. I made no comment.

"Damn it, why doesn't he answer?" Morgan closed the cell phone, quickly reopened it, and punched in some more numbers.

"Andre," he said.

Apparently his film editor recognized his voice, since Morgan didn't identify himself but continued to tell the young man what he wanted. "And use a handkerchief or something to avoid touching any of it directly. Put everything in one of those plastic grocery bags. There's a bunch of them under the kitchen sink."

I smiled. Even though a bit late, it was good that Morgan thought about avoiding more sets of print on the pill container, 7-Up can, and the glass, if he found one.

"That was Andre, my film editor," he said unnecessarily since I'd heard his side of the conversation. "He and the camera crew are still on the lot. He's going to bring the Valium container and whatever over to us."

I wondered who else might be on the lot. "Tommy, can we step outside so you can use that gadget and call your security and ask them to write out a list of everyone who was on the lot at eleven o'clock? That's when you said you went out for food, right?"

Morgan nodded, a sheepish grin on his ravaged features. "I know I should have done this before," he said looking down at the cell phone in his hand as we stepped outside.

"Tell the guard that I'd like to check out everyone on that list first thing in the morning. I know he's probably given all he knows to the police, but I'd like to compare that list with our line-up on the night of the fire."

Morgan made the call, and had just slipped his cell phone back into his pocket when it rang.

Flipping it open, he said, "Tommy Morgan."

A scowl darkened his features and he stared over at me. "What do you mean it's not there?—Did you pull out the couch and look under it?—Well, look again."

I was only privy to Morgan's side of the conversation, but I caught the gist before Morgan slammed his phone shut and pocketed it.

Morgan's hands balled into fists, his knuckles rigid and white, when he said, "Andre said he couldn't find any pills or even the Diet 7-Up can." Biting down on his lip, he continued, "I know they were there when I left. He didn't find a glass either, but I'm not sure if there was one to be found."

******

"Mr. Thomas Morgan," came a voice over the static of the speaker. Morgan and I didn't have to look far to see the doctor emerge from the double doors leading to the emergency room. He was still clad in green scrubs with his feet encased in white paper booties. He was a short, balding man with a serious expression.

"Mr. Morgan?" the doctor asked, attempting to sort out which one of us to address. Morgan introduced himself and then me. The doctor said, "I'm Dr. Anderson."

Overlapping his words, Morgan asked, "Is she okay?"

"Yes, she's resting comfortably in recovery. You can see her as soon as the nurse finds a room for her, but she'll be pretty groggy."

"I'd like her in a private room," Morgan said.

The doctor nodded. "I believe you already requested that. It's being taken care of." Then, continuing with his own agenda, the doctor said. "Mr. Morgan, you said you found a Valium bottle next to Miss Medford, but the toxicology indicated that the drug she'd taken was Prozac, not Valium."

Morgan stared in disbelief. "God, no," he cried out, raising his hands high in the air.

I looked hard at Morgan, mystified by his outburst.

The doctor also looked a bit nonplused, but tried to catch Morgan's eye. Not an easy task, since he'd resumed his pacing.

"Mr. Morgan," the doctor said calmly, "while Miss Medford had taken quite an overdose, unless she was also drinking a fair amount of alcohol, it wouldn't have killed her, just made her very sick. Apparently you weren't aware—"

"Hell no. Dawn doesn't take Prozac; I do. She's been trying to have me cut down."

******

267

We weren't allowed in to see Dawn until she was settled in her private room. This gave us time to ponder over what the doctor had said.

"What was that Valium container all about? Who in the hell took it? And where was the Prozac?" Morgan spit out in shotgun rapidity. With little more than a hesitation, Morgan said, "Excuse me, Barnaby. I'm going to step into the john to give Andre a call. I'll have him check out the medicine cabinet." Before Morgan took off, he said, "I don't think I had more than three or four Prozac left. I've got a new prescription on the way."

When Morgan returned, he looked more perplexed than ever. "My meds haven't been touched. What in the goddamned hell is going on?"

Before we had an opportunity to explore that question, a nurse called Morgan's name and said we could go in to see Miss Medford.

In the hospital bed of her private room, the back had been cranked up to bring Dawn to a semi-upright position. Her face was pale against the white sheets and none-too-glamorous hospital gown. Her eyes were shut, her long mascaraed lashes adding the only touch of color.

Morgan took a fragile white hand. "Dawn. It's Tommy."

She moaned groggily and opened her eyes with what appeared great effort. She looked up at Morgan; then her eyes drifted to me. Confusion masked her pretty, pale features; she struggled to sit up. Her elbow dug into the sheets as she raised her head, but she was weak, and before she uttered a single word she flopped back down, her gaze roaming the room.

Her tongue washed back and forth between her dry lips, and she asked for water. I wasn't sure she would be allowed anything to drink, but poured a tiny sip from the pitcher at her bedside table.

Morgan hadn't moved, just held her hand. "Why, Dawn? Why did you do it?"

Her brows formed a bewildered frown, and she raised her free hand to her temple. "My head hurts," she said. Then taking in the room and our serious expressions, she said, "If it wouldn't sound like something out of a B-movie script, I'd ask, 'What am I doing here?'"

"Oh, Dawn," Morgan said as he kissed the back of her hand.

"Dawn," I said, noting that Morgan was too distraught to be of much use, "it appears you took a powerful overdose of Prozac."

The adrenaline rush apparently kicking in, she pushed herself up and looked at us as if we'd taken leave of our senses. "I've never taken Prozac. I'd never take anything like that."

CHAPTER 53.

When I finally tumbled into bed, it was nearly 4:00 a.m. I knew I had too much on my mind to drift off to sleep any time soon, but for a change I didn't attempt to fight it. My body needed rest, but my mind was wilder than a billy goat's. I mentally went over the night's attempt to end Dawn Medford's life. I harbored no doubt that the person responsible for staging Dawn's apparent suicide, and the other incidents of sabotage aimed at Morgan's movie or the investigation into the death of Lori London, had to be stopped. The crimes over the last couple of weeks were not random, but committed by someone with unquestionable access to the studio premises. It had to be a person whose presence would be expected and whose comings and goings would attract no particular notice.

I made a mental note to talk to the custodial staff, as well as the cast and technical crews in charge of cameras, lighting, costumes, makeup....Then there were the guards, particularly those on the lot at the times in question.

270

It seemed to me that our phantom was beginning to get careless, or at least clumsy. The Valium container had obviously been planted to create the illusion of a planned suicide. While I could understand removing the pill container if the prescription had not been made out to Dawn Medford, the removal of the 7-Up can was more problematic. In fact, it was just plain stupid. If Dawn had been drugged, as I suspected she had been, snatching the can may have avoided detection of the Prozac; but not leaving an empty can in its place pointed directly to foul play and away from suicide. That was the last thought I had before drifting off to sleep.

******

I called Jedediah early the next morning. As the phone rang in my ear, I poured a tall glass of milk and popped a piece of bread in the toaster.

"Hello?" a sleepy voice answered on about the eighth ring.

"I've got a lot of questioning to do at Universal Enterprises this morning. How about accompanying me there?" I looked down at my watch. It was 7:35 a.m. "I'll pick you up in about an hour. I'd like to be there at nine o'clock sharp."

"Barnaby?" Jedediah said, his voice almost a yawn. "What time is it?"

I told him, then said, "Time you jumped in the shower and got that sleep out of your voice. We've got work to do, and that quirky perception of yours might be just what I need."

Just after 8:30 a.m., I pulled up in front on Jedediah's apartment building and gave a short toot. Jedediah came right out, jogging to the car as he shrugged into his navy blazer. His tie was wrapped around the collar of his pale blue shirt and his hair was still damp from the shower.

On the way to Universal Enterprises, I filled him in on last night's drama at the studio. He gave me a few mumbled responses while looking into the visor mirror. He knotted his tie, a striped silk tie in various shades of blue, then asked, "You have any prime suspects?"

"A few, but I'd like to talk with the entire lot of them again and get your take. First impressions are often misleading."

"Fair enough," Jedediah said as we approached the guard kiosk.

"Hello, Mr. Jones," the guard said. "If you don't mind, I need to give Mr. Morgan a call. I'm sure he'll approve your entrance, but he told me not to let anyone in who wasn't approved, and it seems he forgot to put your name on my list."

I shifted the car into park as the guard went back in the kiosk to make his call. "Well, Mr. Morgan," I heard the guard say, "you told me I wasn't to let anyone in whose name wasn't on my list—I understand—So you want me to add his name to the list with the others?—Sure thing." The guard set the phone back on the hook, and in another second the right side of the rococo gate swung open.

"Sorry, for the delay. It won't happen again, Mr. Jones. Mr. Morgan told me to write your name on the list for daily entrance. In the future, as soon as I see you coming I'll open the gate."

I thanked him and headed for the parking area beside Morgan's studio apartment. As I parked the Lincoln, Morgan stepped through the door of his studio apartment and waved a greeting. Jedediah slipped out of the car, tightened the knot is his tie, and was now giving the lot a once-over.

After we exchanged greetings, I asked, "How is Miss Medford?"

"She says she's fine," Morgan said as he held the door open, then followed us into the office area of his apartment. "Apparently she's charmed the socks off all the nurses, and even talked the doctor into signing a release for her to go home today." He shrugged his shoulders but didn't appear too happy about her decision. "I've hired a bodyguard who will be watching over Dawn full time; at least until this film is in the can. His name is Jim Kelsey. He's at the hospital now and will be bringing her home today at 11:30 a.m." He smiled, "That girl is so damn stubborn; she said she wasn't about to stay in that hospital a moment longer. Said she needed to get back to work right away. She even objected to having a bodyguard at first, but I let her know that it wasn't an option. When I explained the bodyguard was not only necessity for her safety but for my piece of mind, she agreed."

Then shifting focus, Morgan pushed a clipboard in my direction and said, "You can use my office for your interviews. I need to spend some time with the boys in the cutting room."

Morgan picked the clipboard back up from the corner of his desk and said, "This list isn't too long since most everyone took off last night well before 8:00 p.m. The only ones still around by 11:00 p.m. were Dawn; Andre Deville, my film editor; and my three top camera men." He pointed down to the list of names. There was Dean Zarkos, who I remembered as the friendly young man with the short-cropped hair; Jon Chevalier, with long, flowing blond hair, whom Dawn described as thinking he was some sort of Adonis; and Chris Montgomery, with the wary, deep-set eyes beneath bushy brows. I'd met all of these men on my very first trip to the lot and had talked with each and every one of them after the fire and incident on the catwalk. I'd also talked with each of the five guards whose names were on the list Morgan handed to me; but I wanted to go through the whole routine again. There had been no new names added, but all of these individuals had been on the lot at the time of both incidents.

"Make yourselves comfortable," Morgan said. "I'd like to meet with my film editor and cameramen to map out our last few scenes, so, if you don't mind, I'd like you to talk to the guards first."

"Sure," I said. "We can do that, but I'd appreciate it if you'd have the others available in an hour or so."

"No problem," Morgan responded. "I just want to make sure everything will be ready for tomorrow night's shoot."

"Dawn will be in shape for that so soon?" I was worried about the young woman, afraid her infatuation for Morgan had blinded her to the dangers.

"She claims she's fine and anxious to get back to work. Tomorrow night's shoot will be inside the Hilltop Café."

"Tommy," I said, my voice reflecting my unease.

"Yes. What is it, Barnaby?"

"That bodyguard you hired. I take it he will have his eye on Miss Medford for the duration of the filming?"

******

The last hour had been tedious. Jedediah and I agreed that we hadn't gained much from the guards. I hadn't really expected to. My strongest suspicion lay with the technical crew, who were privy to Morgan's new storyline for Lori London's final hours. They also had unlimited access to the studio.

Dean Zarkos raced over to Morgan's office, where Jedediah and I had set up our interviews. He was slightly breathless when he said, "I hope I haven't kept you waiting. I sort of lost track of time."

"No problem. We needed a bit of time for a breather," I said. "Dean, I'd like you to meet my associate, Jedediah Jones."

Jedediah extended his hand, and as Dean shook it, he said, "Just call me J. R."

"I was just sick when I heard about Dawn," Dean said.

I motioned him to the soft leather chair. Jedediah and I sat at opposite ends of the couch. We quickly shot past the emotions of last night's near tragedy and asked about his whereabouts around eleven o'clock.

"We were in the cutting room most of the evening, right up till around 2:30 this morning. We were going though the film that hadn't been badly damaged in the fire with Andre. He's the film editor," Dean said. The name Andre, and the fact he was the film editor, was a detail I was unlikely to forget, since everyone kept reminding me. "Anyway," Dean continued, "he had us review what we had that could be salvaged and what scenes we'd have to reshoot."

"I imagine there were times when you weren't all together in that cutting room," I stated.

"Not a whole lot," Dean said, running his fingers over his short-cropped hair. "Every now and then one of us went to the john or took time out for a cigarette. We didn't dare smoke anywhere near the cutting room, but other than that—"

"Was there any disagreement on what could be salvaged?" I cut in.

"There sure was. That's what took so long. Andre's a real perfectionist and pretty much wanted to scrap everything, but there was a lot of good stuff I felt we could use. Mr. Morgan wants a quality movie, but I know he's anxious to finish this film and get it in the can. He'd never approve of any schlocky work, but there were some terrific scenes that weren't damaged."

"Did all of the cameramen agree?" I asked.

"Well, Mr. Jones, I can't really say that. Jon and I were more together than not, but Chris had his own idea. What we liked he didn't, and for the most part the bits he picked out Jon and I thought should be scrapped...."

When Dean left we were alone for just a few minutes before Chris Montgomery came in. When I introduced Jedediah, Chris did not extend his hand. He nodded and mumbled, "I can't be away long, so what do you want to know?"

Gesturing toward the leather chair, I said, "Well, I see you like to get right to the point."

He sat on the arm of the chair, his bushy brows pulled together, his deep-set eyes reflecting no emotion.

"One thing we'd like to know is how you spent your time here at the studio from about 11:00 on."

"I'm sure Dean must have told you," Chris said, but he finally went on to say pretty much the same thing that Dean had.

Jedediah asked Chris about how well they agreed on what could be salvaged from the damaged film.

He didn't respond for a good minute or two.

"You put four guys together, and you'll get four opinions," Chris finally spit out.

"Chris," I said. It wasn't my place to tell him about teamwork. "What's your opinion of this film project?"

He shrugged. "I take the good with the bad," he said. "There are some good scenes and some god-awful shitty ones."

Jedediah loosened his tie and gave me a look. I knew we were coming to the same conclusion. We're wasting our time with this sullen young man. He resented being here and his abrupt responses supplied little if any new insight.

"Well, Chris," I said as I rose to my feet, "you can go on back to work, but if you think of anything we should know, please give us a call." I removed a card from my wallet and handed it to him.

Jon was already outside the door on the porch when Chris walked out. "You're next on the list for the interrogation," I heard Chris say to Jon.

Once the introductions were out of the way, we found Jon's information pretty much mirrored that of the others. As he spoke he kept shaking his hair out of his eyes but showed no signs of the restlessness the young man before him had demonstrated. "I just can't believe that anyone would want to hurt Dawn," he said as we were winding up our interview.

After Jon left, Jedediah stood up and gave an exaggerated yawn and stretched his limbs.

Andre the film editor showed up in the middle of this demonstration. I introduced Jedediah and let him take the lead as I sank back down at my end of the couch.

Jedediah followed the same line of questioning and got most of the same scenario we received from the camera crew.

As Andre fingered his ponytail, his piercing blue eyes remained steady, but when Jedediah came to the question of teamwork and the degree of agreement between the film editor and the camera crew, Andre's glare shifted to me. "We're not techno-nerds—we all work in a creative mode, so you've got to expect creative differences of opinion."

Jedediah, who had been seated at the opposite end of the couch, rose. Now standing, he said, "I understand you don't think there's much that can be saved from the film salvaged from the fire."

"That's right. Mr. Morgan is expecting a blockbuster, and you don't get that by piecing together salvaged film. You want to take a look, and I'll show you what I mean?" Andre challenged. It was a tongue-in-cheek challenge.

Jedediah sat back down on the arm of the couch, and, shaking his head, he said, "You're the expert."

When the door closed behind Andre, Jedediah slumped down in the plush leather chair, the one Andre had vacated. "We're getting nowhere fast! All these creative types say they were together most of the night, but every one confirmed there were portions of the evening some were missing from the cutting room, either going to the john or out for a smoke. Yet no one has a blasted clue when and how long anyone was gone. They can't even estimate a time for their own breaks." He paused. "You know, I've been thinking, that editor and one of the cameramen have French names."

He meant Andre Deville and Jon Chevalier. "Noted that myself," I said. "But, on the other hand, if you're traveling down the road of discovering Montcreif's missing heir, a French name might be avoided, if this so-called heir intends to remain anonymous."

CHAPTER 54.

I spent the next few days interviewing the actual witnesses of Lori London's last days. Those who had worked with her on her final film, those who called themselves her friends, and the handful who observed her at the Hilltop Café on the night of her death.

Now back in my own office, I'd been pouring over the background information Betty had been gathering for the past hour or so on the members of Morgan's technical crew. Their background information sheets were somewhat in order, all but one. The only one that seemed to have large gaps in the details of work history was that of Jon Chevalier. Just as I was beginning to reread the details, Jedediah burst in with his usual gusto.

"You think Chevalier could be our man?"

"I don't rightly know; I'd need a lot more to go on than we've got here," I said, patting the stack of paper beside me.

Then Jedediah went on to reel off the information that I now had in front of me, fanned across my desk.

"Barnaby," he said, "didn't you notice the birth date?"

The personnel records gave Jon Chevalier's place of birth as Chantilly, a small village on the outskirts of Paris. His birth date was September 10, 1981, the same month Lori's dreams of motherhood came to an end.

"Yes, I did. I don't plan to ignore it, Jedediah," I responded, "but I don't feel that jolt of lightning or even a twinge of an 'a-ha.' I might be way off track, but Jon Chevalier doesn't fit the picture I'm carrying around in my head. And he sure as heck doesn't impress me as an angry young man. If Montcreif's son is the one sabotaging Morgan's film, he's got to be doggone brimming with rage.

"I have the feeling that if Chevalier were Montcreif's son, he'd have the means to create an identity that would not send up any red flags. At least, that's my opinion at this very minute." The intercom blared, and I flipped on the switch. "Yes?"

"Tommy Morgan's on the line," Betty announced.

"Thanks, Betty." I looked down at the phone and jabbed the button for line one.

Morgan told me how well everything had gone on the Lori London set over the past few weeks. "Not a hitch," he told me. "We've got some sensational footage. Dawn's turned into a true star, but she still can't get over the fact that I could have believed she'd taken those pills."

"You believe she's telling the truth, don't you?" I asked, knowing he'd had trouble believing anyone could have forced those pills down Dawn's throat without her knowledge.

"I do," he said, his tone without reservation.

"Well, it's the truth," I confirmed. "Biddle called this morning. One of his detectives found the Diet 7-Up can you saw on the floor beside Lori. It was in that big dumpster outside Studio 1. The lab results came out as positive for Prozac. I tried to get hold of you yesterday, but I was told you were at the studio. But since you weren't picking up—"

"Sorry, I wasn't actually in the office, and I had my cell on vibrate since we were filming."

"Not important," I said, "but I knew you'd want to know."

"You bet I do," Morgan said, then after a pause, which he filled with ahs, he said, "You mean to tell me the 7-Up can was in the dumpster all that time?"

"No, they found it the night Dawn was drugged, but Biddle just told me about the lab results this morning. Apparently this phantom of ours got hold of the liquid variety of Prozac. It's not used much other than for older patients who refuse to or can't take the capsules. Since there had to be a prescription, it's being run down as we speak."

Jumping back to the reason he'd called, Morgan exclaimed, "I'm so dammed pleased with the footage we've shot this week, I'd like you to see it."

"When?" I asked.

"How about now?" Before I could respond, he waxed on, "During the last few days, we shot the scene at the Hilltop Café. Well, we didn't actually shoot the inside shots at the Hilltop. They were done at the studio. Even if we could have rented the Hilltop for the shoot, it would have been a bitch to get the lighting balanced. But we did use the actual staircase outside the Hilltop. The one Lori must have taken down to the parking area. We also got some great shots of her inside the Cadillac."

"Not even any minor mishaps along the way?" I asked.

"Other than the hours it took to light the SOB, not a single one!" Morgan proclaimed. "We got rock-solid, super-tight security, but it still seems too good to be true."

"That exactly what makes me nervous," I said.

******

Pulling up in front of the rococo gates of Universal Enterprises, Betty said, "You weren't kidding when you said security was tight."

Besides the guard in the kiosk who was making his way up to my window, there were two men in red windbreakers with the UE emblem, walking to and fro between the gate and the hangar-like studio buildings. Whether they were actually out-of-uniform guards or men Morgan had recruited from his own staff to serve double duty, I wasn't sure.

After the guard had checked and found Betty's name on the visitors' access list, he waved us though as the gate swung open.

"Isn't this the old 'Metropolitan'?" Betty asked. As I nodded, she added, "It looks a lot different from when my parents brought me here as a star-stuck teenager."

The idle chatter came to an abrupt halt when we pulled in beside Morgan's studio apartment. Morgan jogged toward us with expansive gestures. "Follow me," he said as Betty and I emerged from the Lincoln. Turning, he headed in the direction of Studio 1, giving a rapid look back over his shoulder to make sure we were following.

He led us straight into the viewing room, which had just enough light for us to find our seats.

"Sorry, I seem to be forgetting my manners," he said to Betty. "I'm glad you could join us. I can hardly wait for you to see the footage from the Hilltop Café scenes."

"I'm looking forward to it," Betty said. "Barnaby gave me a short rundown of what you're aiming to accomplish in these scenes."

"It's turned out beyond my wildest dreams." Morgan called out, "Dawn?"

My eyes were still adjusting to the dim light and I hadn't yet seen Dawn, who was in the row just below us. Morgan introduced Dawn to Betty, and I added my greeting. Dawn looked much as I'd seen her on the night we first met—her attire every bit as casual.

Morgan signaled, "Roll 'em." The small theater was enveloped in darkness; the only illumination was that emitted from the glow of the large screen.

The camera moved in for a close-up of Dawn seated at the mock-up of the Hilltop Café bar. I blinked taking in her screen image. She was breathtakingly gorgeous. Her makeup and hair were done to perfection, transforming her from the freshly scrubbed ingénue before me into a raving beauty. On the screen, Dawn looked so much like Lori that I felt an ache of recollection. Lori once had the innocence of Dawn Medford. Nigel Montcreif, and her rapid climb to fame had robbed her of much more than she'd gained.

I refocused my attention on the film, watching Dawn, clad in a simple, white, form-fitting dress, her diamond earrings sparkling, as she made her way over to a secluded booth and slipped into the seat across from the mystery man in the overcoat. As I saw her set a glass with a lemon wedge on the table, I wondered what kind of dialogue Morgan had created, since what they talked about was only pure conjecture.

I sensed Betty stiffen beside me. "What is it, Betty?"

She shook her head. "Nothing," she said, totally unconvincingly.

I repeated my question, unable to let it go.

"I'm sorry, Barnaby. It's just that this scene is so much like the one Hal tried to paint for me."

"It's about the only way I see it could be painted with the information we have," I said. I gave Betty's hand a fatherly squeeze.

Morgan had not attempted to add dialogue, which was wise. The scene played a lot better with the cameras panning from a distance. It was just as the bartender and witnesses had observed this exchange. The only spoken words that were in the script to this point were Lori's brief conversation with the bartender and those that were heard spoken by Lori when she gave the mystery man a big hug and told him, "Thank you. You're the best."

I had to agree that Morgan had done a first-class job with this portion of the film, but was a bit uneasy not knowing how Lori's decent down the steep stairs had been orchestrated. I realized that the section with the young man coming on to Lori couldn't be overlooked but found myself impatient with the amount of time it took to get to the outside staircase. Since I didn't have a clear picture of this part of Lori's evening in my mind, I wanted to move along to see how it was played out.

CHAPTER 55.

The screen took on a misty quality as the door leading from the Hilltop Café slowly edged open onto the empty landing of the steep wooden staircase. The only sound to be heard was that of the pounding surf crashing against the shoreline of the deserted strip of Malibu Beach. The camera artfully panned along the sandy shore, the phosphorescent, purplish-foam of breaking waves, then seamlessly moved to the calm still water beyond, capturing the moon's reflection as it glinted off the surface.

Slowly, the camera refocused on the form of a woman on the landing. She was clad in a floor-length fur coat. Knowing Morgan's obsession for authenticity, particularly for this, the most important movie of his life, I was certain the coat was sable. He labeled this a "reality film." The coat had to be a replica of the one Lori had taken such pride in. The generous collar of the fur had been turned up, brushing the bottoms of her earlobes.

The hazy backlighting from the doorway of the Hilltop Café obscured the features of the young woman, revealing only her pale blonde hair, which cascaded over and past her shoulders, creating a soft halo around her face. As she tottered slowly across the landing, her tortoise-like steps appeared unsteady.

She stood for a few seconds, then leaned forward, precariously reaching out for the railing and grasping it as though her life depended on it. Gripping the stair rail with both hands, she took one hesitant step, then another, her hands crisscrossing with each descending step. Even through the dimness of the night setting, the splintery wood railing appeared treacherous and was most likely riddled with a multitude of potential hazards.

After every two or three steps, the young woman stopped, rubbed her temples, and swung her head cautiously from side to side as if to clear a foggy brain. Near the bottom of the staircase, she stopped, staring down as the camera focused on her lovely face. What it revealed was an expression of utter bewilderment.

As the light played across her high cheekbones and perfect features, my mind flashed back to the many times I'd gazed at this same troubled countenance on the features of the young Shirley Demstead—the fragile young girl who had grown up without the affection she'd craved so desperately; a life with no father and a part-time mother who'd never allowed her daughter to become a real part of her life.

The face I now stared at on the wide screen was not at all unfamiliar. It was one I'd seen many times in the past. The girl Hal and I had known so well had often mirrored this same depth of vulnerability throughout her early days as she'd embanked on that stairway to stardom. Even after she'd reinvented herself as Lori London, the actress who'd grown into a star of international fame, the insecurity of the young child had remained deep inside.

I felt a visceral jolt as this heart-wrenching scene spread across the wide studio theater screen. I no longer saw Dawn Medford; I saw Lori London. This was the scene leading to the penultimate one, on the night Lori's life had been brought to an abrupt end.

The cameras stayed focused on Lori's frail form and enormous blue eyes long enough to feel her pain and the depth of her puzzlement. A puzzlement I was sure had come from the wooziness that she must have felt wash over her. Knowing she'd consumed nothing stronger than tonic with a slice of lemon, her head must have been reeling from more than the drug I'd assumed she'd been slipped. This had been my vision of Lori's final hours—a vision I was now privy to seeing fleshed out and brought to life through this moving enactment.

The next image flashing across the screen revealed another reason for Lori's inability to take in the events of that fatal night as they slowly unfolded. Two or three stairs from the bottom of the staircase, a massive silhouette filled the screen. It was the figure of a tall man in a dark, calf-length overcoat.

There was no dialogue; none was needed. The eerie strains of anxiety-producing music swelled to a crescendo as the camera zoomed in for a close-up of Charles Stafford, the actor who had been cast as Nigel Montcreif. I wasn't actually clear whether Morgan had the guts to risk using the Montcreif name or not. As Lori's gaze tried to focus on the man, I remembered Dawn's description of Charles Stafford, whom she truly liked and respected, as well as how she said she'd been "literally blown away" by the ability and performance of the mature silver-haired actor.

The camera narrowed in on the man, then expanded to a view excluding everything but the arms of the man as he reached up and wordlessly scooped the dazed young woman off her feet. The camera then flashed to the limp body of the unconscious form in those long arms as the wide screen faded from gray to black. Then with breathtaking speed the house lights blinked on, flooding the theater with a blinding brilliance.

CHAPTER 56.

On the grounds of the Montcreif Estate, Tommy Morgan was flying high. After the unparalleled footage captured from the outside night shoot on the staircase and adjoining parking lot of the Hilltop Café, he had high hopes that they were finally on a roll. The outside lighting at the Hilltop had gone without a hitch. The lighting crew had done a masterful job creating a misty oceanside ambiance, totally in synch with his visualization. He'd anticipated no major screw-ups for tonight's shoot—at least not in the form of outside lighting. But he was wrong. This was turning out to be one of the most hellish days of his life.

Setting up the lighting at the Montcreif Estate was a whole new ballgame. Outside in the driveway and inside the spacious three-car garage, Murphy's Law was in full swing, and the lighting technicians were mad as hell.

Tommy had been at the Montcreif Estate for hours with nothing to eat and nothing to drink other than bitter black coffee from the thirty-cup aluminum pot the lighting crew had set up inside the garage. He could visualize exactly what he wanted to achieve in this scene, but he was having a devil of a time translating his idea to either of his technical crews. The lighting setup for the scene had been going on since 10:00 a.m., and he was still far from satisfied.

Outside shots were a bitch. Key to the film's success was making sure the light level was kept up, while keeping in mind the pitfalls. Too bright, the whites got blasted out, and too dark produced a grainy image without much color. The trick was to create a play of light and shade on the objects in the footage before revealing depth, form, and mood. He'd had enough experience to know just how important getting the lighting right was. Good thing they'd started early. He thought they'd had a sufficient supply of professional lights and plenty of reflectors. But during the first hour he saw that wasn't the case. He had to send a couple of his men out to a local studio rental agency for an additional Redhead. He smiled, remembering when he first came into the business and heard the term Redhead used for these standard pro-lights, he mistakenly assumed it was because the backs of the light cans were painted sort of a reddish orange; but he soon learned that the next step up in power for professional lights was referred to as Brunettes, and the most powerful were called Blondes. The more powerful the light the more heat they produced. Well, he always considered blondes hot stuff.

"Hey, Eric," he called out to the lighting techie, who had his arms wrapped around two or three large reflectors. Morgan had seen only the silver and white reflectors being set up. "You have plenty of the gold and whites?" Gold warmed up skin tones.

"Still in the truck," Eric shouted back as he continued over the grass area beside the driveway.

The white Cadillac was parked at the entry of the driveway since their city permit to close off the street did not allow them to set up before 2:00 p.m. They'd concentrated on the proper lighting for the driveway. They couldn't do a lot with the garage until they captured the shots of Lori's drive into the garage. That would have to be done when the Cadillac was in the garage.

The day was overcast, and Morgan could feel the ocean chill deep in his bones. He wore beige chinos with a red crewneck sweater under a blue windbreaker embossed in red with United Enterprises. His entire crew had been given similar windbreakers in reverse coloring, red with blue lettering.

Just when he thought he'd obtained an absolute balance in the lighting setup, at least as much as could be tested before dusk, he turned to his film crew for feedback. A jillion subtle changes surfaced and required action. That wouldn't have been so bad if they'd managed to come up with a united front, but that had been far from the case. What surprised Morgan most was that it seemed he was most often in agreement with Dean and Jon—they seemed to share his vision.

Dean had come up with using the neutral density filter to combat a washed-out effect on the white Cadillac.

While he'd been touting Andre's skill as a top-notch film editor and admired Chris's skill behind the camera as well as his compulsive pursuit to absorb the skills required to become a film editor, today neither of these young men had presented many ideas that were in tune with his vision. They weren't even in sync with each other in their suggestions.

The lighting techies were getting bent out of shape hearing suggestions from so many directions. Maybe he should have followed the normal protocol for setting up this take. The camera crew wasn't normally on board during the initial setup, but Morgan had wanted perfection. What he'd gotten was a big fat headache. As he continued to observe the childish antics of his crew, their unrelenting clashes of creative insight, he felt as if a heavy wire had been twisted tightly across his head.

"What in the hell do you think you're doing?" Andre's face turned a brilliant red as he shouted out to Chris.

Chris glared back at the film editor from the top rung of a metal ladder. Why couldn't Andre have stayed back in the cutting room where he belonged? He'd never worked on a crew where the film editor was allowed to impose himself on the other technical specialists. Morgan's presence was tough enough to stomach, but it was his cockamamie film. "I'm just disabling the motion detector," he shouted back to Andre.

"No way," Andre shouted as he jogged over to the ladder. "Reconnect that wiring at once."

Chris continued to dismantle the motion sensor. The ladder began to sway, and he looked down to see Andre hands on the ladder.

"Cut it out." Chris's voice was deep with menace. "Go back where you belong," he said through gritted teeth, his hands gripping the slanted wood bar bracing the rooftop.

Morgan raced over to the two men, who were acting like juvenile delinquents. "Stop," he shouted. "What in the hell do you two think you're doing? This is a movie set, not a goddamn preschool."

For a timeless moment neither spoke, then Andre began, "This turkey-brained idiot is trying to disable the motion sensor."

As Chris came down the ladder, he flashed the film editor the finger out of Morgan's view, and said in an indignant tone, "This light is too bright. It will distract from the shot."

Morgan looked up at the light. "How do you know how bright it is?" It wasn't dark enough for the light to have been activated.

"I've got the same type at home," Chris mumbled.

Morgan looked back up at the motion-sensitive light, then at Andre. "He could be right."

"If it turns out it's too bright, we'll use one of those pink fishnet covers to tone it down," Andre offered. "When Lori London drives up, she should activate the motion detector."

Morgan listened to the two banter back and forth for a moment or two longer, then said, "We'll check it out at dusk. For now, leave it as it is."

******

When Detective Scott and I arrived at the Montcreif Estate just before dusk, everything was quiet. The technical crews had not yet returned from dinner. Only Morgan, Dawn, and Charles Stafford were in view. They were standing in the driveway, deep in conversation.

Dawn wore a replica of the simple white dress that Lori had worn on the last night of her life, a sable coat draped over her arm. There seemed to be some sort of a disagreement but it appeared that no tempers had flared, and neither Morgan nor the actors seemed aware of our presence before we came within a few feet of them.

"Good evening," I said.

Morgan turned his head in our direction. "Barnaby, Detective," he said, giving us an expansive smile. Excitement sparkled in his eyes. "So glad you could make it. This is going to be one phenomenal scene."

Dawn and Stafford chimed in. I was relieved that Morgan had abandoned his original idea of "absolute reality" and had let Dawn in on the fact that the ignition was rigged so that it could not be turned off. I just didn't cotton to his original plan. Dawn was turning into a real professional. I had faith that she could conjure up the appearance of panic. She didn't need to experience it first-hand.

The crew began returning. The lighting technicians got right to work adjusting the lights for the waning sunlight. One of the staging crew members had backed the Cadillac into the street shortly after it had been roped off in compliance with their city permit. The air filled with conversation and last-minute adjustments as Dawn slid in behind the wheel and nodded her head.

I noted that Morgan had not scripted Montcreif as the driver nor shown how he'd managed to rouse the unconscious Lori London enough to be able to drive. I hadn't seen the scene after her descent down to the parking lot, which had been shot two nights ago. I wanted to ask Morgan how the drugged Lori, whom we'd seen Montcreif swoop up in his arms, had been able to drive, but knew this wasn't the time to distract him with questions.

All four of the cameras were rolling, capturing various angles as Dawn drove the Cadillac slowly into the driveway.

"Cut," Morgan shouted when the car reached the middle of the driveway.

Dawn got out of the car to stretch her legs, while two of the lighting technicians ran over to the car.

I must have had a quizzical expression on my face, because Morgan said, "They're adjusting the light in there. Have you ever noticed night shots in the interior of a car? The audience wouldn't see much if we didn't light it up. For this shot and the one from the parking lot the other night, we used a portable light. It's aimed down to bounce off a reflector in the back seat, and voila, the interior has sufficient light to pick up expression as well as form."

When the car was ready, Dawn slipped back inside.

Morgan peered into the garage ready to shout the next "Roll 'em," when he heard Chris shout, "Hold it."

Morgan spotted the coffee pot on the work counter as Chris unplugged it and rechecked the garage to make sure all the lighting equipment was out of sight. Morgan didn't look happy about the oversight as Chris carried out the coffeepot, but said nothing.

Again, all cameras were activated, catching the out-of-focus expression on Dawn's face.

Dawn pointed the mock-up remote door opener at the garage door while one of the prop men activated the real one. The door lifted slowly, and Dawn drove in. Unexpectedly, the door crashed down an instant later, leaving everyone but the young actress on the outside.

Morgan exploded over to the door. He hadn't even bothered to call cut. "Dawn. What in the hell's going on? Somebody open the goddamned door."

The prop man picked the remote back up and pointed it back at the door. He pushed the square white button. Nothing happened. He stared down at the remote and began punching the button repeatedly. "I just put new batteries in," he said, more or less to himself, then took off in search of more new batteries.

I sprinted over to the large door Morgan was attempting to lift up.

Scott shouted out, "I'll call 911 for the fire department." He pulled out his cell phone.

We heard the roar of the Cadillac's engine followed by the squeal of spinning wheels emerging from inside the garage. This was a far too much reality for my taste. I glared over at Morgan, and as if in answer to my unspoken question he said, "I don't know what in the hell's going on but we've got to get this door open."

It sounded as if the Cadillac's wheels were spinning, unable to get traction; just what we figured had happened on the night of Lori's murder. But how could that be? The ignition had been rigged, but every precaution had been taken to eliminate risk. Besides, it was only colored water, not oil, that was pooled on the garage floor around and beneath the car to create the illusion of oil. Or was it?

We tried brute force to lift the door. Scott jogged over to lend a hand. Then it seemed full-scale pandemonium broke out, with Charles Stafford and the whole crew joining us, trying to lift the door. It wouldn't budge.

With the remote non-functional, the garage door had to be deactivated from inside. I ran around to the back of the house, Scott hot on my heels, while Morgan's crew members scattered and were running aimlessly in every direction.

Dodging between the script-strewn tables and scattered chairs abruptly vacated by various crew members, at last I reached the kitchen door adjoining the garage. It was locked, and I could see little through the glass window at the top of the door. Scott and I nearly cracked heads as we simultaneously tried to see though the small window. Other than a blinding glare from the headlights, which illuminated nothing but the back wall, the garage was pitch black. I could barely make out the outline of the Cadillac, but saw no sign of Dawn. But why? "When I'd checked out the garage electrical system on my first entry, I found the light stayed on for five minutes after the door was closed."

"That's right," Scott confirmed. "That's how they're supposed to operate."

"The electricity's been switched off," we shouted in unison.

Scott backed up a few feet into the kitchen. "Move aside, Barnaby. Let me see if I can get through." With a running start, Scott thudded against the door full force with his shoulder and upper arm. The door didn't budge. "Holy shit," Scott yelled as an explosion of pain shot up his arm.

"Fuse box is out back," I said, and made a beeline for the back of the house.

CHAPTER 57.

Dawn's hands tightened on the steering wheel when she heard the garage door slam shut behind her. She threw the car into park, but as she expected, the engine continued to roar. She picked up the remote garage-door opener and pointed toward the large double doors. It was too dark to see, but she was pretty sure her direction was right. Nothing happened. She tried again, then quickly guessed that the electricity had been turned off. Then it dawned on her that the object she held in her had was a mock-up, a mere prop rather than the actual remote.

Knowing the ignition was rigged to stay on, she slipped out of the car and started gingerly over to the door adjoining the house. Aware of the oil-colored water that had been spread on the floor around the Cadillac, she slipped off her shoes to avoid getting them wet, but nearly lost her footing on the very first step. This couldn't be water beneath her feet. It was something slick and oily, not what the script called for. She managed to regain her balance and avoided a nasty fall into the oily substance. Frantically she tried the door, turning the knob first one way and then the other. It was locked. She tried again, twisting it one way and then the other with all her strength. It didn't give one iota. Think, think, she commanded her brain.

She heard the commotion at the massive garage door, but was sure no matter how many men tried, they'd be unable to lift the door from the outside, particularly now that she knew there was no electrical power. She looked up to the emergency bar on the garage-door apparatus. It was too high for her to reach, and it was too dark to see if there was any kind of ladder or stepstool around.

She was utterly alone. It was up to her to find a way out. She'd be darned if she'd let Montcreif, or whoever, destroy Tommy's film. The vapors from the car engine were getting to her, making her dizzy and sick to her stomach. Without taking as much as another second's thought, she slipped back in the driver's seat, closed the door, and moved the arm of the gear from park to drive, intending to slowly smash into the back wall, just as in the script. But this time she wasn't acting. This was a matter of life or death—her own life or death. She didn't want to hit the wall hard enough to hurt herself, but she did want to damage the car—to kill the blasted engine.

The car hit the wall hard enough to knock out the headlights and send the wheels spinning.

Her cool demeanor disappeared and she floored the accelerator. She hit the accelerator so violently it jammed at full throttle. She tried to throw the gear back into park but she found she couldn't. Next she attempted to pull it into neutral. No luck. It was stuck in drive. Worse yet, when she smashed the headlights, the garage was plunged into complete darkness. She tried the overhead car light and the dash lights. Nothing worked. She felt herself beginning to grow weak. The beginning of a headache was growing stronger by the second and she felt more than a bit nauseous.

She couldn't die, not now when she had so much to live for. Tommy seemed to have become far more attentive since that awful night when she ended up in the hospital. He no longer called her kid or Lori. Inadvertently, her brain turned to the effect her death might have on Tommy Morgan. She wouldn't allow Montcreif to destroy the man she loved. He couldn't survive the guilt if she didn't come out of this alive. She felt across the car seat for the sable coat, raised it to her face, and breathed in the scent. Then, stretching out across the seat, she covered her head and took a few shallow breaths. She took in the clean scent of the coat and tried to block the sickly exhaust fumes, but she was getting so very, very sleepy.

******

I raced to the fuse box while Scott had a go at breaking the glass in the peek window. There was a padlock on the outside of the fuse box. It hadn't been there before. I pulled out my Smith & Wesson and shot the padlock at close range. From the corner of my eye, I caught a glimpse of movement. It was Lieutenant Biddle, who'd apparently moved to the back of the house when he heard all the commotion.

He and Morgan rounded the corner of the yard, ran past me, and thundered up the back stairs.

No words were spoken; we were all intent on rescuing Dawn Medford.

The lock was still intact. It was one of those dang locks that defied even bullets. Frustrated, I raced to the tool shed. Rummaging though the tidy array of tools, I found an axe. Just what I needed. Hoping I wasn't too late, I hot-footed it back to the kitchen, straight to the door adjoining the garage. Scott had broken the small window at the top of the door, but it didn't accomplish much other than to bring a gust of fumes into the kitchen. Biddle and Scott stood back while Morgan attempted to get a bit of leverage with a broom handle. No one dared fire a shot at the door lock.

"Step back," I shouted, as I swung the axe back to attack the garage door. The wood splintered.

Scott reached for the axe and said. "Let me give it a try."

I didn't object. After a few more swings, the door was splintered enough for Morgan to try a shoulder block. He crashed through to the garage and charged straight over to the Cadillac, nearly losing his footing in the oil. But somehow he managed to stay upright. He thrust the car door open.

From a distance, we heard the wail of fire engines.

Morgan saw Dawn's petite form stretched across the seat, the sable coat covering her head. Tossing the coat to the floor, he impulsively placed his hand below her nose. To his great relief, he felt soft breaths tickle his palm and expelled the breath he hadn't realized he'd been holding.

Gingerly wedging his hands under Dawn's semiconscious form, he lifted her from the car and carefully made his way across the oil-slicked floor.

CHAPTER 58.

Lieutenant Biddle and Detective Scott had gone out to meet the uniforms and the backup from the Hollywood Precinct, which had arrived shortly after we broke into the garage. I stayed back to lend assistance to Morgan as he carried Dawn's limp form toward the ragged kitchen door frame.

I held the remains of the door open, then walked ahead, straight through the kitchen and dining room to the living room. I pulled the dust cover off of the closest sofa.

As Morgan was laying Dawn on the sofa, a team of four paramedics burst through the open front door. A tall muscular man in uniform addressed Morgan. "Sir, if you'll step aside, we'll take over."

"Oh, sure," Morgan said in a shaky voice. He stepped back, his eyes never straying far from Dawn's pale face.

The paramedics went right to work. In seconds they'd set up the oxygen and placed a mask over Dawn's face.

******

Outside in the driveway of the Montcreif Estate, Biddle filled the police officers and his own men in. He instructed them to go over the crime scene thoroughly, to bag a sample of the substance on the garage floor, and then meet with him in the dining room.

The detectives took off to the back of the house and through the kitchen to the garage. The fire department had been called, but for now there was no electricity. One of the detectives had armed himself with two of their powerful portable lights. The men wasted no time. "Over here," a detective shouted. A beam of light was shot his way, revealing a short ladder, which he picked up, as the light followed him to an area beneath the garage-door mechanism. He climbed the ladder and released the emergency bar. Outside, uniformed officers from the LAPD lent a hand, assisting the detectives in pushing the massive garage door open.

A tall, wiry detective took the second light to the car, released the hood from inside the car, and began pulling wires until the engine shut down. "I'll be damned," another detective cried out, barley avoiding a pratfall in the oily substance. He knelt down and rubbed a bit of oil between his thumb and index finger. "This doesn't look like oil. It is oil."

Two fire trucks pulled up alongside the paramedics van. Firemen wielding axes headed for the garage door, then froze as they watched the door being lifted. Taking in the situation, Biddle walked over to the fireman who seemed to be in charge. "Lieutenant Biddle, LAPD," he said, then added, "Hollywood Precinct," as he handed him a card.

"Tom Nix." He extended his hand. "It appears you have everything under control."

"Not quite," Biddle said. "The electricity has been shut off, and the fuse box is locked shut with one of those indestructible padlocks."

"Where?" the fireman asked.

"Follow me," Biddle said as he led them to the back of the house.

******

In the living room, Dawn pulled the oxygen mask off. "I'm okay. Please believe me. I don't want to be taken to any hospital."

Morgan moved in between two of the paramedics and grasped Dawn's hand. "Darling, you've taken in a lot of carbon monoxide. I don't want to lose you. Please—"

"Tommy," she cut in. He had called her darling. "I didn't breathe as much of that stuff as you think, and I don't need to go to the hospital."

Still grasping her hand, he met her eyes. "Dawn, I love you. Please, for my sake let them get you checked out. You have no idea how much carbon monoxide you may have taken in. And you sure can't tell me you're ready to go out dancing."

Dawn slowly shook her head—a head that was reeling, not from carbon monoxide, but from those words she'd longed to hear. Tommy had said he loved her. Could this really be happening?

"Tommy, please listen to me. I'm okay. Although I'm not quite ready to go dancing, I bet I will be in less than an hour."

Morgan sighed. Looking up at the paramedics, he said, "I guess she's not going to take advantage of your hospitality." Before they had a chance to object, he continued, "I'll get my doctor to come over here now and make sure she's as unharmed as she seems to thinks she is."

******

I'd spent the last hour or so in the dining room, questioning everyone who had been around when this drama was being enacted. Morgan and Stafford were within eyesight throughout the filming of this last scene. Lighting, camera, makeup, and wardrobe consultants were within earshot, ready to step in when needed, but many of them had drifted off at various times during the evening. Accounting for their time was as difficult as it had been at the scene of the arson. If only I'd paid stricter attention to who was missing at precisely the time the garage door slammed shut. It seemed that everyone was in place, but there had to be at least one person missing. The electricity had been on when Dawn hit the remote to enter the garage, then switched off instantly once the car was in the garage, trapping Dawn inside. There was no way in tarnation to cut the electricity or clamp on a padlock remotely. Our phantom had managed to escape detection for the moment, but I had a feeling he'd about run out of his clump of luck.

CHAPTER 59.

Lieutenant Biddle reopened the Lori London case. The sets at the studio and on location were being well policed during the shootings or reshootings of all the remaining scenes, right up to the final wrap-up, which would be in the next six weeks. So far, all had gone without incident, but I knew only too well that this was too good to last. We were experiencing the tranquility before the storm.

Dawn was giving the performances of her young life. She'd dreamed that one day Tommy would overcome his morbid fascination with Lori London, but when it happened she found it hard to believe. She wanted to keep pinching herself to make sure it wasn't just a dream. But it was true: Tommy's fixation on the ghost of the dead actress was a thing of the past.

She was the one who now shared a wholesome and growing love with Tommy Morgan. He had asked her to marry him and, of course, she'd said, "Yes, yes, yes." They planned to honeymoon in Spain after the premier. Tommy Morgan's new obsession for *The True Story*

Behind the Legend of Lori London had nothing to do with a ghost from the past. It had everything to do with Dawn Medford, the actress he intended to make a star, and the woman who would soon become his wife.

******

While preparation for the upcoming premier filled the days at Universal Enterprises, I spent my time narrowing down the list of suspects, eliminating those least likely to be involved.

The fact that the Lori London case was officially reopened hadn't made any difference in my working arrangements with Scott. The case had been turned over to the Cold Case Team, and Scott had a full-time job learning the ropes as one of the new kids in plain clothes. Fortunately, he never seemed to tire of moonlighting, so we could continue to brainstorm.

Friday night about 7:00, Scott arrived at the office. I had an open folder spread across my desk with the details we'd gathered on the cast of characters who had been present during all the mishaps over the last several weeks, when Scott came in carrying bags of Chinese food. I stacked the papers and placed them to the side while Scott spread out his selected dishes.

"You brought in enough to feed the entire cast at United Enterprise," I said with a smile in my voice.

"It's not easy to order Chinese food for two." He grinned. "But what we don't eat tonight can be tomorrow's lunch." Scott filled his plate, then picked up the first folder.

"What do you think of that film editor?" He strummed his fingers across the folder marked Andre Deville.

"Personally, he leaves much to be desired. But somehow I don't think he's our guy."

"Because?" Scott probed.

"While it's no secret that surly young editor is no team player, and he's made it clear he isn't sold on Morgan's concept, I—"

Scott jumped in, finishing my thought. "But since he's the one with the most access to the film, why take the risk of being caught in an act of sabotage?"

"It seems we're trotting down the same trail, Craig." Scott had spouted out my theory to the letter. "If Andre were the one intent on destroying this film, why not just expose the film? I know a little about the processing of movie film, and there's a lot that can go wrong, particularly since the editor does a lot on his own and not necessarily in the presence of anyone else. If he were our man, it seems he could just wait till the movie was a wrap and do his dirty deeds at the end. What's the point in destroying one scene at a time? A scene isn't that difficult to reshoot. But to wash out the entire film...."

We were about to fold up our tents and head for home when I picked Chris Montgomery's folder up and flashed Scott his picture. "What's your take?"

Scott looked at the picture of Chris Montgomery for a long beat, then said, "I wouldn't choose him for a best friend." Scott grinned. "Sorry, Barnaby. That guy kind of gives me the creeps, but I can't put my finger on anything specific. He just seems strange. He's so quiet; he scares the shit out of me. Out at the studio on two different occasions I turned around and he was right on my heels."

"He's the one I'd like to keep my eye on next Saturday at the premier." I couldn't name anything specific either but thought Chris Montgomery bore watching.

"Expecting trouble?" Scott asked.

"Aren't you?" I asked. It was rhetorical, since we'd gone over all the possible scenarios, and I had no doubt that he was as convinced as I that the premier would not go without incident.

"With all the coverage we've planned, I'd say it's damn near impossible for anything to go wrong." He paused. "Listen to me; I'm taking the company line, but after what happened during the first take at the Montcreif garage, we'd better be prepared for anything."

I nodded, "I'm taking nothing for granted."

******

Jedediah raced into my office just as I was getting ready to turn off the lights and head for home.

"Barnaby, take a gander at this," he said, his voice full of the excitement. As if he'd found that proverbial needle in a haystack, he shoved a piece of paper in my direction.

I glanced down at the article he'd found and printed from his computer.

Dr. PETER LYNCH—WHEREABOUTS STILL UNKNOWN

Dr. Lynch, the preeminent medical authority on stem cell research, has not been seen since June of 2001. Dr. Lynch, formerly on staff at Sloan-Kettering and Cornell University, was to begin human trials at Laurel University in Los Angeles, where he had accepted a position as chief of staff for the small private hospital.

After successfully coaxing stem cells from mouse embryos and developing them into brain tissue, Lynch achieved amazing results—a cure for a Parkinson's-like disease in mice. Dr. Lynch claimed that brain stem cells, as well as other stem cells found in bone marrow and skin tissue, would be our hope for the future. His human volunteer trials were to have included and be centered on the replacement of damaged brain cells for victims of three specific groups: those with Alzheimer's, Parkinson's, and spinal cord injuries.

On the night of June 10, Dr. Lynch had delivered an inspiring lecture to fourth-year medical students in the 300-seat auditorium on the campus of USC. According to reliable witnesses, Lynch left the auditorium at approximately 9:45 p.m. Mrs. Lynch reported that her husband called her about that time on his cell phone, telling her how well his talk had gone and that he was on his way home. He never showed up, and she has heard nothing from him since.

To date, there have been at least four known break-ins at Laurel University in the medical facility where Dr. Lynch had lined up the volunteers for his select study. Lynch was replaced by Dr. Richard Wigod, who has taken on the challenge of these studies. He reports that some of the stem cells that had been coaxed from human subjects have turned up missing....

The article went on to give the merits of the stem cell potential, along the lines of McCormack's dissertation at Pelican Bay. I looked at Jedediah.

"Are you thinking what I am thinking?" he asked.

I nodded. Had Montcreif set up his own private hospital, as he had in the south of France—an exclusive hospital with only one patient?

CHAPTER 60.

Tommy Morgan had selected the Warner Theater on Hollywood Boulevard for the premier of *The True Story Behind the Legend of Lori London*. He could have chosen one of the more modern theaters, but he'd always had a special feeling for the Warner Theater, and it seemed the perfect setting for this film. Klieg lights were placed beside the red carpet where Morgan, Dawn, and Stafford would most likely be giving interviews. Beacons of light crossed the sky above the theater as I handed my car keys to the valet.

Betty and Jedediah had offered to pick me up, but I didn't want to be a third wheel to either Jedediah and his date or Betty and her escort. Besides, I wanted my own car.

I didn't have to scan the crowds long. Betty and her escort spotted me and were walking in my direction. I'd known the tall, broad-shouldered man with silver hair long before Betty had become an eligible window. Geoffrey Cane was a former client and city councilman. Betty looked very attractive in her long, form-fitting velvet gown, a Tadashi that she'd modeled for Jedediah and me a couple weeks ago to get our reaction. She looked every bit as glamorous as any movie star. I gave Betty a quick hug and had just reached out my hand to shake Geoffrey's when we were greeted by Jedediah and his latest girlfriend.

Feeling a growing excitement in the crowd, I turned in time to see Tommy Morgan and his rising star, Dawn Medford, as they emerged from the back seat of a vintage pearl white Rolls-Royce. The chauffeur waited for a moment to make sure his passengers were out of harm's way, then drove on down Hollywood Boulevard.

Stunning in a red, strapless Valentino gown, Dawn floated seamlessly onto the star-studded walk beside the dashing Tommy Morgan in a well-tailored tuxedo. Morgan gazed at her with unabashed pride. As she took his arm and started down the red carpet, a black Jaguar swept up to the curb. The debonair Charles Stafford slid out from behind the wheel, handed his keys to the valet, and joined his co-star and producer on their stroll down the red carpet. Stafford's silver hair glistened, and he looked at home in his tuxedo. Microphones were thrust toward each of the glamorous trio as they began making their way into the theater. Dawn was gracious and effervescent as she talked with the reporters; Stafford was gentlemanly and polite; while Morgan appeared brusque and wary.

As reporters crowded in to interview the handsome trio, our small group was ushered into the reserved section that had been taped off for celebrities and Morgan's special guests. We fit into the latter group. Betty's eyes sparkled as she and Geoffrey took their seats. Jedediah's young date was awestruck. "Oh, J. R.," she said, "I just can't believe I'm actually right here with all these stars." Jedediah took on a casual air as if it were no big deal, but I knew he'd been anticipating this moment for weeks. I was as uneasy as Morgan had appeared earlier, and took the seat nearest the aisle.

From our vantage point, we were able to observe the eager crowd fill the theater. Typical of Southern California, there was no particular dress code. The crowd was decked out in everything from tuxedos and couture gowns to more sedate cocktail attire, and as could be predicted, a few arrived in sports jackets and blue jeans.

A frail old woman wearing a black, full-length taffeta dress and pushing a man in a wheelchair stopped beside an usher and presented her invitation. "Could we go as near the front as possible? I'd like my son to be able to enjoy the show from his wheelchair."

The usher solicitously helped wheel the chair down the aisle to a position of vantage, across the aisle and a row down from where we were sitting. The man in the chair appeared to be a veteran. He wore an overseas cap and a military jacket that bore a multitude of ribbons. A blanket covered his lower body, but it was obvious he was legless. Dark glasses concealed most of his sallow features.

I kept my eyes pinned on the two of them and heard her excuse herself to go to the restroom, in a voice that was unnecessarily loud. She patted her son on the shoulder, and said, distinctly, "I'll be right back." Pulling a rather large handbag from the back pocket of the wheelchair, she disappeared up the aisle, passing within a couple feet of me.

I felt something was not quite right and walked down to have a word with the veteran.

"You okay, buddy?" I asked. He didn't answer right away, so I patted his shoulder as I'd seen his mother do and repeated my question. Still no reply. Something about the feel of his shoulder brought me to full alert. I reached over and lifted his cap and his glasses fell to the floor.

It was a dummy. I started up the aisle after the woman, then stopped abruptly. On a hunch I returned to the dummy and ripped off the blanket. By then I was surrounded by security. Beneath the wheelchair there was a bundle of dynamite sticks, crudely wired to a cheap alarm clock.

A man in a nearby seat gasped, "My god, it's a bomb!"

The echo of "a bomb," reverberated throughout the theater. The sound echoed off the ornate theater walls, throwing the crowd into uncontrollable panic.

As the theater began to clear out, I ran back to the wheelchair to get a better look. Something about the dynamite sticks didn't ring true. Then a picture flashed before me, and I got it. What I was looking at weren't dynamite sticks; they were ordinary highway flares. "It's a ruse!" I shouted to the security and police officers nearby, the ones that weren't involved in attempting to control the stampeding crowd. I bent down on one knee, disconnected the wires, and hollered, "Lights!"

The house lights came on full force. "Find the woman in the long, black taffeta dress," I shouted while scanning the crowd. My eyes traveled to the balcony and fixed on an old woman in black taffeta, battling against the tide of the thundering crowd in search of escape.

I wound my way through the audience-packed aisle, then turned into a row of seats and found I had less trouble stepping over the seats, one row at a time, rather than battling the crowds flowing down the main aisles.

The old woman had made it to the projection booth by the time I climbed to the balcony. Fortunately, the projectionist had locked the steel door as instructed, and by now the crowd had dispersed from the balcony. As I got within a few feet of the woman, I saw she was reaching into her bag for something. Maybe a real incendiary bomb.

I caught hold of the back of her long dress and tried to get my hands on the handbag. In the ensuing struggle, the old woman's wig fell to the floor, revealing dirty blond hair pulled back and held with a rubber band. It was Morgan's surly cameraman, Chris Montgomery.

"Get the fuck out of here," Chris snarled. He lost his hold on the handbag as I wrenched it free. Chris ran for the fire escape as I gingerly steadied the handbag. I sure didn't want it to hit the floor.

I pulled out my Smith & Wesson, which I'd taken from the inside pocket of my tux and slipped it in the waistband of my pants the instant I'd discovered the wheelchair was a hoax.

Chris had just stepped on the first rung of the ladder of the fire escape when it gave an eerie creak, broke off, and clattered to the ground. Chris was hanging onto the rail from the floor of the landing by one hand, then two. I slipped my gun back in my waistband, gripped the railing, and reached down to give Chris a hand. He didn't reach toward my hand; instead, he looked straight down. For a terrifying moment I thought he was going to let go and fall to his death. His gaze returned to me, and he hesitantly let go of the rail with one hand and reached toward my extended hand. I heard Detective Scott calling my name. "Out here on the fire escape," I called back. I heard his feet thud onto the landing before I saw him.

He reached down and caught hold of Chris's elbow, and with tremendous effort, we pulled the angry young man back onto the landing. When Chris was steady on his feet, Scott pulled his Beretta from his shoulder holster, whirled him around, and cuffed him.

"Thanks, Craig," I said, a bit winded.

"Only in the movies can that maneuver be done by one person—not in real life."

I smiled. "Just trying to save an old man's pride?"

"No way. I would have had a hell of a time on my own."

"Well, thanks anyway."

I looked over at Chris Montgomery, his eyes fixed on the peeling orange paint of the fire-escape landing.

"What is your real name?" I asked.

"Chris Montgomery," he said, a malevolent glare in his eyes.

"Do you want to give that another try?" I asked.

His reply was utter silence. He continued to focus his gaze on the floor or the laced, old lady shoes on his feet.

"I guess we'd better take him on down to the precinct. Maybe that will improve his memory," Scott offered.

"Go fuck yourself," the young man with the unkempt ponytail hissed.

"How about we have our talk inside on the balcony?" I said. It was darn cold out on the fire escape. "We've got a lot to talk about."

Reluctantly the young man who was going by the name of Chris Montgomery followed us. Scott took hold of his upper arm and pushed him down in one of the theater seats while the two of us stood, the balcony rail to our backs.

"How about if I tell you a story about a beautiful young actress and the man who made her a star," I stated. It wasn't meant to be a question.

"I never did believe in fairy tales."

"This is no fairy tale, I can assure you, Nigel Montcreif III." I enunciated "the third" slowly and clearly.

With a glare that could melt marble, he said without conviction, "Who in the hell is that?"

"The game's over," I replied. "Now let me finish my story. The actress and the producer were once lovers, but circumstances changed, and their relationship hit troubled times. The actress wanted to pursue her own dreams, but when she found she was going to have the producer's child, she—"

"Took off and left them both." The young man's face was as red as the velvet seat upholstery.

I waited a beat. "Who told you that?" Obviously I'd hit a nerve. He'd blown his cover.

"It's the goddamned truth." He paused. "All right, I was born with the name you said, but I haven't used that name since I was a kid."

"You've gone by the name Chris Montgomery?"

"My name is Neal Montcreif. Now are you satisfied?"

"Not by a long shot," I said.

"Why are you out to sabotage this film?" Scott asked.

A whirlwind of expressions crossed and changed on the young man's unpleasant features.

"Excuse me, Detective Scott. Do you mind if I pursue the past before we get to the recent crime wave?"

"Well," Scott said reluctantly, "go ahead."

Young Montcreif adjusted his position in the theater seat.

"You say you've gone by the name Neal Montgomery, and yet you went to work under the name Chris Montgomery on Morgan's payroll."

"That's right." He offered no more. I was guessing this was going to be a long night, when I heard more feet thudding up the stairs.

"All right, let's get straight to the point. I know that your father did not die at sea."

"Prove it."

"Eventually, that's exactly what I intend to do. Through the little black book that Tanya Guttenberg kept we've been able to piece a great deal together. I don't care how long it takes, I don't intend to drop the ball this time around, but I could use a little help, rather than your roadblocks, to cut the time frame."

"Well, Mr. Jones, if you happened to be right—I'm not saying you are. But if you were, do you know how old my father would be by now?"

"Probably somewhere in the early to mid-nineties," I said.

"Right," young Montcreif shot back, "And how many ninety-year-old men do you know that are in tip-top condition?"

"There's no statute of limitations on murder," I said, keeping my voice in a low and monotone.

"You don't have a prayer of proving that. Besides, if he did murder that bitch, she had it coming."

"Is everything under control?" Biddle asked. Three of his detectives were backing him up in case there was any trouble on the balcony.

More footfalls could be heard on the stairs. Jedediah bolted in and breathlessly asked, "You okay, Barnaby?" An appearance of consternation played across his rough, youthful features.

I assured everyone that I had things under control. "Go on back to your young lady and Betty," I said.

"Stephanie and Betty are with Geoffrey," he shot back.

I nodded my approval.

I turned to Biddle. "Where is Tommy Morgan?"

"He said he was taking Miss Medford home, then coming back here."

"Leaving her home alone?" I asked. Before Biddle replied, I said, "Forget it. I forgot about the bodyguards he has on round-the-clock protection. We have things under control, so you might as well run along and enjoy the rest of the evening."

"Are you sure?" Jedediah looked apprehensive, but when I reassured him he quickly disappeared to join the others.

Biddle and Scott remained.

"Lieutenant Biddle," I said, "I'd like you to meet Neal Montcreif, Nigel Montcreif's son."

"You don't say." Biddle did not extend his hand, but looked at me with amused incredulity.

"Do you mind if I resume my line of inquiry of the events over the past several years?"

"You've got the floor," Biddle said, still trying to take it all in.

"Now, Neal. Let's get down to the business."

"I've got nothing to say." A pinched expression appeared on Neal's face as his brows formed a single bushy line.

Biddle was about to interject, when I said, "In that case, let me finish my story."

"I'm not interested in any fiction," young Montcreif stated.

"Good, because I'm not serving any."

A smug look settled on his face. "Well, get on with it. You've got a captive audience," he said, leaning forward and raising his handcuffed wrists as high as possible, which wasn't too high at all.

"As I was saying, when this young actress found that she was going to have a baby, she decided nothing was more important and did her best to piece back together her relationship with the producer. She wanted this baby so much that even though she was a major star, all she wanted was to be a wonderful mother to her baby."

Young Montcreif glowered with rage. He leaned forward, trying to rise from the chair.

Scott shoved him back down by his shoulder. "Cool it."

"Thought you said you weren't dealing in bullshit."

"Not exactly my vocabulary," I said, "but in essence, that's correct."

"What do you take me for? I know what happened. Not only did this 'lovely young actress' of yours fail to curtail her climb to stardom, but the instant this so-called 'baby of her heart' was born, she took off without even laying eyes on me."

I couldn't help but note his shift from baby to me. This was one angry young man. He'd been lied to with the same brand of cruelty dished out to his mother. "That's just not true, Neal."

As if on cue, Tommy Morgan thudded up the staircase to the balcony.

In the next hour or so, though not an easy sell, Morgan and I told young Montcreif the true story of his birth, about how his mother had been deceived—not only made to believe that her child had been a stillborn, but also put through the ordeal of burying an empty coffin—one she was led to believe held the body of her dead baby girl.

"Baby girl?" Neal wailed.

"That's what she was told." Morgan picked up from the day Lori learned that her child had not been stillborn and how she vowed she'd never rest until she rescued her son and was allowed to become the loving mother she'd always longed to be.

It was clear that young Montcreif knew his father had murdered his mother. He'd been led to believe his mother was a cruel, self-absorbed movie star who cared nothing for him, never even wanted to lay her eyes on him. The Lori London he learned about at his father's knee had deserved to die, and his father should be held blameless. Ridding the world of her wickedness, he should be applauded, not punished.

At the end of our hammering away at the facts, young Montcreif's expression reflected doubt and a heap of suspicion. I could feel a shift in his demeanor and knew his long history of admiration mixed with a bit of ambivalence toward his father shifted. He looked confused, as if he wasn't sure if we were the ones trying to deceive him or if he'd been deceived since childhood.

CHAPTER 61.

"I don't buy it," Neal said, "but I'll take you to see my father. That is, if you'll get these off so I can discard this garb." He leaned forward, jerking himself to his feet and again trying to raise his handcuffed hands.

Biddle nodded to Detective Scott, who removed the keys from his pocket and unlocked the cuffs.

After shedding the female garments he'd worn over jeans and a T-shirt, Neal was ready to lead us to his father.

"We can take my car," Biddle said.

Neal shook his head. "I'd rather walk."

He led us down the stairs from the balcony and out into an alleyway beside the theater. We passed several swarming patrol cars as we started up the hill toward Franklin. Not much farther, Neal stopped in front of one of those spooky Hollywood mansions built in the '20s.

Neal took out a large ring of keys, located the one he wanted, and let us in. We cautiously followed him up a creaky staircase. As we were led down a wide hallway into a large room, I noted the unvaried decor of the place. It was a Lori London museum—every inch of wall space was papered with posters of her movies, and lobby display cards were set up on large easels. Large glass cases lined the walls with displays of Lori's costumes and jewelry, photographs, and other memorabilia of every description.

Beyond the mementos, I saw a virtual maze of mirrors arranged in sequence, at angles to allow a viewer to look around corners and beyond. In a series of reflections, I saw a room reminiscent of the shrine in Tommy Morgan's castle-like home. From behind, I heard an intake of breath and saw that Morgan's face had turned ashen.

The sole occupant of the room was a kneeling figure in a black, ornately embroidered oriental kimono, head bowed before an altar on a dais supporting a life-sized nude statue. The figure was flanked by Taj Mahal-shaped brass incense burners, each wafting upward a thin veil of incense. From somewhere beyond came the delicately tinkling sound of glass wind chimes punctuated periodically by the deep, majestic resonance of a temple gong.

The nude statue was, of course, Lori London.

The figure slowly rose, genuflected, backed away from the altar, and disappeared from sight, appearing immediately via reflection from another angle.

The frontal view revealed the desiccated face of a very old man and a suggestion of an evil strength.

Apparently able to see Neal and me from that angle, he spoke. His voice was echo-chambered and was accompanied by a smile projecting nothing short of malevolence.

"Montcreif," I called out.

Ignoring me, he said, "Felicitations, my son. I see you have brought a worthy sacrifice—the nosey detective. I've been expecting you." From under his kimono, I saw him whip out a sawed-off shotgun.

In the maze of mirrors, it was hard to tell which was real and which was an image. Ducking sideways, I drew my gun from my waistband.

The blast from Montcreif's shotgun reverberated throughout the room, followed by the sound of shattered glass falling to the floor. Apparently, Montcreif had taken aim at my reflection in the mirror, and hit the image dead center.

Behind me I heard a static blare from Biddle's walkie-talkie. "You hear something?" came a voice from one of the patrol cars, then a response from another, "Like a shotgun blast?" Biddle was nearby, but I hadn't a clue where Scott and Morgan were.

I ducked down and, crawling low to the floor with my gun in hand, I heard the wail of police sirens and the unmistakable sound of the shotgun being reloaded from close by.

As Montcreif and I continued our game of cat-and-mouse among the mirrors, I wondered where in the heck Neal had disappeared.

I also wondered whose side he'd be on, as I made my way silently beneath the drapes beside the altar. Montcreif must have heard me because he whirled. We fired simultaneously. I saw that my bullet had winged Montcreif, but the bulk of the blast was taken by Lori's life-sized statue, which fell from the stand and knocked the gun from my hand.

Montcreif smiled and, seizing his advantage, shifted the shotgun to his good arm. He was about to blow me away. From out of nowhere, Neal took a flying leap at his father.

In the struggle for the gun, it went off. Montcreif took the full charge straight into his gut and crashed to the floor.

Neal stood over his father, a stunned expression on his face. I made my way through the mirrors to find the others. Mystified, I had no idea where everyone had gone.

After a few twists and turns back through the maze of mirrors, I saw Biddle struggling to get to his feet, his hand on one side of his head, with a narrow trickle of blood oozing through his fingers. On the floor beside him was a small statue, which lay in two large pieces. It took no Einstein to figure out what had happened, but he appeared to be okay, so I asked, "Where are Morgan and Scott?"

Still dazed, Biddle pointed to a solid steel wall dividing the room in half. I felt all around, trying to see if there was something to push or slide.

"Chris—I mean Neal," I called out. "What's with this wall?"

Without a word, the grief-stricken young man walked to the altar and pulled a lever. The steel wall slid open. Morgan stood there, frustration and rage registering on his face. "A few more days like this," he said, "and Dawn will have to be wheeling me around in one of those blasted wheelchairs."

"Where's Scott?"

Morgan shrugged.

I heard the wail of sirens from the black-and-whites, but Scott was most likely calling in the heavy artillery from the fire department.

In the next few minutes, the house was bustling with policemen, firemen, detectives, and paramedics. Biddle dismissed the paramedics and called for the M.E.

Neal Montcreif looked dazed as a detective again cuffed his hands behind him. I felt an ache of sorrow for this young man who'd been raised on lies and hatred and had been twisted into a murderer and perhaps a kidnapper. The feeble attempts at arson and minor break-ins weren't life threatening. Killing his father was an accident, but Tanya Guttenberg was another story; so was drugging Dawn Medford, and there was still the mystery of the missing doctor. LAPD was not about to close this case, and neither was I.

CHAPTER 62.

Tommy Morgan and I left the Montcreif hideaway at the same time. He was anxious to get back to Dawn. I headed off to meet with Lieutenant Biddle and Detective Scott on their turf.

When I arrived at the Hollywood Precinct and gestured back to Biddle's office, I saw Scott seated comfortably across the desk from Biddle, a steaming cup of coffee in front of each of them.

"Where's Neal?" I asked.

"Cooling his heals in an interrogation room," Biddle offered.

"Because?"

"I think he needs a little time to reflect," Biddle said.

"Still thinks we fed him a pack of lies?" I asked.

"He says so," Scott interjected, "but I don't think he really believes it." Shaking his head, a baffled expression on his face, he added, "He kept mumbling something about a puppy. When I tried to get more out of him, he just cradled his head on the table and began sobbing like a baby."

"A puppy?" I repeated.

Biddle shrugged as he rose from the desk chair and walked around his desk. "I think we've given young Montcreif sufficient cooling-off time. So let's get on with it." Then, turning his gaze directly on me, he said, "I assume you have a few questions of your own."

I followed Biddle out of the office.

The tiny interrogation room was claustrophobic. There was no large window or roomy interior. The six-foot-long brown Formica table stretched nearly wall to wall in a small eight-foot-square room, with little maneuvering space to squeeze between wall and table to reach the opposite side.

Since there was no way more than two could occupy the small space at one time for the questioning of Neal Montcreif, Biddle chose the interrogation room that had been wired for sound and video for our initial questioning. Though the room was exactly the same size as the other interrogation rooms, our interview could be viewed from the adjoining room. A major remodeling had been scheduled at the Hollywood Precinct later in the year. For now, we had to make do with the present facility.

Biddle and I went into the room with Neal Montcreif, while Scott looked on via a color monitor in the next room. I was still in my tux but would hardly have blended in with any fancy black-tie shindig at this point. My trouser legs were covered in more than a bit of dirt from crawling on the floor and I'd ripped a five- or six-inch tear in my jacket sleeve. Biddle hadn't come out much better in his

Hickey Freeman suit, and while he'd torn nothing, his suit was far from presentable, and he sported a thick gauze strip held with white adhesive tape on his head. Bits of dried blood decorated the outside of his dressing and suit jacket.

Since I uncovered a connection between Dr. Peter Lynch's disappearance and his contributions to brain stem cell research, Biddle let me take the lead. As soon as Neal Montcreif was seated on the opposite side of the table and the door of the interrogation room swung shut, I wanted to get straight to the questions I needed to have answered by the remaining member of the Montcreif family, but first, I had to test the young man's mind set.

"Neal, I realize you've had a traumatic evening and I regret—"

"Save it, Mr. Jones." Looking up to meet my eyes, he bit down on his lower lip. His hair was tousled and hung down around his shoulders, rather than in the usual ponytail, and the whites of his eyes were yellow with tiny red veins. "I'm afraid I didn't really grow up until tonight. I wanted to believe that my father was the innocent victim of a vicious woman who broke his heart, so I overlooked all the signs of his own maliciousness since I was a child...."

I listened, praying that Biddle would not divert his ramblings and request that he get to the point. But Biddle was too smart; he also knew Neal had to get it out before we'd get anything concrete.

"Anything that I loved would somehow disappear. For as long as I can remember, my dad had to be the focus of my entire world...."

When he finally came to the story of the puppy that was taken from him when he was only about seven, I wondered how that moving recollection could have remained buried for so long.

Neil wiped his eyes with the sleeve of his shirt. "The old man told me I was imagining seeing puppy fur at the bottom of my bathtub. But I wasn't. I saw the black and white hairs around the drain. I guess deep down I've always known he drowned my puppy, but I really didn't want to believe it. To believe that would mean he didn't love me, and I…."

By the time Neal came to the end of his childhood memories, he tossed his head back and looked me in the eye. "Okay, so what do you want to know?"

"I know that you were just a young child at the time of Lori London's death, and still pretty young when your dad was reported lost at sea, but try to fill us in on what you know or have picked up over the years."

Neil held nothing back. "Around 1998," Neal said, "my father was diagnosed with Parkinson's. He was desperate to find a cure, said he had no intention of letting the disease turn him into some feeble old man. He was obviously concerned over the physical aspects of Parkinson's, but feared the mental deterioration even more. So when he found out about the research being conducted at Sloan-Kettering and Cornell University, we made anonymous donations to the program, hoping to speed their progress."

"You're referring to the brain stem cell research?" I threw in to make sure Biddle was not out of the loop.

"Yes, the researchers had come up with some pretty phenomenal results in combating the disease and controlling the tremors in control groups of mice. Lynch and his team had successfully replaced damaged cells in mice that had the Parkinson's-like disease with the brain stem cells from healthy mice. And he'd not encountered a single case of rejection.

"When we found out the first human trials were scheduled to be conducted using fetal brain stem cells in 2000...."

Neal went through the procedures, much like Terry McCormack had on our visit to Pelican Bay, and the reporter had detailed in the article I'd read—the one telling of the doctor's mysterious disappearance. "Neal, what do you know about a Dr. Peter Lynch?" I asked.

The young man looked down at the Formica table top and was quiet for more than a beat.

When he looked up his eyes were full of tears. "I didn't want anything to do with kidnapping the doctor and refused to get involved at first. But my father was a very convincing man. He insisted there was no other hope for him in warding off the ravages of the disease. He also ground in the fact that Parkinson's could be passed on, and as his son, I was at risk. He said it was more than likely I'd develop the disease in later life."

"Is that a fact?" I asked.

Neal clinched his fists, turning his knuckles a bony white. "Hell, I don't know. It's controversial, but nobody argued with my 'old man.'"

Running his tongue over his dried lips, he asked, "Is it possible to get a drink of water?"

Biddle opened the door of the interrogation room and called out to one of the members of the cleaning crew to get the water.

Neal stretched and readjusted his position in the stiff-backed plastic chair. As soon as the water appeared, he extended his hand, took a sizable swig, and continued. "Since my father was supposed to be dead, he wasn't able to talk his way into being a subject in the human trials. Even with the impressive false IDs he'd obtained, he was turned down flat. We talked with Dr. Lynch personally, since he was the big gun for limited human trials. We asked him to include my father in his initial trials. Father offered the doctor mega-bucks, but the doctor was adamant that he'd already screened patients for the initial trial and he was restricting his research to those with more severe cases than my father's. He let us know that he couldn't be bought, and more or less blew us off. So my father set up his own private hospital in the Hollywood Hills." Neal shrugged his shoulders as if to say, "What choice did we have?"

"You kidnapped the doctor?" Biddle exclaimed, leaning across the table and resting his palms on the table top so that his face was within a couple inches of Neal's.

"Where is the doctor now?" I asked.

Neal gave us the address and directions, then dug in his pocket and pulled two keys off his key ring.

Biddle and I had not taken a seat. We'd been standing against the wall in front of the table. But now in a rare show of fury, Biddle pulled a chair out from our side of the table and twisted it around so that its back banged against the table. Raising one foot to the seat on the chair, he leaned forward. "And just how have you managed to keep the doctor? Is he chained to a bed or—"

"No. Of course not. I'm no monster. The doctor has a lot of mobility. He can go anywhere in the hospital and his quarters that he likes. He can even go outside to the porch." Neal's former surliness returned.

I frowned. "So what keeps him from leaving?"

"He has one of those ankle alarms. You know, like the ones they use at those residential places for old people. If he goes beyond the perimeter it sets off an alarm."

"So you have 'round-the-clock security?" Biddle asked.

Neal nodded.

Biddle continued the questioning, getting all the details regarding the captive doctor, then asked Neal to outline the method of deactivating the alarm on the ankle guard and dispatched a unit to pick up the doctor.

Biddle excused himself to call Dr. Lynch's wife.

Other than the one minor flare-up, Neal seemed quite docile since accidentally ending his father's life. Strictly out of curiosity I asked, "Were the stem cell transplants successful?"

Neal shrugged. "His tremors didn't get any better, but they didn't seem to get any worse." He took a breath and bit down on his lower lip. "As for as his mental condition, I'd say it was definitely declining. I wasn't sure if we were getting defective brain stem cells or not, or if the transplants weren't actually as effective in human subjects as they were with the mice." He picked up his water glass and drained it.

I pulled out one of the chairs and sat across from the young man and asked the question that was most pressing on my mind. "Neal, I know you were just a kid when your mother was murdered, but how much do you know about your father's role in her death?"

"What do you want to know?" Neal spread one hand from temple to temple, massaging around his eye sockets. "The bastard was proud of it. I can't believe that he lied to me. My whole fucking life is nothing but a pack of lies."

"Well," I said, "I think I know that he paid his crew to lie about his whereabouts at the time of Lori's death."

"Right," Neal confirmed. "He also had a helicopter at his disposal with a pilot he paid damn well. A pilot who just happened to die after he picked my father up from what was supposed to be my father's death at sea."

"Died? How?"

"He dropped Father off at our private airstrip in Ventura, refueled, and took off again. The plane blew up right off the coast of Ventura and ended up in the Pacific Ocean. The 'accident' was never reported."

"Other than the death of the pilot, I sort of surmised the rest. What I don't know is how he killed Lori."

"She died of carbon monoxide poisoning after he drove her into the garage," he said, as if I were a particularly dull child.

"I know that part," I said. But how did he get her into the car? I know Morgan's movie scenario, but it doesn't jibe with the police reports. If your father had drugged her drink, a tonic and lemon—"

Neal met my gaze straight on and with a tilt of his head repeated, "Tonic and lemon? Is that the truth?"

I nodded. "There were plenty of witnesses to back that up."

Biddle walked back in. "At least we have one happy ending. The Lynches may not run out of conversation for the next month or so."

Neal picked up where we left off. "The old man said she was a lush, but she'd gone on the wagon that night, so I think he had to knock her out."

"There were no signs of physical abuse and the toxicology reports were clean—they found no traces of drugs," Biddle chimed in. "There was alcohol in her bloodstream, but a pretty low count."

"I figure Montcreif took care of that after she was sort of out of it, forced a little booze down her throat; but it's tough to get anything down an unconscious person's throat. Figure that's why there was a low count." I added, "So what could he have drugged her with that wouldn't show up in the toxicology report?"

Neal gave a rueful laugh. "He didn't actually tell me about drugging my mother, but I know what he did to my stepmother, the woman I thought was my real mother until he killed her." He paused, inhaled deeply, then said, "Okay, here goes. He fed me a whole cock-and-bull story about how my stepmother planned to get rid of me by sending me off to some fancy boarding school in England."

That jibed with Morgan's account.

"Anyway, he told me he had to stop her from sending me away, so he had to kill her. She was a teetotaler and my dad told me he didn't know of any drugs that were free from detection, but found out an overdose of insulin was the way to go."

"Couldn't that also be detected?"

"Yes, but only if they were looking for it, my father told me. What the insulin does is lower the blood sugar. But unless someone is on insulin, it's unlikely the coroner would test for it."

I'd check that out with some of my doctor friends, but I thought maybe this young man had worked out the answers to my most frustrating conundrum.

Mentally filling in the scenes that had been left out of the celluloid version of Lori's last night, I was fairly certain the insulin injection could only have been given outside the Hilltop Café, most likely in Lori's Cadillac. Montcreif could have used any number of mild drugs to make Lori a bit woozy, but he'd need privacy to jab Lori with the insulin needle and make sure he hit a vein. I bought into Morgan's movie rendition of Lori's departure down the steep staircase and Montcreif presence, convinced that scene was more fact than fiction. But the possibility of Lori driving herself home, I couldn't swallow.

"Neal," I said, looking into his deep-set eyes, "did you father mention driving Lori's car back to the Venice estate?"

Neal nodded. "He said she was out of it, so it was no problem getting her to let him driving her home, then leaving her in the closed garage with the engine running."

"Did he mention how he got away from the crime scene?"

"No, but I imagine he had a spare car. There was never any shortage of wheels, and the old man never left anything to chance."

"Thank you, Neal; that answers most of my questions. I'm real sorry for all the trouble you've got yourself into," I said, "but there's not a whole lot I can do to help you. The murder of Tanya Guttenberg threw your case over the edge."

Neal looked back down at the table, rubbing one thumb over the other, then looked up.

"Mr. Jones, I know it doesn't make much difference now, but I didn't mean to kill Tanya Guttenberg. I just meant to scare her, but she started screaming and her voice was louder than a sonic boom. I heard a car pull up and had to shut her up before anyone heard her. I pulled that damn scarf too tight. That's not an excuse, I know, but it's what happened. I've been my own worst enemy, but I really want you to know that I never intended to kill Miss Medford. I just set it up to look like a suicide."

"And you did that, hoping it would scare her?"

"Morgan was the target, not Dawn. I wanted him to abandon the film," Neal said.

"You wanted that enough to risk Miss Medford's life?" I asked.

"No," Neal said, his voice rising. "People just don't die from an overdose of prescription drugs. That's only in the movies, just like someone slashing his or her own wrists. That rarely works. That's one thing I learned from my dad."

I raised a brow. "It seems to me that a fair number of people have died from drug overdoses."

"Street drugs, sure. But not too often on prescription drugs, unless they're mixed with a large amount of alcohol. Usually before anyone can take enough to kill themselves, they start heaving them up."

Biddle confirmed the facts young Montcreif had laid out, and I excused myself, leaving the rest of the interrogation to Biddle and Detective Scott.

******

Two weeks after the original night set for the premier of *The True Story Behind the Legend of Lori London*, Morgan had it rescheduled. He'd paid through the nose to get the Warner Theater because it had been previously reserved by the Backstreet Boys. Morgan had dealt directly with their manager. He'd arranged and paid for the Dorothy Chandler Theater, which had only become available due to a last-minute cancellation by Whitney Houston. Tommy Morgan had his heart and mind set on the Warner Theater and would accept no other for his premier.

"To hell with the cost," he told reporters. He felt it was worth every penny, even after he'd paid for the cost of both theaters. He even

344

picked up the cost of the publicity for the Backstreet Boys' change of venue—double the cost they'd already invested. And as the pièce de résistance, he offered to set up a private viewing for the group, their production crew, and business manager.

The evening was a huge success, attracting an even larger crowd than the first time around. Morgan's public-relations specialist had done a phenomenal job with the publicity, but what brought it over the top were the headlines spread across the top of all the major and minor newspapers in Los Angeles. The unraveling of the true story behind this sizzling cold case had even made its way onto the front page of the *New York Times*.

Tommy Morgan set out to produce a blockbuster, and a blockbuster was what he'd created. Dawn Medford, a formerly unknown young actress, had been catapulted to instant stardom with rumors of Academy Award nominations. Tommy Morgan's name was being bandied about for best producer, Dawn Medford's for best actress, and Charles Stafford's for best supporting actor. That was the supposition. The Academy Awards were a good ten months away, but I had a feeling that win or lose at the actual awards, Morgan and Dawn had come out winners. At the wrap party in Tommy Morgan's castle-like estate, the shrine to Lori London had been disassembled and every memento it contained had been donated to the Academy of Motion Picture Arts and Sciences.

Tommy and Dawn Morgan had their whole lives ahead of them, and the ghosts of the past had finally been laid to rest.

******

By Monday evening, I was actually enjoying my solitude. Betty and Jedediah had been real troopers over the past couple of months, and I'd sent them both on vacation. I didn't get any arguments. They deserved a vacation. We all did. I would be taking off on a fishing trip tomorrow but had a bit of office catch-up to get out of the way. I'd reviewed Jedediah's reports on the status of our routine cases and was satisfied I was up to speed.

Now, wrapping a thick rubber band around the file that bore Lori's name, I smiled and picked up a wide felt-tipped pen and wrote across the cover "Case Closed," and set it in my outbox for storage in the archives in the basement cabinets.

"Well, we did it," I said aloud as if Hal were beside me. "You were right, and together we proved it." I smiled, feeling a bit silly hearing my voice echo in the empty room, but I meant what I said. Hal's belief that Lori could not possibly have committed suicide but had been murdered had preyed on my mind until I was able to carve out some time and spur myself into action. Without his yellow Post-it with the words "recheck the ignition," I'd have been without a tangible lead for a lot longer.

Although I had cared deeply for Lori, I realized now that I had devoted myself to clearing her name and wiping the suicide label from the records as much for Hal's sake as for Lori's, maybe even more so. Hal deserved closure, and though many calendar pages had been turned over, the case was now officially closed, as it should have been some eighteen years ago.

After locking the office, I was looking forward to the long-overdue fishing trip I had planned with my old cronies. As I began my journey home, I impulsively took a detour down Hollywood Boulevard and parked by the Warner Theater. The marquee announced, *"The True Story Behind the Legend of Lori London—6th Smash Week."* I noticed a rather long line at the box office. The sight brought a smile to my face as I sauntered off down the street.

At Lori's star I paused and started to walk away. A few feet beyond, I saw a flower stand set up outside the food market where a Mrs. Mirabelle Reese had told a reporter of the annual rose that appeared on Lori's star on the anniversary of her death. I pulled out my wallet, looked at the red roses, but decided to purchase a single pink carnation instead. The annual dropping of a red rose, I was sure, had come to an end. I would begin a new tradition, celebrating not the anniversary of her death, but the days of her life. Lori had loved carnations, and pink had been her favorite color. I bent down, placed the carnation in the middle of the star, and then began a peaceful stroll to my car.

From somewhere in the distance, I heard the saxophone continuing to speak of sweet, poignant loneliness of times gone by.

THE END

EPILOGUE

The words to an old song often play though my mind as I think back over the past year—*"What a Difference a Day Makes."*

Tommy Morgan and his wife Dawn are as much in love today as ever. While Dawn did not win the Academy Award for her first starring role, she has most certainly made a name for herself and is considered one of today's major stars. She's had offers from several major studios, more than she could possibly accept, even if she wanted to. She is not thinking of giving up her career, but definitely has other priorities and is limiting her number of films. Eight months after she and Morgan returned from their month-long honeymoon in Spain, she delivered twin boys, and she's determined to spend "quality time" with them. Tommy Morgan, Dawn's husband/producer, has been quoted by reporters from all forms of media to be in full support.

In a recent interview published in *Cosmopolitan*, Dawn Medford-Morgan is quoted as saying, "Tommy and I want a lot more children." And when asked how she thought that might affect her career, she said, "If Catherine Zeta-Jones can do it, so can I. In fact, since I'm confining my roles to those my husband produces, my schedules can be flexible." Later that same month, when interviewed on *Larry King Live,* she responded to his question about whether she was worried that limiting her motion pictures to only one producer might stifle her career, she said, "No way. Tommy's the best." And somehow, as I listened to her being interviewed, she made me a believer.

******

Detective Craig Scott reached his goal of being transferred to Homicide with a promotion to Detective II in record time—the youngest detective in that department. And owing to his high energy level and need for little sleep, he is working on his second novel. His first one, entitled *Take a Second Look,* hit the bestseller list and remained there for a record thirty-two weeks—an almost-unheard-of record for a new author. Only three novels of recent years could boast that kind of staying *power—The Bridges of Madison County, The Notebook,* and the Harry Potter series. Scott's was the first mystery by a first-time author to achieve that distinction. His novel was a fictionalized version of the Lori London case. "Names and locations have been changed to protect the 'guilty,'" Scott was quoted as saying in jest. His novel gave all the facts—more actual facts than were in Tommy Morgan's award-winning documentary. He thought of writing a nonfiction book on the case. Neal Montcreif had told him he'd give him a release to write it as he saw it, but Scott decided on fiction. "I'll stick to the facts and the absolute truth on the job," he told Oprah during a TV interview, "but in my writing life, I enjoy fiction. It's my one chance to get away with lies and create fascinating characters. On the job, a job I wouldn't give up for the world," he added hastily, "I deal with characters as they are. In fiction, I'm more or less in charge."

When Oprah asked what he meant by "more or less," the camera flashed back to Author/Detective II Craig Scott, who looked as if the answer was clear. "I can bring a character to life, but once that happens, I find the character often takes off on his or her own agenda and I'm left to follow their lead." He stopped abruptly. "Sorry, Oprah. I remember the first time I heard something similar from that former policeman who wrote *Die Hard*. Thought he'd lost it until I got there myself." The camera flashed to a commercial break.

******

During the last few months, I've gone to Folsom Prison to see Neal Montcreif twice. While it would be stretching the truth to describe his life as having a storybook ending, I found Neal was no longer the angry young cameraman I'd met on the Lori London set; he'd come to terms with the past, forgiven his somewhat-deranged father, and set about learning all there is to know about his mother. Lori must be resting easier now that her boy is on the road to recovery. While serving a life sentence for the murder of Tanya Guttenberg, he's made a dramatic turnaround in attitude. He became a model prisoner and worked himself up from the lowly job of cleaning latrines to an assistant cook in the prison cafeteria. If he continues chalking up that day-for-a-day work time, he might be out of prison before his fortieth birthday. But what I found most amazing, as well as ironic, was what he confided to me on my last visit. "Barnaby, I used to be so full of hate. Nobody has to tell me that the things I did were wrong. I know, and I pray every day I will do enough good in the rest of my life to someday find forgiveness, from myself as well as from others."

While serving his time at Folsom, the prison made famous by the late Johnny Cash, Neal said, "I feel I was sent here for a reason." He paused, stared down at the floor as if searching for the right words—words that did not come easily. Finally he continued, "You may think this is corny or overly dramatic, but I don't know how else to express it. This is the first time in my entire life I've actually felt a real sense of purpose and acceptance."

******

I might say that since the sizzling cold case of Lori London was closed—as it should have been two decades ago—the offices of Barnaby Jones Investigations are back to normal, and we are back to working with our routine clients on routine cases. But in this business, I've found that seldom is there any such thing as a routine case.

ABOUT THE AUTHOR

Buddy Ebsen's best known characterization is that of "Jed Clampett" patriarch of that celebrated piece of Americana *The Beverly Hillbillies*. His second best known is the television sleuth "*Barnaby Jones*."

Prior to that he was "Georgie Russell," Davy's pal in the Walt Disney classic *Davy Crockett*.

Surprisingly, Buddy had never intended to be an actor. His goal in life was to be a doctor. However, after completing two years of pre-med studies at the University of Florida and Rollins College, the Florida landboom collapsed, affecting the fortunes of the Ebsen family.

Since Ebsen senior was a dancing teacher, he had taught all his children his trade. Buddy shuffled off to New York to try show business, arriving there August 4, 1928. His Broadway credits include: *Whoopee* 1928, *Flying Colors* 1933, *Ziegfeld Follies* 1934, *Yokel Boy* 1939, *Showboat* 1945 and *Male Animal* 1953.

His film credits include: *Broadway Melody of 1935* with his dancing partner, sister Vilma, *Broadway Melody of 1938* with Judy Garland, *Born to Dance*, the Shirley Temple picture *Captain January*, *Banjo On My Knee*, *Girl of the Golden West* 1938, *Parachute Battalion*, *Night People* with Gregory Peck 1954, *Between Heaven & Hell* 1956 with Robert Wagner, *Attack*, *Breakfast at Tiffany's* with Audrey Hepburn 1961, *Mail Order Bride* 1964, *The One & Only Family Band* 1968,

The President's Plane is Missing, Fire on the Mountain 1981, *Stone Fox* 1986, to name a few.

His creation of *Cabaret Dada*, a musical was inspired by the Dada artistic revolt as a protest against World War I. A song from that show was selected for world-wide broadcasting in seven languages by the Voice of America. In 1968, he won the Honolulu race in his 35 foot catamaran, "Polynesian Concept."

Buddy had painting lessons as a child but this introduction to art did not flower until his later years. From casual pen and ink sketches of old Duke and Uncle Jed he was encouraged by his wife, Dorothy, herself a painter, to try oil.

This led to a brisk sale of originals and three limited edition serigraphs of 300 each, *Hong Kong, Sea Power*, and *Sedona* presently 90% sold out. The Uncle Jed Country limited edition series of ten paintings represent a return to, and the development of his original inspiration Jed Clampett and Old Duke.